THE GATE-CRASHER

Mary Baker

Copyright © Mary Baker 2025

THE GATE-CRASHER

The right of Mary Baker to be identified as the author of this work has been asserted by her in accordance with the Copyright, Designs and Patents Act 1988.

ISBN: 978-0-9933277-8-0

All rights reserved. No part of this publication may be reproduced, stored in a retrieval system, or transmitted in any form or by any means, without the prior permission in writing of the publisher, nor be otherwise circulated in any form of binding or cover other than that in which it is published and without a similar condition, including this condition, being imposed on the subsequent purchaser.

A CIP catalogue record of this book can be obtained from the British Library

Published in Great Britain by Cam Publications

Printed and bound by Witley Press Ltd
www.witleypress.co.uk

To

Brian James

20-2-1948 — 13-1-2024

A kind-hearted Cornish man through and through

Also by Mary Baker

Light Airs

Seventh Child

The Dummy Run

A Purposed Overthrow

The Live Ringer

The Purpose of Playing

Dentist Imperial

General Revenge

Death of a Ten Pound Pom

Fridays

Eight Years Earlier

A Very English Republic

Seeking Tansy

Aftermath

1

"Great reporting this week, Char. Your traffic-reduction article's an absolute humdinger. Yep, you really tore into the scheme. That'll keep those Town Councillors under pressure." Translation: it's what you should have done, but didn't.

Charlotte Paxton wondered what copy the *Clarion*'s editor was hoping she would file. Fistfights in Polrenek's Council Chamber? A police raid on the Mayoral house? Planning applications in envelopes stuffed with fifty-pound notes?

Son of the newspaper's owner, Gideon Penry had once found himself attending a staff-management course, and never quite recovered. Motivation through praise was his gleaned mantra, which meant kind words and a smiling editor told recipients that they were perilously close to unemployment. Gideon also believed nicknames create a friendly atmosphere in the workplace. "And, Char, let rip again on potholes. My car is practically a write-off. That reminds me. Next week we'll have a little chat about your future."

Smoothing back fair hair so glossy, it might have been manicured along with his fingernails, Gideon tried to make his threat sound like a mere throwaway line, but Charlotte knew better. Spice up her Council reportage, or never again darken the *Clarion*'s doorstep.

Formally clad in suit and tie amidst often unkempt employees, Gideon and his forthcoming little chat bustled further down the corridor, living proof that background outranked talent. He had been sent to oversee a minor Penry business venture, presumably because dear old Dad hoped to forget his younger son's existence. And who could blame Papa?

Charlotte told herself that she would resign, and deny Gideon a chance to play the unassailable boss. After all, Charlotte Paxton was twenty-five, halfway to fifty, not an insecure adolescent. OK, so she still regretted not inheriting her mother's flaxen allure, but dark-blue eyes and brown hair were acceptable. And Charlotte was tall: taller than Gideon. And the Town Archivist had praised her article lamenting a demolished sixteenth-century Inn. She would get another job. Perhaps. Maybe.

A former orphanage housed the *Clarion* among its tenants, but that dour granite building was close to Polrenek Promenade, and Charlotte felt like an escapee waif able to breathe freely again. Brisk winds were agitating the Atlantic into choppy surf, while gulls circled a sky puce with imminent rain, but the freshness of a Cornish autumn was invigorating. Charlotte could now scorn Gideon's finicky disposition, and to hint that fate might be on her side, a bus arrived at the stop just after she did. Even more providential, there were empty seats and no foul-mouthed teenagers weaponizing backpacks. The weekend was close, which offered time for leisurely meals and binge-watching TV drama. She would also start a job search, and possibly pre-empt Gideon's axe.

"Staying indoors on a weekend? You're young. You should be at parties, having fun." Her mother's voice was still in Charlotte's head, their wrong-way-round conversations replaying again and again.

"I've got to study," Charlotte had long ago wailed in protest. "If I don't pass this exam, I'll never get a university place, and my life will be ruined."

Yet even death was unable to silence Melanie's ambition to transform her daughter into a gregarious butterfly. As fair and fragile-looking as any porcelain doll, Melanie hid her resolute nature behind a demure mask, and had therefore inevitably attracted domineering suitors who would flee in shell-shocked confusion after the real Melanie at last went bananas. Now her feisty ghost was determined to browbeat Charlotte into making the same mistakes.

"It won't work," Charlotte's mind informed Melanie, as the bus reached their destination, just when drizzle became rain. "It won't work, Mum. I'm a romance disaster zone, exactly like you."

"Hoods wreck your hair and the shape of a jacket," Melanie's spirit retorted. "You should carry an umbrella."

Charlotte tried to outpace the phantom by scurrying round a pavement lake in front of Victorian houses that had tumbled down the social ladder with a thud by morphing into numerous small flats. Charlotte was unusual in having had the same address for fifteen years amidst moving-in-moving-out strangers, and accustomed to anonymity in the district, it was a surprise when she heard her name called.

"Charlotte Paxton! Amazing to see you again. It's been yonks."

Charlotte turned and saw an unknown female get out of a car: an expensive car. The woman was stylishly dressed, blonde, rake-thin, and bejewelled: more Gideon Penry's world than anyone Charlotte knew. Unfurling an umbrella that matched her blue coat, the fashion plate tiptoed on azure stiletto heels toward Charlotte, who thought how much Melanie would have adored the colour coordination.

"Oh, calamity! I've aged beyond recognition. You can't place me. I'm Nadine. You must remember me."

Indeed Charlotte did, and knew fate was switching sides when it tossed up Nadine Napier. Seven years of adult life made no difference. Charlotte still hated Nadine Napier. "You had light-brown hair."

"And the moment I was freed from school, I became Goldilocks. Pass each hour productively, as Miss Polnan used to say," laughed Nadine. "Good seeing you, Charlotte. Brings back the old days in glorious Technicolor. Wonderful to bump into a childhood friend."

Then Nadine Napier should go and bump into someone else. Sullen adolescence had returned with full-force rancour, and only the restraints of civilization held Charlotte back from punching Nadine's smirk to oblivion.

"We all missed you at the school reunion last night. Such fun to meet up once more." Nadine laughed again, employing the same exultant trill that had so often taunted her victims. "Didn't you get Gabby's email?"

"No," lied Charlotte.

"She sent it to the *Clarion*, but I bet an idle secretary just deletes your messages. Never trust people to do their jobs. A stupid surveyor didn't check the guttering when he did his measurements for my new windows, and the top three wouldn't open. They might as well have been nailed shut. I had to threaten that useless firm with the law to get their shoddy work replaced. Your secretary will be another lackadaisical incompetent."

Secretary? Nadine had plainly never worked in provincial journalism, but Charlotte could hope that her imaginary *Clarion* eminence might impress one swaggering bully, late of Farfield Manor School for Girls.

"We were disappointed that you didn't show up last night." Nadine was either deluded or suffering from amnesia. Nobody at the reunion would have given Charlotte Paxton a thought. "It was like time travel. Only minutes seemed to have gone by since we were last together. Gabby even brought her ouija board. Remember our séances in the reference library?"

"I don't think so." The school's reference library had been where Charlotte went to revise. She would have left the instant Nadine and cronies appeared, with or without ouija boards. "In fact, not at all."

"You were too incredibly hard-working, and it's paid in shoals. Look at you now!"

Oh yeah, look at Charlotte Paxton, dripping wet in sodden jacket and jeans, just off a bus, while Nadine Napier plus car exuded wealth. But Nadine always had, even in school uniform, and she was still mocking a quarry. People never changed. "You went to art college, didn't you?"

Nadine gave a would-be grimace, before her tinkling laugh yet again exasperated Charlotte. "Sadly, I was a student drop-out in my first year, so the great fashion house I meant to found didn't happen. Oh, you know me!"

Yes, Charlotte did. The other students must have outshone Nadine, who would be unable to tolerate a life in the shade. "What did you do then?"

"The usual. Marriage, divorce, second marriage with second divorce imminent. You're right to avoid the domesticity trap." Not much of a trap when Nadine was launched on escape number two, still flamboyantly rich. She could afford to sound complacent: afford it in every sense of the word.

"Well, I've got to get going before I drown," said Charlotte, to end the old-pals-chatting pretence.

"Hang on a sec. Weird coincidence that we should run into each other. I've got some stuff that might interest the *Clarion*, and now I can simply present you with a budding scoop. Wait a mo. It's in the car."

How handy. Less coincidence, thought Charlotte, than a tedious joke concocted at the school reunion. Did Farfield pupils ever grow up? Not in Charlotte's case, and she was offended by the assumption that a one-time scholarship girl should be considered so easy to dupe.

"They're jealous of your brain," Melanie's voice declared. "The school wouldn't accept them until their parents forked up thousands every term. I never had to bribe anyone. Farfield Manor wanted you."

Alas, Charlotte was realistic. A good memory, rather than intellect, had slid her through exams, and now she was a bedraggled mess next to immaculate Nadine, who produced a large brown envelope from her car.

"You'll check each page, won't you?" she said, making the question an order. "Let me know what you think. My phone number's inside."

And that phone number would be the first thing torn up, Charlotte promised herself.

Having thrust a hoax at her prey, Nadine got back into the car, mission accomplished. No more need to make believe old chums had had a joyous get-together. The sucker could be dismissed. "Great catching up, Charlotte. Call me, and we'll arrange a coffee."

"Absolutely," replied Charlotte. Absolutely not, she thought.

"Must dash. But ring me when you've gone through the documents." Then Nadine hesitated, apparently doubtful. She had always been a good actor. "It's true that journalists never reveal their source, isn't it?"

"My lips are sealed for all eternity."

So Nadine Napier planned to distance herself from any flak that might head in a patsy's direction. Cunning Nadine, hence typical Nadine, but she had underestimated Charlotte Paxton.

Then Nadine's car was hurtling down the street, as though fearsome fiends were in pursuit. Of course she would be a self-assured driver, ready to blame any unfortunate pedestrian who got in her way. No hanging around at bus stops for Nadine Napier. She probably inhabited a mansion. But Charlotte had her own realm as well, and it was just across the road: a ground-floor flat inherited from Melanie, and more valued than ancestral acres. Farfield Manor School was history, and one rain-speckled envelope could go straight into the recycling sack. Charlotte Paxton would never again be made to look a fool. Goodbye, Nadine Napier. Go to hell. And stay there.

*

Out of sight, but not out of mind.

Charlotte told herself that she was meant to be a journalist, albeit limited to reporting Council squabbles or chapel fêtes, and curiosity was fundamental to the job. Charlotte retrieved Nadine's envelope, and spread the contents over her kitchen table. Figures on page after page in neat columns, presumably the supposed accounts of a supposed company, but genuine or not, they told Charlotte nothing. Quite clearly, Nadine wanted revenge, perhaps on the soon-to-be ex-husband or even on a potential third spouse who also had had the gall to reject her. Unless it was a simple wind-up? Likely, given Charlotte's long and unpleasant acquaintanceship with Nadine Napier.

Hawk Enterprise was the name heading Nadine's documentation, and Charlotte did an internet search on her laptop as ambulance or police sirens wailed outside, disrupting the normally unheard flow of traffic.

Experts in location filming, a website announced. Avoid legal hassle with our expertise in gaining permits to film, our expertise in finding suitable accommodation, our expertise in catering for film crews. Do the creative work, and leave everything else to us.

So *Hawk Enterprise* plus its expertise did actually exist, unless Nadine had paid somebody to fake a website, and Nadine Napier would delight in pretending she was connected to the glamorous showbiz world. Classic Nadine fantasy.

Charlotte had made a sensible choice to drop rubbish paperwork into her recycling sack, and she gathered up the pages, returning them to their envelope, satisfied to trust instinct and ignore the attempt to send a hapless stooge on wild-goose chases. Farfield Manor School was categorically in the past, where Nadine Napier also belonged.

2

Gideon Penry had yet to adorn the building, when Charlotte arrived at work, so she was able to focus on her job without being hindered by a motivational pep-talk. In the days before a paper went to bed, the premises ought to be frenzied hubs of excitement, but again Polrenek had let its journalists down by remaining humdrum, and the grandly-styled newsroom was still two desks in a drab-ochre cubicle. Other staff writers were working from home, and had been ever since the Covid Pandemic revealed a first-rate Gideon-avoidance strategy.

The *Clarion*'s print edition was nearing its Saturday publication, and several online stories needed an update, but Charlotte's Council coverage must have been given an OK, notwithstanding Gideon's veiled criticism, as no handwritten invitation to visit him for a little chat in his office was on her desk. Their next little chat would end Charlotte's *Clarion* career.

"He wants me to do a series of investigative reports," said Adam Rigg.

"What about?" asked Charlotte.

"A minor detail Gideon left up to me." Months earlier, just free of college and looking half-starved despite a diet of chips and cheeseburgers, Adam would have received Gideon's command with ecstatic glee, anticipating national acclaim for his explosive reportage. He had been defeated by law-abiding Polrenek, and his leonine auburn hair was now a tame short-back-and-sides, which made him seem practically emaciated. "There's nothing to investigate in this docile place. Even cyclists refuse to ride on a pavement. OK, I'll admit it was fishy the Mayor's cousin won that Christmas-hamper raffle, but after exposing their chicanery, what's left?"

Hawk Enterprise? Charlotte, only four years Adam's senior, felt old and jaded in comparison to his dreams. "Have a dekko at Daniel Henver, our wannabe MP. Great wealth hides great crime, and so forth. No family can accumulate that much money without a scandal somewhere."

"Almost certainly, but as Henver owns this building, Conrad Penry might baulk should the *Clarion* be threatened with eviction."

"True. And à-propos threats, Gideon mentioned inviting me to one of his little chats."

Adam shook his head, aping dejection as he waved Charlotte goodbye. "Oh well, there are other jobs."

"Yep, an entire world of work exists beyond the *Clarion*. I could be employed by any superstore in the land. I was phenomenal on checkout as a student. Rivalled the speed of light as I shot items through, and my finesse at shelf-stacking is unparalleled."

"Just as well," said Adam.

"Too right." Charlotte switched on her laptop, and emails began jumping onto the screen. Most would contain details of imminent jumble sales or book fairs, but one stood out from the pack. It had been sent by Gabrielle Henver: Gabby of the ouija board and séances in a reference library. On Nadine's behalf, her crony was investigating whether or not the *Hawk-Enterprise* trap had been sprung.

Well, both Gabrielle and Nadine were going to face disappointment. Charlotte Paxton was now an adult, and able to keep them at a distance. They could contact her, but responding was Charlotte's choice, not theirs, despite the Gabrielle ploy of entitling her email TERRIBLE NEWS. Perhaps the ouija board had foretold that nail-varnish suppliers were going on strike or Gabrielle would have a bad-hair day.

Scorning childish dramatics, Charlotte opened the message, but had to read it twice before the words made sense. Then she jerked back, her chair scraping on floorboards.

"What is it?" Adam demanded, eager for gossip. "What's happening?"

"She's dead."

"Who is?"

"Someone I knew at school. But I saw her yesterday. Nadine can't be dead."

Adam hastily modified his voice to a sympathetic tone more in keeping with the circumstances. "A close friend of yours?"

"No. I hated her."

Adam was taken aback at such a departure from convention. Glossed-over *Clarion* obituaries had become his norm and, according to them, the dead were all exemplary humans. "You're in shock. I'll get you a cup of tea."

Even something far stronger than tea was unlikely to cushion Charlotte's stunned disbelief, as she re-read Gabrielle's email yet again. *Nadine killed. A mugging. Yesterday afternoon. Phone me.*

Charlotte gazed at the mobile number, but what could be said to Nadine's co-conspirator? Awkward commiserations? Lies about Nadine's kindness and empathy? Better to delete Gabrielle's message, which had doubtless been copied to all acquaintances. She would not notice Charlotte Paxton's failure to reply.

"Careful," said Adam. "It's hot."

"What is?"

"Your tea." Journalistic obligation his excuse, Adam did a quick survey of Charlotte's laptop screen, as he placed the cup beside her. "A mugging? I didn't bother with the police website when I came in. There's usually nothing on it worth the effort. Was she a local?"

"I guess so. Nadine used to live in one of those villages down the coast, but I don't know if she moved into the actual town later on."

"Yet you saw her yesterday."

"For a minute or two, that's all. We bumped into each other. I hadn't seen her in years." It was a new experience for Charlotte to find herself being cross-examined, and she thought of the many interviewees who must have wished reporters would leave them alone. But if Nadine had remained a local, Adam was doing his *Clarion* duty.

"Her surname?" If it bleeds, it leads. The pitiless newsroom axiom would be running through Adam's hopeful imagination.

"Napier at Farfield Manor, but she might be known by her husband's surname now: her second husband."

"*You* went to Farfield Manor School?" Adam was thunderstruck at so exclusive an establishment permitting lowly Charlotte Paxton to breathe its upper-crust air, and he gawped as if never before having seen her.

"Polrenek has since retrieved me," said Charlotte, unwilling to pretend sorrow at Nadine's death, even though a disturbing reminder that her generation was identical to any other. They would all inevitably perish.

Adam left Charlotte to cup-of-tea solace, and he went to study the police website on his own computer. Gabrielle's email now seemed to fill an entire laptop screen, and Charlotte deleted the message, trusting she could delete all her links to

Farfield Manor at the same time. She had a job to find, and schooldays to forget.

"A busy newsroom. That's what I like to see," Gideon announced from the doorway. "What's our latest?" Adam stood up, hurried across to Gideon, and began speaking in a whisper that Charlotte was supposedly unable to hear. "A fatal mugging. Schoolfriend of hers died. Minutes after they'd been talking. Charlotte's devastated."

"Oh." Gideon's normal torrent of words hit a drought. He yearned for intriguing Polrenek stories, but Charlotte's proximity to the potential crime-wave was a definite *faux pas*. "Terribly sorry, Char. I'll be in my office if you need me, Ad. Yes, terribly sorry, Char. Terribly."

"Maybe Charlotte ought to go home," suggested Adam.

"Yes, yes, Ad. Whatever Char wants. Whatever," Gideon mumbled, escaping down the corridor to seek refuge from any embarrassingly emotional scene.

"You should go home, Charlotte," said Adam. "I'll deal with the Nadine write-up. And don't worry about Gideon. He won't dare summon you for a little chat this side of the New Year."

So Nadine had done Charlotte a favour, in Adam's view. He was close to becoming a journalistic cliché.

*

She had hated Nadine, and once spent many hours silently ill-wishing a teenage tormenter. If they had not met on the previous afternoon, Nadine Napier would be no more than a name long since outgrown. But they had met, and Charlotte could see the adult Nadine: a Nadine emphatically alive and confident she would remain so.

The bus trundled away, and of course Charlotte was approaching the very place where Nadine had parked her car. Yesterday's rain was now a misty drizzle, but puddles still spread across uneven paving and the potholed road. If an afterlife did exist, Nadine's ghost would refuse to haunt such a down-market area, and within weeks, within months, Charlotte might repress the memory. Perhaps.

Arriving home, she flopped onto a chair, glad to unwind at last. Charlotte opened her laptop, and Nadine did some breaking and entering, because Adam had updated the *Clarion*'s online edition. Scanty police info meant that Nadine was consigned to a paragraph, despite the headline claiming she was from a prominent local family. Not prominent enough for Charlotte to have come across Nadine's parents during *Clarion* commitments, but they had paid Farfield Manor's exorbitant fees, and being rich certainly counted as prominent in Polrenek.

"I can't believe you'll be going to Farfield, even though it's where you belong, strictly speaking," Melanie had said, while she studied prospectus photographs of a Victorian-replica baronial hall. "This looks so like those boarding-school stories I read as a child."

Mercifully, Farfield Manor was a day school, and escaping its tentacles had been possible every afternoon, particularly as Charlotte was deemed too poverty-stricken to own a mobile phone. Had Nadine exulted in ridiculing those she considered lesser beings? Or simply thought her victims lacked a sense of humour? Maybe bullies never realized they were bullies. Unimportant. Nadine was gone.

"So get out of my head, and stay out," Charlotte ordered Nadine, but several knocks on the front door were still welcome. Even religious zealots would be preferable to memories of Farfield Manor. However, zealots usually hunted in pairs or packs, yet the young woman was alone and too fashionably dressed for a sales pitch. She might seek charity donations, but the stranger would garner no bank details from journalist Charlotte Paxton who had written a warning piece about scammers only three weeks earlier.

"Yeah?" asked Charlotte, sounding more belligerent than necessary.

The woman was perplexed, gazing at Charlotte in bewilderment. "Don't you know me? I'm Gabby: Gabrielle Henver."

Charlotte was tempted to slam the door, but civilization again prevailed. Nadine had become a blonde, and Gabrielle's brown hair was now coal-black, which made her blue eyes more noticeable, presumably the intentional effect. Like Nadine, Gabrielle had always strived to be conspicuous.

"Is Fenella with you?" Charlotte glanced down the road, her heart juddering in automatic apprehension. First Nadine Napier, then Gabrielle Henver; of course Fenella Beckett would turn up next. And so what? It was time Charlotte Paxton freed herself from the malevolent trio's power: high time

"I don't see Fenella a great deal these days. She never goes anywhere. Didn't even come to Farfield's reunion." And suddenly Gabrielle was crying, the false Fenella unimportant. "Poor Nadine. She had such trouble over those windows. Then her husband left, and today I heard he's shacked up with that sneaky Yeo kid. Do you remember Eleanor Yeo at school? She was positively plain. It's so dreadful. At least Nadine was spared that news."

"Yeah," muttered Charlotte, to dodge parading a show of distress over Nadine's fickle spouse, never mind her windows.

"Can I come in?" sobbed Gabrielle.

No! Absolutely not, screamed Charlotte: a gutless internal shriek.

But Gabrielle required no permission, and was already inside as though she had an official right of entry, perhaps to scorn cheap furniture or the heirloom deficiency. Nadine would have delighted in an opportunity to sneer. "I can't think straight. I don't know what to do."

"When in doubt, do nothing," said Charlotte, annoyed to realize she was quoting their former headmistress. Farfield Manor infiltrated her brain much too often. She had nicer memories. Why were they being stifled? "Make haste slowly, and all that."

"What? Oh, poor Nadine! And you didn't phone me." Gabrielle added a piteous little-girl whine to her voice, implying that Charlotte had inexplicably declined to rally round the friendship flag.

"I thought you'd want some space," lied Charlotte, wishing she had the nerve to remind Gabrielle of their schooldays enmity. After all, who could demean journalist Charlotte Paxton? Apart from omnipotent Gideon.

"And nobody's phoned me," wept Gabrielle. "Nobody!"

Unsurprising, in Charlotte's view. Nadine and her gang had never endeared themselves to a wider circle. Best to hustle the visit nearer its end. "What are you doing now? You went to college in London, didn't you?"

"Nadine and I shared a flat, but when she came back home, I did too. It'd be no fun there by myself." Predictable conclusion from Nadine's shadow. Gabrielle was a purposeless wreck on her own, and rapidly moving close to distraught. "I was meant to get married last summer, but —"

But fiancé fled in terror? "Sorry it didn't work out."

"Men are all cheats." A sniffing Gabrielle began to rummage through her handbag, no doubt the latest in designer bags, and she dredged up what was probably a designer packet of tissues. "By the by, those documents Nadine gave you. Are they here?"

"They're in the *Clarion* newsroom," replied Charlotte, conscious of her recycling sack under the kitchen sink. "Our investigative team will look at them. Did Nadine work in films? Do you?"

"Films?" said Gabrielle, astonished by the question. "Nadine didn't have to work. Nor do I. A trust-fund babe: that's me."

"Lucky you."

"Yeah, though Dad's threatened to disinherit me, if I don't start making an effort." Gabrielle smiled, confident that her financial future was secure. "I told him it'd be immoral to snatch wages from someone desperate for cash. He wasn't impressed, but never mind him. Tell me about your job. Do you have a separate office? Where does your investigative team work?"

"We're mostly in the newsroom," Charlotte replied, hoping Gabrielle's imagination saw a black-and-white 1940s film with raincoated reporters crying, '*Hold the front page!*'

"Must be fun, writing up the local scandals and secrets." Evidently Gabrielle had never once encountered an edition of the *Clarion*.

"Well, I could reveal what Polrenek's Mayor had for lunch the last time I interviewed him, but journalistic integrity silences me."

"No, you can't ever reveal your sources," agreed Gabrielle. "Nadine said you couldn't. Huge dump, that old orphanage. The *Clarion*'s top floor, isn't it? I thought those attics were haunted, when I was a kid. Dad took me to see the place, before it was converted into offices, and told me my great-great-great-grandpa founded the orphanage, although family legend maintains there wasn't an iota of charity in him. Dad's theory is that great-great-great-grandma just wanted a steady supply of servants."

Wannabe Parliamentarian Daniel Henver owned half Polrenek, and claimed he could trace his ancestry back centuries. Charlotte had no idea who Melanie's great-great-grandparents were, but it was very possible that her antecedents had been among that steady supply of servants.

"And now Nadine might be a ghost, like those attic orphans," sighed Gabrielle, tears again choking her. "I left flowers around the corner, but nobody else had. I couldn't get any nearer because of police tape. Nadine was telling me she'd just met you, then — then the signal broke up, and she was gone. Mobiles are useless in Polrenek. Useless!"

Gabrielle slumped her shoulders in a manner that would have been reprimanded at Farfield, but the school was no longer in Charlotte's mind. She had heard ambulance or police sirens while examining the *Hawk* accounts. A blue-light run for Nadine?

"Around the corner?" queried Charlotte. "You mean, from *here*?"

"You didn't know? I thought journalists knew everything. It happened on the Trevail site. Her car's still there. You've got to go and leave flowers as well. Then my roses won't be all by themselves. Makes it seem no one cared in the least about Nadine."

Gabrielle's tone was dismal, not accusatory, but her words made Charlotte uncomfortable. She would never buy flowers for Nadine. She would never regret not buying flowers for Nadine.

"But I mustn't keep you talking." Gabrielle gulped back tears and stood up as readily as if a tedious visit could be crossed off her list of chores. "I'm glad you can't tell the police Nadine was your source. They're so nosey. Great to be in contact. There's nothing like an old friend."

And Gabrielle Henver was nothing like an old friend to Charlotte, who could shut her front door on an unwanted guest. No need to contact the police. Charlotte knew zilch about Nadine's mugger, and the *Hawk* tease had been stymied. Unless Nadine's husband had set up *Hawk Enterprise*? Unless he got rid of his wife? Too melodramatic. Charlotte lived in Polrenek, not a crime-ridden city.

*

"I must be next in line for the chop. Gideon's spying on me," Adam remarked, surveying his desk. "Shame there aren't servants here to run round after him. He never puts a thing back."

"My desk's had the Gideon experience too," said Charlotte. "Wonder why he bothered? I won't survive his little chat. Anyhow, he can't sack you as well. Someone's got to fill Saturday's *Clarion*."

"Yeah, but I've already been cursed by fate. My girlfriend wants a trip to Italy, and thinks I should pay my share of the expenses."

"So would I. Incidentally, Gideon's also been through the wastepaper bin," added Charlotte, noting that part of its contents had fallen underneath her desk. "Whatever was he looking for? Unless you lost some copy, and checked the recycling?"

"I'm efficiency personified, so never mislay copy. And I tidied this room with my own fair hands yesterday evening. Gideon had whined that the place was a mess." Then Adam frowned as he foresaw plots against him taking shape. "Gideon will swear I ignored his edict. He *is* booting me out."

"Evidence can be removed from a crime scene," said Charlotte, gathering errant paper scraps and returning them to their bin. "Even Sherlock Holmes couldn't get you convicted now."

"You underestimate Gideon. He's —"

"Well, *I* didn't!" Rosalind Webb's voice declared from the corridor. For decades she had coerced local businesses to buy advertising space in the *Clarion*, and was a woman so self-confident that even Gideon meekly kowtowed to her. "You dare to accuse *me*? You have the gall to —?"

"No, Ros! No! Absolutely not! I never did. I never would!" Gideon was fraught. Perhaps Rosalind bore an uncanny resemblance to one of his sterner childhood nannies. "I just mentioned somebody's broken the lock on my office door."

"Then don't say it in that tone," ordered Rosalind, storming into the newsroom. Even indignation was unable to make her look anything but perfectly groomed: dark hair faultless, jacket and skirt pristine. She might be close to retirement age, but sheer energy made her seem years younger as she strode around with the vigour of an athlete. "Gideon's had the cheek to say I go about kicking in doors. But staff members are always at fault, according to Gideon Penry, so don't listen to him, either of you."

"I didn't blame anybody," Gideon protested. "I only said the lock was broken, Ros."

"Ham-fisted, that's your problem," retorted Rosalind. "Charlotte, do a puff-piece acclaiming the Lambert firm and its invaluable contribution to Polrenek prosperity. Edward Lambert's dithering over the cost of their adverts. You know what's needed."

"Lambert: the guiding light in freight transport?"

"Perfect! Thanks, Charlotte. You see, Gideon, other people actually work here, while you charge around, smashing up the premises."

"I don't. Somebody broke the lock —" But Gideon quailed beneath Rosalind's derisive gaze. "Well, locks can just break, I guess, although —"

"There is no *although*," decreed Rosalind, departing in victory.

"Well, whatever broke the lock, someone moved papers on my desk, and the filing cabinet isn't closed properly." Gaining courage, now that Rosalind had left, Gideon turned to Adam. "I don't suppose you —?"

"Suppose nothing," said Adam, amused by Gideon's drama. "When I want info, I go online. I might think of trying to hack your computer, but not your office door."

"Have any files gone AWOL?" Charlotte asked Gideon, before he could start accusing her of larceny.

"Somebody was in my office," Gideon maintained, ignoring the question. "I sensed it immediately."

"And, this morning, we knew our desks had been searched." As Charlotte would face unemployment within days, confronting Gideon was no problem. She could even pretend to be a Rosalind. "Both Adam and I realized straightaway that someone had been rummaging around the newsroom. I thought it was you."

"Me?" queried Gideon, taken aback that anybody should imagine an underling's property might hold the slightest interest for him. "Why me?"

"You're wrong, Charlotte. There *was* a prowler in here last night," said Adam, to curry favour with the boss. "Our interloper must think we've gathered incriminating evidence against him."

"A burglar would have to bypass the security codes to get in," Charlotte pointed out. "Yet it was all OK when I arrived."

"An inside job," said Gideon, awed by the prospect. "Is another tenant under your microscope?"

It seemed improbable that a Polrenek greetings-card manufacturer, travel agent, osteopath or baby-clothes designer could generate copy compelling enough to prompt such lawlessness, but Charlotte looked at Adam, who was gazing at her.

"Perhaps Kay or Gerald's onto something," Adam suggested, but with scant belief in his words.

Kay Lytton, long-time *Clarion* gardening and sports expert, had refused to return to the office after Covid-Pandemic restrictions were lifted. A second refusnik, Gerald Tate, bore the imposing title of culinary correspondent, but stories that interested them would involve recipes, soil, wielding bats or hitting balls: subjects unlikely to spark criminal activity. However, landlords could set up security systems before a tenant moved in, and presumably had an override code to facilitate evictions should rent not be forthcoming. Charlotte recalled Gabrielle's enquiry concerning the *Hawk* whereabouts, and felt certain that a mystery could be solved.

"Gideon, was there always a lock on your office door?"

"I had one put in, when I came here. Why?"

"Did you tell Daniel Henver?"

"No reason to." But Gideon sounded wary, as if an accusation of infringing the lease might follow.

Henver. Hen. Hawk. Was *Hawk Enterprise* connected to Daniel Henver? It would be typical of his arrogance to assume he could blithely search office desks without alerting their occupants, and Gideon's lock must have been an inconvenient hitch. Yet would Nadine rat on a friend's father? Definitely, in Charlotte's opinion. Had there been a random mugging? Or retaliation? Or did Charlotte watch too many TV series?

"You know what's going on," said Adam. "You know why this place was searched."

"I'm probably wrong," conceded Charlotte, "but I was given paperwork that could have been left in here overnight. The documents came from an unreliable source though, and I didn't take the info seriously."

"What paperwork?" Adam demanded. "How big a story?"

"Don't know. Just some accounts, but I couldn't spot anything wrong with them. At first glance, that is," Charlotte added, hoping to seem less cavalier when handed potential scoops. "I was planning a second look at the figures, when I had a bit more time."

"Excellent!" Gideon was impressed, and Charlotte began to hope she might keep her job after all: an unexpected helping hand from Nadine, whatever the *Hawk* had or had not done.

"Only Daniel Henver could silence the alarms, I reckon. And all Polrenekers know the guy's a crook." Adam said, eager to escape the usual *Clarion* provincial-town monotony. "As Gideon hadn't told him about those extra door locks —"

"One lock," amended Gideon. "And I bet there isn't a syllable in the lease forbidding additional security measures."

"Charlotte, can I see this paperwork?" Lauding charity quiz-nights and school concerts had plainly got to Adam, but a story that might include burglary to reclaim dubious financial records would bring zest into his life. "I understand accounts. My Dad has a shop, and I often help him sort out his tax forms."

"Then you know more than me," said Charlotte, glad to offload Nadine's malevolence and possible Henver guile. She would be too prejudiced for a cool appraisal of evidence. "Drop by my flat sometime, and you can inspect the documentation."

"I'll go home with you this afternoon," said Adam, impatient with even that delay. "Would your source talk to me?"

"No!" Her reply was more abrupt than Charlotte had intended.

"What about over the phone, quite anonymously?"

"I'm afraid not. But an unreliable source, as I said, and one doubtless keen to make trouble."

"For Daniel Henver?" Gideon had been mulling over the name, and was now less enthusiastic. "Henver's influential. I mean, he stood for Parliament in the last election, and only lost by a few thousand votes. If we upset him, it might impact our advertising revenue. He could pressurize local firms to boycott us."

Yet Penry *père* had bought the *Clarion* partly to frustrate a Henver assault on Westminster, according to Rosalind, so Conrad would not object to a campaign against the *Clarion*'s landlord. There were other offices to rent in Polrenek.

"If the accounts are from a dodgy source, it's liable to be a non-story," added Gideon, as further career protection.

"Then why was somebody in here last night?" asked Adam. "And why didn't the alarms start shrieking?"

"Because there wasn't an intruder." Gideon did his best to appear decisive, but Adam's sceptical gaze forced him to continue. "That's what Ros said, and she's never wrong. Door locks do break, and Char told us her source could be iffy. That's right, isn't it, Char?"

"I can't deny it."

"Then we're in agreement," Gideon said, relaxing. "We forget Daniel Henver. Update the *Clarion* website, Ad. And Ros wants that Lambert article, Char. Back to work, everybody."

"You're the boss," Adam declared, sitting down in a show of humble obedience. "Need any help with your redoubtable freight transporters, Charlotte?"

"No, it's fine. I'll give you my copy in an hour or so, Gideon."

"Excellent! Don't hesitate to consult me, if a snag arises." Gideon rushed away, presumably to summon a locksmith and obliterate evidence of their nighttime visitor. An editor's wish to kill a story was his staff's command, but Adam held a contrary view.

"If there's something really big hidden in those documents, we could sidestep Gideon, and sell our copy to one of the nationals," said Adam, picturing his name emblazoned in Fleet-Street bylines galore. "And it must be big, when Daniel Henver's so clearly rattled. Why else would he come here, frantic to retrieve his paperwork?"

"Assuming he did," Charlotte replied, her prime suspect Gabrielle.

"Who else could switch off the alarm system? Only Gideon's clandestine lock held our Daniel up. And Henver won't care about the residents' petition for a zebra crossing in Meriasek Street or the chapel-roof fund. No matter how ropey your source, I want to examine that paperwork."

"OK, but it could be a hoax."

"And it could be the biggest scandal in this area since — since — well, since forever," Adam claimed, rather optimistically. "If Henver's that desperate to grab back his accounts, the story must be huge. I trust you've got those documents hidden in a secure place?"

"Actually, they're among my recycling."

"Good plan! Henver wouldn't lower himself to root through the débris in your garbage bin." Adam nodded his approval of Charlotte's cunning, and she smiled.

"Recycling isn't garbage, and after Gideon's jumping-on-the-bandwagon editorials about our doomed environment, you ought to be up on the distinction."

"My girlfriend deals with saving-the-planet stuff." Adam shrugged, indifferent to a *Clarion* call to arms. "My time's important."

"The more you mention your girlfriend, the more I pity her."

"She knows I investigate topics of national consequence." Adam shrugged again, his nonchalance reminding Charlotte why her latest relationship had ended so abruptly.

"Anyway, your bin theory's wrong. Henver, or somebody, scrutinized the office recycling last night. Why else would all that paper have been tipped onto the floor?"

Adam gasped in agitation, visualising a shortcut to fame and fortune snatched from his grasp. "We've got to reach your place as soon as possible. Get a move on with that freight-transport nonsense."

*

Adam seized Nadine's envelope, and shook its contents over Charlotte's table, where the pages spread fan-like in a graceful arc. "You've checked *Hawk Enterprise*, haven't you? Does your source work there?"

"No." When Charlotte had last examined the documents, a siren went wailing down the road. Perhaps an ambulance attempt to save Nadine. A futile attempt.

"But these are just accounts," said Adam, disappointed. "Haven't you got anything else? A letter or —?"

"No, that's the entire stash. I can't fathom the significance, but you might be able to."

"Me?" Adam flipped through several more pages, shaking his head in defeat. "Why me?"

"Because your father runs a shop, and you do his tax returns. Isn't that what you told Gideon?"

"Yeah, but I had my fingers crossed at the time. Dad actually works as a bartender in the golf club. I bet Daniel Henver patronizes it. I'll ask Dad about him. Anyhow, my girlfriend's good at sums. I'll get her to check the arithmetic and whatnot."

Presumably after girlfriend had organized the recycling, thought Charlotte. "I couldn't find a link between Daniel Henver and *Hawk Enterprise* online, but I only did a quick search. If it hadn't been for Gideon's lock, I wouldn't have connected the Henvers to whatever this might be."

"A first for Gideon to help the *Clarion* uncover scoops."

"Assuming it *is* a scoop. And assuming Gideon didn't bash in his own lock, as Rosalind maintains." A passing shadow at the window made Charlotte glance up, and she added with sudden urgency, "Grab those papers and leave via the kitchen. Hurry!"

"Why? Has a jealous boyfriend arrived to wallop me?"

"Worse. Far worse." As Charlotte spoke, a knock on the front door turned her voice to a whisper, "Gabrielle Henver."

"Daniel's wife? Daughter?" Adam demanded, shoving the *Hawk* documentation back into its envelope with clumsy haste. "How do you know her? Is she your source?"

"Of course not. We were just at the same school. She put in an appearance yesterday too. It was her friend who got mugged."

"Oh, Farfield stuff," said Adam, mimicking an over-refined accent, but he was wary. "Is this a conflict of interest for you?"

"I loathed Gabrielle and her crew, but she might get suspicious if it's a Henver *Hawk* on view in my flat. Go!"

A second and louder knock at the front door sped Adam on his way, and Charlotte ran to answer her summons.

"Am I disturbing a visitor?" asked Gabrielle. "I heard voices."

"Then I should sue the double-glazing firm," replied Charlotte, trying to sound relaxed. "I had the radio on. A ponderous political discussion squandering electricity."

As on the previous visit, Gabrielle assumed that knocking on a door gave her the automatic right to enter a house, and she headed for the front room, flopping wearily onto a chair. Perhaps tired after her wakeful night searching *Clarion* offices? "The police keep on and on at me. They seem to blame Nadine for leaving her car, yet she couldn't know a mugger was hanging around, any more than she'd arrange to meet someone by the ruins of an ancient inn that practically fell down. And why Nadine phoned me doesn't matter. We were always ringing each other."

"I think you're just being asked the standard questions."

"Then they should ask them sensitively," snapped Gabrielle.

"I'm sorry. Would you like coffee or tea or something?" Was she actually feigning hospitality? Even a pretence of civility betrayed Charlotte's teenage years.

"I feel sick if I eat or drink." Traumatic events ought to hit ordinary people, not those in a gilded Henver world. Maybe it was the first time Gabrielle had encountered grief in her comfortable life. "Incidentally, that paperwork Nadine gave you. Is it still in your *Clarion* office?"

Gabrielle attempted casualness, but the tension behind her words was palpable, and Charlotte became doubly vigilant. "All out of my hands now. Our investigative team are assessing the info. At their London HQ."

"I guess your editor finally decides whether or not to print a story. What's he like?" demanded Gabrielle, forgetting her supposed indifference. "Where does he hang out?"

"Not a clue. Above my pay grade to mingle in his rarefied circle."

"Does he take stuff home to help him decide?"

Were more Gideon locks in danger of being clobbered? "We never bring copy home. Never. The *Clarion*'s lawyer would blow up."

"Who's he? Or she?"

"We use quite a few. Here, there and everywhere. Even in London," claimed Charlotte, to foil a Henver crime spree targeting Polrenek solicitors. "Depends on their field of expertise. Again, this is far above my pay grade. Why are you interested? Is it vitally important to get this story in the *Clarion*?"

"Nadine thought so. But Nadine was — well, she was Nadine. You know that."

"Yes," said Charlotte. "Yes, I do know that."

However, in death, Nadine had lost the power to overrule an acolyte, and Gabrielle was ready to defy her once-assertive friend. She wanted that paperwork back, and if breaking and entering were required, then Gabrielle Henver would break and enter.

"Why was Nadine so eager to go public with the *Hawk* story?" asked Charlotte. Particularly when Henvers might be involved, she did not add.

"I don't know a thing about it. And I'll have to sprint. My hairdresser will be waiting for me." Gabrielle stood up to leave.

No *Hawk* documents in the flat, and apparently none in Polrenek either, *ergo* stupid to waste any more of her time with Charlotte Paxton.

3

Her weekend off, and yet there was Adam at Charlotte's front door, brandishing a copy of the latest *Clarion* as cover for his visit.

"Safer than phoning you," he said, as if their mobiles were routinely hacked. "I spoke to my Dad, and you'll never guess who was with our esteemed editor last night at the golf club."

"I didn't know Gideon was a member."

"He isn't. So tell me who invited him to wine and dine there."

"Not the slightest idea," declared Charlotte, before realizing that she did know. Of course she knew. "Daniel Henver!"

"Our lock-basher himself, plus wife and daughter." Adam sauntered into the front room and sat down, pleased to note Charlotte's astonishment.

"Gabrielle was with them?"

"Your buddy in person, and being most attentive to a flattered Gideon. Either he was their stooge from day one, or Mata Hari's out to ensnare him." Adam grinned, basking in the shrewdness that had led him to an apparent conspiracy. And should Adam Rigg be the journalist who exposed corruption in Polrenek high society, even better.

"Gideon wouldn't have locked his office door, if he were part of Henver shenanigans," said Charlotte, unable to picture

Gideon deviously conniving with anyone. Gabrielle, or maybe Daniel, had decided on a new stratagem to obtain certain documents.

"Does Gideon know you gave me the *Hawk* stuff?" asked Adam.

"He doesn't, but Gabrielle thinks an investigative team has it."

"Ah, the enticing Gabrielle!" remarked Adam, smirking at what he took to be an inadvertent blunder. "So she *is* your source."

"A definite no to that. Source told her I had the *Hawk*."

"While gloating over Henver panic," concluded Adam. "Well, that explains why Daniel annihilated Gideon's lock. Can I co-lead your investigative team? It sounds brilliant. And I've already recruited my girlfriend as an assistant to decipher the *Hawk* figures."

Girlfriend would have little else to do on a Saturday, thought Charlotte. The next recycling collection was Tuesday. "Gideon isn't keen on a Henver story. He'll be even less keen, if it jeopardizes free feeds at the golf club."

"Or seduction by your friend Gabrielle."

"She's no friend of mine," Charlotte stated. "I'm facing the sack anyway, but Gideon could turn on you as well. Be careful."

"Charlotte edits my raw copy, and alters every single word, I'll whine. She's the sole culprit. But Gideon can't be planning to kick you out. Charlotte Paxton's got a byline in this week's rag. The freight-transport gush to keep penny-pinching Lamberts sweet."

"A byline! And I didn't check my laptop." In case she saw Nadine's face looking back at her. Charlotte snatched the *Clarion* Adam held up, and began a page-search for her name's moment of glory. "Rosalind must have insisted. She'll want the Lamberts to think it wasn't a puff-piece churned out by some anonymous hack."

"Who cares?" said Adam. "Bylines are bylines. When I get one, I'll have the article framed. And Rosalind won't let Gideon sack you, if your golden prose makes the Lambert crowd resume coughing up for adverts."

By Charlotte Paxton, the print read. Melanie would have sent cuttings to everyone she knew. "At least my ship will go down with the flag still flying, should Gabrielle whinge to Gideon about me. And that's a possibility, Adam. Our editor's no fearless warrior, battling for integrity and truth."

"Then we'll do it instead, and sell our sensational copy elsewhere."

Adam was right to be optimistic. If a good story did exist, and Gideon baulked, other editors might pay attention. Yet that scenario seemed to belong in somebody else's life. Occasionally, the teenage Charlotte had found herself gazing around in bewilderment at Farfield Manor's Victorian opulence as though never before having seen it, and she had felt disorientated to be trespassing amidst such splendour. Charlotte Paxton was a gate-crasher, and when the mere sight of a byline in their provincial *Clarion* thrilled her, storming the national dailies was beyond belief.

"I never did trust that source," said Charlotte.

"Let me judge for myself," Adam pleaded. "You could introduce me as a casual acquaintance, with no link to the *Clarion*."

"Impossible."

"Oh, you're too ethical for words," grumbled Adam.

If he knew that her source had been killed minutes after handing over the *Hawk* accounts, his conspiracy-fed imagination might go haywire. But would Adam be so very wrong? There was a convenient lack of CCTV around the Trevail site, yet *Whistleblower Murdered* felt too dramatic for a *Clarion* headline, and Charlotte suspected that time spent with Adam Rigg could end up mangling her brain.

*

Charlotte opened the front door, and was taken aback when an unknown man thrust a bouquet of pink roses at her.

"Just to say thanks," he declared.

"I'm afraid you've got the wrong address." He definitely had. Men Charlotte knew would consider floral tributes an unwarranted extravagance. They also wore denim jeans with anoraks, not bespoke suits, and never gave the impression of being wealthy.

"You're Charlotte Paxton, aren't you?" The smile was a Hollywood one, his pale-brown hair the only jarring note. It should have been sunshine-blond or raven-black. "I'm Edric Lambert, dispatched by my father to thank you for that brilliant account of the firm's history. My Dad's planning to send copies to all prospective customers, and we simply had to show our gratitude."

She was an impostor, accepting his bouquet under false pretences. Her article had been cobbled together with the sole aim of looting Lambert coffers via sycophantic guff, and the ruse had worked spectacularly well, going by the bouquet's size. But it ought to be awarded to Rosalind, not a money-grubbing hack. "How did you know where I live?" asked Charlotte, uncertain of the correct response.

"Like a journalist, I have my sources." Edric smiled again, this time in self-congratulation, but if he had spoken to Rosalind, her wiliness would have first secured Lambert advertising for another year.

"Well, thanks for such lovely flowers."

"A mere token. You've no idea how pleased we are with your work. Could I take you out to dinner this evening?

Additional proof of our appreciation?" Edric made his words a question, but he was handsome and in the money: therefore confident that no Polrenek woman would ever choose to spurn Edric Lambert.

"Go!" ordered Melanie's voice in Charlotte's head. "Look at him. What more do you want?"

After her speedy trawl through Lambert history, Charlotte knew that twenty-eight-year-old Edric (son of Edward and Richenda) was unmarried. Seemingly nice, affluent and single. What more did Charlotte want? Well, not a repeat of her mother's fate with an over-privileged man.

"One dinner, that's all the guy's talking about," Melanie reminded her daughter. "And you've nothing else to do this evening."

"My work's not that good," Charlotte told Edric. "I just put facts into print. The Lambert firm's been so crucial to our local economy, there are even streets named after your family."

"I think that might have less to do with acclaim, than my grandfather bribing Town Councillors," remarked Edric. "You were extremely tactful concerning him, and the entire clan breathed collective sighs of relief. I'll call for you at seven."

A statement, not a suggestion. Self-assurance differentiated his world from hers: the same demarcation Charlotte had felt at Farfield Manor. Infuriating that an overrated school made her believe she was a second-class citizen, unworthy of bouquets and dinner invitations.

"See you at seven," agreed Charlotte, as Edric began strolling away.

At least Melanie's ghost would be happy.

*

"Are you interviewing me for the *Clarion*?" Edric asked, smiling at Charlotte's attempted small talk. "Yes, I work for the company, and will take over when my Dad retires, if we're not bankrupted by the Government. Let's talk about you instead. Your job is far more interesting."

An attractive man, the scent of flowers, an expensive restaurant, and Chopin nocturnes gently accompanying muted conversation. Either she was an incomparable wordsmith, or the Lamberts expected additional grovelling from a subservient *Clarion*.

"I get to attend Council Meetings, Magistrate Courts, charity fêtes and school concerts," said Charlotte. "Not the most fascinating way to earn a wage. And our editor thinks my writing lacks clout."

"Gideon Penry's an idiot. You made freight transport sound riveting, and your local-government pieces are unparalleled." Edric was obviously another Polrenek citizen who never read the *Clarion* on a regular basis.

"I'll call on you for a reference when I'm job hunting."

"You won't have to hunt. Any newspaper would snap up someone with your talent. You could get a job anywhere."

Mockery? The lessons learnt at Farfield Manor were not forgotten that easily. Farfield Manor had no intention of allowing itself to be forgotten. "I've lived in Polrenek since birth. Staying with the *Clarion* would be OK by me."

"Are you part of its investigative team?"

Charlotte had wondered about Edric's endeavour to ingratiate himself, and now his motive was plain. Also mortifying. The dinner invitation had not been an accolade to her work or a compliment to her irresistible charm. He was Daniel Henver's representative. "I'm merely the all-purpose hack. Our investigative team concentrate on in-depth analysis."

"Who are the team?" A show of polite interest. Edric was good at imitating casualness.

"Their identities are secret," replied Charlotte, struggling to keep her voice solemn. "Complete anonymity. More freedom that way."

"I wouldn't have thought there were enough big stories in Polrenek to justify the expense," remarked Edric.

"Our team's an independent unit, and works for whichever news organisation does the hiring," Charlotte said, to spin her yarn further. "They scrutinize evidence and then validate. Or not."

It sounded plausible, and Edric was apparently swallowing the hogwash. "Like detective agencies?"

"Yes, a specialized national service. In London." With luck, the bunkum might help reduce Henver larceny and preserve Gideon's newest lock. Charlotte was pleased to be deceiving a deceiver.

"I'd no idea *Clarion* staff were so very — so very professional," Edric commented. Gabrielle might cross-examine Gideon about his famous investigative team, but if he erupted in the newsroom, Charlotte could laugh merrily and maintain she was teasing Edric. Gideon would not be amused to hear of *Clarion* advertisers taken for a ride, but as Charlotte was facing the sack, she had little to lose.

"I expect haulage firms have their support groups too," she said, and Edric sighed in regret.

"Not that spellbinding. Did you always want to be a journalist, even at — even at school?"

Even at Farfield Manor? Had he just stopped himself mentioning the school Charlotte had not named? Maybe Edric Lambert knew everything about her, courtesy of Daniel Henver.

"I didn't really have a plan." Except to escape from Farfield Manor with examination results surpassing everybody else's. "At university, I did a stint on the student rag, and a piece I wrote about Old Mother Trevail's Inn was reprinted in the

Clarion. Its previous editor took a few more history articles, and I ended up gate-crashing my way into a full-time job there."

"Must be great, not having your entire future mapped out from birth." Edric's tone held a touch of wistfulness, but he slotted so neatly into his fortunate background that any regret would be a charade to portray himself as a dashing young rebel: a rebel who had never rebelled.

"What job would you have chosen instead?" asked Charlotte, waiting to be told astronaut or beachcomber.

"I wanted to please my Dad. That's it, I'm afraid. He was the freedom fighter who lost his final battle, and surrendered unconditionally to my grandfather. I just went along, agreeing with everybody. I hate a fuss." And that might explain why Edric had obeyed his Henver command to ascertain the precise location of Charlotte Paxton's investigative team.

"Nothing wrong with peacemakers," said Charlotte, as Edric tried to look apologetic for ambition shortcomings.

"I'd never succeed as a journalist."

"Good. There's already enough competition for jobs."

"You wouldn't have to worry about competition from me." Edric smiled, once more faking ruefulness. He was content with his life and the choices made, whether for him or by him: the same complacency so often encountered at Farfield Manor. However, Charlotte could now be smug too. She was not fooled by Edric's smooth talk. All his questions had concerned the *Clarion*. Charlotte herself was of no interest to him. Melanie could forget match-making.

*

Again security-obsessed-possibly-paranoid Adam was at Charlotte's front door. Soon he would begin to suspect that her flat might he bugged.

"Wasn't there a note with those documents?" Adam demanded, glancing up and down the street before he hurried inside. "Some sort of hint what to look for?"

"You've got the entire batch, complete with original envelope," replied Charlotte. "Why? Does your girlfriend think a page has gone missing?"

"No. The sums add up, according to her." Hence his girlfriend had let him down, Adam's tone implied: let him down badly. She ought to have found a glitch out of sheer loyalty. "What did your source expect you to uncover?"

Adam glared at Charlotte, now a hostile witness withholding information, and she became defensive. "I warned you the source was unreliable. It might even be a hoax."

"Then why would Henver ransack our newsroom and trash Gideon's office? You've got to get more gen from that source."

"Perhaps we should give the paperwork to an accountant," said Charlotte.

"We can't trust anybody. Henver knows we're on his trail." Adam scowled in frustration, the whole world out to thwart him. "Ever heard of a Rufus Olsen?"

"Nope. Is he linked to the enterprising *Hawk*?"

"In charge, if you believe its website. A pseudonym, I reckon, but his company doesn't appear to be much sought-after. Three sunk-without-trace epics are proudly listed, and that's it. Not the highest-flying hawk." Adam dropped onto a chair, the impasse defeating him.

"Maybe a hawk that only exists on paper? Has it gobbled any lottery or governmental grants?"

As Charlotte spoke, Adam bounced back onto his feet, hope blossoming anew. "Of course! That's it! Henver concocted Rufus Olsen and his hawk to swindle taxpayer dosh."

"Could be," conceded Charlotte. "Although I'd say Henver's too rich to bother with handouts."

"The rich are never too rich, in their opinion," decreed Adam. "Henver wouldn't be rolling in it, if he weren't avaricious. And his family isn't exactly celebrated for benevolence."

"A great-great-grandfather founded Polrenek's one-time orphanage in the very building where we work." Yet that particular historic gem had come from Gabrielle, another unreliable source.

"I bet the orphans were a tax dodge, and great-great-grandpa Henver collected donations while starving those poor brats." Adam began to pace the room, his imagination aflame with fraud, bylines, and London editors pleading for him to join their staff. "I'll tell my girlfriend to research Government grants, particularly the pandemic ones. There were millions of crooks swindling money then."

"If the story's got legs, your girlfriend ought to have her own byline," commented Charlotte.

"Oh, she's not into things like that." Girlfriend's amateur status was dismissed by the scornful wave of an arm, as Adam continued to march around the table. "And she's got more free time than me. I'm always busy."

"Free time galore? That sounds good. What's her job?"

"She doesn't have one," said Adam. "She's a student."

"Majoring in business studies, I hope, or accountancy. Either would be handy at the moment."

"No such luck," griped Adam. "She's doing medicine. Aims at paediatrics."

Charlotte was taken aback, having pictured Adam's downtrodden girlfriend as a pathetic waif, submissive to his every whim. A future doctor preparing to deal with all manner of human trauma was an entirely different person. "Why are you making her waste whole hours on *Clarion* trivia?"

"Our work isn't trivial," Adam protested. "We could be unearthing a crime: possibly multiple crimes. We might even topple Daniel Henver's corrupt empire. Incidentally, he and his wife plus daughter were again wining and dining Gideon last night. I don't think we can trust our dazzled Gid. He'll kill the story, if we run it by him."

"There is no story yet."

A fact that Adam pooh-poohed, and Charlotte knew that he could be right. Something had galvanized the Henvers into action, and Gabrielle was attempting to captivate Gideon. She would quash any input from *Clarion* staff members, because women did not usually target Gideon Penry.

"Until you've got actual evidence of sleaze, Gideon's feasting companions are insignificant," said Charlotte. Equally unimportant was Edric Lambert. No call to tell Adam that she too had been wined and dined after a Henver directive. Whatever Nadine had sought to achieve, Gabrielle was endeavouring to outmanoeuvre an ex-friend.

*

Charlotte could find only one local Rufus Olsen. He had recently bought a house in Polrenek, but there were no explanations given on social media for the move, and no bragging self-promotion accompanied by photos of an ideal lifestyle. Yet he had been present at the occasional charity bash, and those pictures showed a fetching man in his early thirties, dark-haired and gym-toned. The people around him were also expensively dressed, also clutching champagne glasses while they sighed over warfare or famine victims: a Henver world. Perhaps Rufus had been paid by Daniel for use of his name. Perhaps Rufus himself was the *Hawk* determined to snaffle tax-payer money. Whichever, nothing seemed to link him to Gabrielle, but Nadine had presumably known Rufus, and known him well enough to gain access to his paperwork.

Charlotte then went to the *Clarion*'s online edition (pausing only to savour her byline) but Adam's paragraph about Nadine was barely updated, and the police were still appealing for doorbell or dash-cam footage. Nadine's widower, her absconding second spouse, was businessman Terence Piper, but no further details of him or his business were supplied.

Farfield Manor, two husbands, a few words in their local newspaper, and that was the end of Nadine Napier. Not much to parade after twenty-five years, and an ignominious departure for someone who had deemed herself loftily above the *hoi polloi*. That a nonentity like Charlotte Paxton should outlive Nadine might feel close to an affront in Napier circles.

*

Charlotte was strolling home, grocery bags in hand, when she came to an abrupt halt. Outside her front door stood Gideon Penry, gazing at the flat as he waited for an employee to acknowledge his arrival. Why not sack her by phone? Or had Gideon been dispatched by a Henver? Charlotte's instinct told her to retreat, but that would leave uncertainty, and she was curious.

"Hi, Gideon. No need to risk uncharted territory. You can sack me tomorrow, when I reappear in the newsroom. Or am I banished forever?"

Gideon swung around, his smile unctuous. "If I sack you, Char, Ros would throttle me. The Lamberts are now shelling out for bigger and better adverts. I just wanted to check something with you. And I was in the area."

"Yeah?" Charlotte paused, expecting enlightenment.

"It's work-related, but also a private matter." Gideon was obviously unwilling to say more until safely indoors, a possible indication that Adam's paranoia might be contagious.

Charlotte reluctantly ushered her guest inside and after dumping groceries on the kitchen cupboard, she darted back into her front room, where Gideon had sat himself down at the table, and was eyeing Charlotte's computer speculatively.
"What's the problem?"
"I gather you've got an investigative team looking at some documents, yet I've been told nothing regards all this. Are you a stringer for another paper? One of the London dailies?"
"Terrifically impressive if I were, but the *Clarion* has my total fidelity." It sounded good, even to Charlotte, and Gideon was mollified.
"I knew I could count on you, Char. Can I see the documents? Are they here?"
"In London. With specialized researchers. I did mention it to you, but as the source was unreliable, I didn't waste any more of your time on potential trivia. Leads so often fizzle out."
"But who are your investigators?" asked Gideon.
"Strict anonymity," Charlotte stated. "As usual."
"Yes, of course," Gideon agreed automatically, but he had not given up. "I'd like to take a look at what you have so far, even before any copy's filed. Did you scan the documents into this laptop?"
"I wouldn't ever leave a device lying around, if it had *Clarion* work in it," declared Charlotte, hoping her sternness rang true. "Security's vital. After all, someone broke your lock, and smashed down the door."
"Ros doesn't think so." However, Gideon was pleased with the idea of being important enough to have adversaries frantic to raid his office and purloin the contents. "Where exactly are these accounts now, Char? Have your investigators got them all?"
"Yeah, all," Charlotte said firmly. "But as soon as the paperwork's returned, plus analysis, it'll be on your desk. Then you can decide if there's a story worth chasing."

"My decision. Yes. Excellent!" Gideon stood up to leave, but hesitated before remarking with elaborate casualness, "You were at Farfield Manor, weren't you, Char? A friend of mine went there too. Did you know Gabrielle Henver?"

"Everybody knew her," replied Charlotte.

"A popular girl?" Gideon was caught between emotions. He yearned to hear sky-high praise of Gabrielle, yet would face competition for a popular woman, and Charlotte felt sorry for someone who had yet to realize he was being manipulated by Henvers.

"Gabrielle would hold séances in the school library with her ouija board," said Charlotte, dredging memory for an innocuous comment.

"She's psychic?" Gideon was dazed by so startling a revelation, very distant from the earthbound Penry viewpoint.

"I'm not sure how psychic Gabrielle is, but most teenage girls want to hear that they've got a glorious future of success and romance. She might simply have enlarged on their hopes."

"So Gabrielle doesn't actually believe in all that —" The word *rubbish* was deftly fielded by Gideon, lest Charlotte convey his scepticism to the ouija-board oracle. "Well, all that paranormal stuff."

"Haven't a clue what she believes. You'll have to ask her."

Gideon looked wary at the prospect of broaching such an *outré* topic, but the more cautious he was with Gabrielle, the better for him, in Charlotte's opinion.

*

And the less contact between Charlotte Paxton and Edric Lambert, the better for her. Evidently the Henvers wanted additional gen.

"I have to be in London until next weekend, but I'll take you out on Saturday."

"I'll be working," claimed Charlotte. Difficult to assess Edric's reaction over the phone, but he sighed in apparent disappointment, perhaps at letting Gabrielle down.

"What about Sunday?"

"It'll depend what happens on Saturday."

"That sounds intriguing. A big story?" prompted Edric.

"Sorry, but I can't discuss it," said Charlotte, as though she regularly provided the *Clarion* with earth-shattering headlines. "All a bit up-in-the-air doubtful right now."

And that might disturb the Henvers. It seemed to bother Edric at any rate. "A local story?"

"Every *Clarion* article is local," Charlotte pointed out. "As you'll already know, I'm sure. Doesn't Polrenek's entire population read the paper from front to back page each week?"

"Oh, naturally." Edric paused, for once indecisive. He must have assumed Charlotte would grab the slightest chance to see him again, and she was proud to be contrary.

"Fool!" scolded Melanie's voice.

"I'll phone on Sunday," Edric decided. "Your schedule might be more clear-cut then."

"Possibly." Definitely, if Gideon intervened. Either way, Charlotte could leave her phone switched off all weekend.

"And you're meant to be so clever," grumbled Melanie, overlooking the unfortunate consequence of her own foray into a rich man's world.

*

"Rufus Olsen," Adam proclaimed, delivering his lecture to an audience of one in Charlotte's flat. "No local connection that I can trace, yet our guy appeared fully-grown in Polrenek last year, but the Olsen business career began almost a decade ago with his own advertising agency. Then there's a second website, and the bloke's now a showbiz agent representing actors and models, which must mean Rufus bled wannabe-superstars dry."

"And the lucrative experience made him gravitate toward movie companies," Charlotte concluded.

"But he hasn't worked much in films or TV. The gent's all bluff."

A showman with nothing to show. The con artist Nadine had hoped Charlotte would destroy, while Gabrielle was shielding him. "No wonder he hangs around the richest people here."

"More like he freeloads off them," jeered Adam. "I found a few Rufus pictures online, and my Dad recognized him at once. Not a golf-club member, our Rufus, and yet Dad's often seen him there, swilling down champagne and devouring pricey food as long as the bill's covered by someone else."

"A gate-crasher," said Charlotte, amused to remember the Farfield insult mocking scholarship girls, and she warmed to Rufus Olsen, whatever his activities.

"Bet the guy has tinned soup and tap-water at home, while he dreams up the next get-rich-quick scheme," declared Adam, forgetting his own get-famous-quick-in-London goal.

"Well, at least Rufus must have a vivid imagination," Charlotte remarked. "And he's the perpetual optimist. Always a plus."

"Re: optimism. Gideon's still hanging around your chum Gabrielle. He asked me if I knew what you're currently working on, and where you store documents. Not the foggiest to both questions, I replied, but Charlotte will be back in the newsroom tomorrow."

"Gideon couldn't wait that long. He was here earlier, and wanted details of my investigative team. He also wants the *Hawk* paperwork."

"That is, Daniel Henver does. OK, I'll print a copy, and Gideon can have it. But how on earth could you afford to hire one investigator, let alone whole teams of them?" scoffed Adam. "Gideon will know you were lying."

"Gideon's never had to worry about paying bills. It won't occur to him that other people might hesitate before throwing money away."

"Maybe," Adam conceded. "But Gideon's a Henver puppet."

"Who's bewitched by Gabrielle. He won't fret over detail."

"Our Gid will wake up when she dumps him," predicted Adam.

"Yeah, but you're in the clear. Gideon regards me as the sole stasher of documents. He thinks you're from a shopkeeper family, and doesn't suspect there's an undercover Dad at the golf club, scrutinizing a Penry romance."

"True," agreed Adam, indifferent to Charlotte's potential banishment, while he could remain safely and gainfully a *Clarion* employee until London job offers began flowing in.

*

Was Gabrielle in love with Rufus? Charlotte had difficulty picturing Gabrielle Henver in love with anybody except Gabrielle Henver, which might be a left-over prejudice dating back years. Equally juvenile to imagine Gabrielle vowing never again to speak to Nadine after a quarrel. Yet, whatever the reason, they diverged when it came to Rufus Olsen. Perhaps Daniel Henver had asked Gabrielle's best friend to act as *Clarion* go-between in an attempt at separating his trust-fund daughter from a penniless charlatan.

Yet now the *Hawk* accounts had to be retrieved, and Gabrielle was surprisingly in collusion with Daniel. Could Rufus be blackmailing Henver? Hooray for gate-crashers, thought Charlotte.

4

Her days off felt close to a false memory. Charlotte was back in the *Clarion* newsroom, with six Council Meetings to attend that week, and diamond-anniversary revels looming. The decision to sack her had evidently been postponed, maybe thanks to Gabrielle's influence over editorial resolve.

"Great to see you, Char." Gideon managed to sound almost genuine, but he had sped out from his office as though her arrival triggered an emergency alarm. "Loads going on. Next Saturday's edition will be chock-a-block. Incidentally, Char, those documents we were discussing. Have you got hold of them yet?"

"Not so far," replied Charlotte, avoiding Adam's sardonic glance.

"Don't forget to give them to me the very minute they're here," said Gideon, eager to inform Gabrielle that her wish was granted. "Tell your investigative team to get a move on. Phone them now."

"OK," agreed Charlotte, picking up her mobile and preparing to mimic a call.

"Better go outside," advised Adam. "The signal's patchy in here today for some mystifying reason."

A most convenient mystery, and Charlotte stood up. "I won't be long, Gideon."

"No problem, Char. Take all the time you need." On condition that you return in minutes, reporting that courier and paperwork have been dispatched. Gideon's unspoken command was clear. However, his chance of a warm relationship with Gabrielle would end, when the *Hawk* accounts were in Henver possession. Rufus Olsen held the puppet-strings that danced Gideon.

Atlantic winds buffeting her, Charlotte stood on the Promenade, and mimed a call to the imaginary investigators. Gideon was unlikely to be watching, but still Charlotte felt under observation if only by optimistic gulls on alert to snatch chips and ice-cream cornets, even though pickings would be meagre so late in the holiday season.

What could she tell Gideon? That Hawk documents were on their way. She had no alternative. Chalk-white gulls shrieked and circled in purple clouds above ocean depths: a joyous display of liberty that scorned Charlotte's wingless captivity. She had to continue bluffing Gideon, or admit her famed investigative team was a myth. It meant Gabrielle would triumph, rather than Nadine, and Charlotte wished she could somehow stymie them both. Ally with Rufus?

"Will those accounts be here soon?" Gideon demanded, bouncing back into the newsroom when he heard Charlotte open its door.

"Later today. By courier. But it'll depend on traffic and so on, naturally."

"Naturally." Gideon was impatient but accepted the reply, lacking a personal ouija board to forewarn him that any document-handover would lead to his swift abandonment by Gabrielle. Charlotte was going to face the resultant storm, and she thought again of Polrenek gulls, apparently so free, drifting in arcs above a turbulent Atlantic: their own churlish boss.

"What's the joke, Charlotte?" asked Adam, too innocently.

"No joke. I was thinking about gulls. There are at least a hundred of them outside."

"They're definitely no joke," said Gideon. "One dropped out the sky, and snatched a white rose from my hand yesterday."

"Must have mistaken it for an ice-cream cone. Carry a bluebell or crimson tulip next time," advised Adam.

A single white rose. Gideon was an unsuspected romantic, and one hopelessly smitten by Gabrielle. The pillaging gull had had more sense. "They're a protected species," said Charlotte. "Seagulls, I mean."

"We need protection from them," Gideon stated, the memory of his lost rose still rankling.

"Gulls were on earth before humans, and they can't possibly damage the planet as much as we do," Charlotte pointed out, uncertain why she was recklessly bickering with the proprietor's son.

"Given their diet of chips, pasty and ice-cream, gulls will end up extinct long before we are," predicted Adam, whose own diet could rival that of any junk-food addicted gull.

"Char, do a piece about scavenger birds blighting Polrenek," ordered Gideon, ready to unleash a second War of the Roses. "That'll bring in a good reader response. Everybody hates gulls."

"I don't," said Charlotte. Stupid to argue, when Gideon was on the verge of sacking her. Lucky she had bid the *Clarion* farewell weeks ago in her mind.

"I could do a scary feature about killer gulls," offered Adam, to soft-soap the rose-bereft Gideon. "Babies snatched from their prams. Pensioners cowering at home. Schoolkids attacked. I'll terrify Polrenek."

"No!" Rosalind decreed from the doorway. "We're not alienating either Tourist Board or Council. Too many jobs rely on holidaymaker dosh."

Gideon might officially sit in an editorial chair, but the final word belonged to Rosalind, and Charlotte was rescued from her own foolhardiness. Better to find a shiny new job, before handing Gideon an excuse to dispense with Charlotte Paxton immediately.

"Gulls are atrocious," maintained Gideon, his feeble last stand in a battle already over. Advertising income reigned supreme.

"As far as the *Clarion*'s concerned, we have no problems in Polrenek, apart from those inflicted on us by national government. Everything here is beyond reproach, including our seagulls." Rosalind spoke decisively, and Gideon capitulated at once. The single-rose gull would never experience press intrusion in its life, while Rosalind was at the *Clarion*.

"That school chess tournament," Gideon announced, to regain a little authority. "You're covering it, Ad."

"But I never learnt to play chess," objected Adam. "I don't know the first thing about it."

"You only have to name participants, and say they're enjoying the contest," instructed Rosalind. "If Jethro takes a few dozen photos, next Saturday's *Clarion* will fly off the shelves as proud parents grab multiple copies."

"Exactly!" declared Gideon, who would doubtless claim the strategy as his own. "You can't fail with school stuff. And, Char, get Jeth to that diamond-wedding celebration. Those Carricks are a big family."

"The daughter sent in a gorgeous picture to go on our anniversaries page. You'll adore it, Charlotte," added Rosalind, smiling as she visualized yet more airborne editions flying out newsagent doors. "Bride in spidery false eyelashes and beehive hairdo that towers over the groom, who appears to have balanced a mop on his head for the occasion. I can imagine their children laughing uproariously each time that photo resurfaces. File a really long piece, Charlotte: how the couple met, where they worked, changes in Polrenek over decades, the usual flannel. It should make a double-page spread with pictures."

Gideon must have been tempted to remind all present that he, not Rosalind, was the actual editor, but his phone began to ring. Releasing it from a pocket, Gideon glanced at the caller ID, before hurrying off to seek seclusion and perhaps, if he were gullible enough to believe Adam, a less sporadic mobile signal. "Gabby, hi!" they heard Gideon say, his tone elated. He could now assure Gabrielle that the *Hawk* would soon land.

"Girlfriend?" queried Rosalind. "Gideon?"

"Gabrielle Henver," reported Adam. "Don't put money on it lasting."

Good advice, thought Charlotte. And the odds were also against her finishing the week as Gideon's employee, but with Nadine Napier as a source, Charlotte knew she ought to have left the potentially fraudulent *Hawk* in her recycling sack to vanish on collection day. Recalling Nadine sent Charlotte to her computer, but there was no police update. Presumably a mugger remained at large.

"I'd best notify Conrad before gossip does. He'll hate the idea of his son courting Daniel Henver's daughter," Rosalind was saying.

"My Dad would be over the moon if I captured an heiress," said Adam. "Do I have a chance with your school-pal, Charlotte?"

"Gabrielle Henver was no pal of mine, but she might regard you as a holiday after Gideon."

Rosalind laughed as she went back to her office, giving Charlotte the opportunity to reclaim Nadine's dodgy bequest. "Adam, I can't waffle much longer. I need the *Hawk* stuff. Or at least a copy of it. Gabrielle won't stop pressurizing Gideon."

"OK," Adam said amiably, stretching an arm under his desk for a rucksack and then rummaging through its interior. "Here you are. One iffy *Hawk*, and original envelope too."

"I didn't think you'd cooperate so easily," Charlotte admitted, glad to salvage her job, albeit temporarily.

"Why wouldn't I oblige? I haven't parted with anything except the envelope. What you've got are photocopies of photocopies. Although some figures might bear only a slight resemblance to the original numbers, but I doubt Rufus will spot a little tweaking here and there."

"Then why attempt to hoodwink the poor guy?" asked Charlotte, amused by Adam's endeavour to muddy waters that could in reality be crystal clear.

"Oh, just in case. You never know. Anyhow, I bet Rufus will simply grab a shredder the moment Gabrielle shows up. And she won't quibble, because our Gabby can now free herself from the amorous Gideon."

And vow eternal devotion to Rufus, a possible felon? Gabrielle would be wise to discard both men, but *Gabrielle* and *wisdom* were ill-matched words. Charlotte had her own worries. "What if Rufus does check we've returned the correct paperwork? He hasn't any reason to trust us."

"No reason to trust *you*," said Adam. "He isn't aware that I exist."

"Not the most reassuring of remarks, especially if Rufus tells Gabrielle to kick up a fuss with Gideon."

"Inform Rufus he's got the photocopies you were given, and add journalists don't reveal their sources," Adam replied, consequences that someone else might have to face not his problem. "But Rufus won't complain. It'd draw attention to whatever he's hiding."

"Which is?" queried Charlotte, promising herself never again to share into with Adam. "What's the horrific truth behind *Hawk Enterprise*?"

"Not sure yet," Adam conceded. "But there must be something. Why else would your source bother?"

Because the source had been born a troublemaker. "As I've said from the start, it could all be a hoax."

"A hoax that made Daniel Henver raid our newsroom, before smashing his way into Gideon's office? And why would a hoax encourage Gabrielle to aim her seductive prowess at Gideon?"

And why should Edric Lambert target Charlotte Paxton? Adam was right. A story had to lurk behind Nadine's abrupt reappearance and her equally abrupt disappearance. "After studying the *Hawk*, did your girlfriend reach any conclusion at all?"

"That our relationship needs an adjustment, but she's forever saying that," reported Adam, impervious to the irrelevant when his future might soon contain a high-flying career far from Polrenek. "She'll get over it. Or not. A useless mathematician though, as I told her. She still maintains those *Hawk* sums add up."

"Maybe they do, but they're not the figures on Rufus's Inland-Revenue form," suggested Charlotte. Revenge via tax-officer scrutiny? Had Rufus rejected Nadine for Gabrielle? "You might have the real *Hawk* paperwork: its secret accounts."

"Of course!" gasped Adam, his expression brightening with sudden inspiration. "And there's one way to learn more. I'll replace the ex-Gideon. Introduce me to Gabby. I've no objection to an older woman."

"Older women throughout the land will rejoice at your magnanimity," Charlotte commented, picturing Gabrielle's reaction to older-woman status. "No surprise your girlfriend's reassessing you."

"I've told her I might need to go undercover when investigating a lead. The next time you plan to see Gabby, tell me, and I'll show up by an amazing coincidence."

"I don't plan to see Gabrielle ever again," Charlotte vowed, glad that all recollection of her would evaporate from Henver minds after the *Hawk* soared back either to Daniel or Rufus.

"Stick close to Gideon. He'll arrange to meet Gabrielle when the paperwork's in his hand. Join them, and Gideon will have to introduce you. Treat Gabrielle to a dose of your fatal charm."

"And get sacked. I'll wait until Gabby chucks him. But I can trail our boss today, and then see if Gabby leads me straight to Rufus."

It was all so easy in Adam's view. A scoop would automatically bring him the brilliant future he craved, but Charlotte was now an older woman with no greater expectation than reporting Council decisions or the history of freight-transport companies. Even post-*Clarion*, she would apply to other local-news outlets, and think herself lucky to find a job anywhere. Older women surrender to reality.

"I'll persuade Gabby that she's being used by Rufus," said Adam. "It's true. What man would dispatch his girlfriend to coax Gideon into handing over documents?"

"You."

"We're not discussing me," retorted Adam. "What's Gabby keen on? Music? Films? Books?"

"Not an inkling. She's got a ouija board though."

"Spiritualism?" Adam looked as taken aback as Gideon had done. "She believes in all that gibberish?"

"Don't knock it. Gabrielle and her spirits might put a curse on you during the next séance. We older women can get a bit narked at times."

"Olsen's chasing money," Adam concluded, unable to credit any other motive for pursuit of weirdo Gabby. "Yeah,

Rufus plans to swindle Henver. Or marry his daughter, and skedaddle with her inheritance. Or both."

Gabrielle certainly had rotten luck when it came to men, thought Charlotte. Dumped by fiancé, and then a fortune-hunting gate-crasher orders her to seduce Gideon Penry. Could tender matters get any worse for Gabrielle? Indeed they could, if next in line turned out to be the *Clarion*'s Adam Rigg.

*

Every few minutes, Gideon found an excuse to go back into the newsroom, and ask with phony casualness, "Char, have those documents got here yet?"

`Charlotte would respond by inattentively shaking her head, as she went through reader comments about the previous Saturday's edition, until Adam grew more and more impatient.

"Give Gideon the damn paperwork, and let Gabby ditch him."

"I want Gideon to think my investigative team's London-based, and so its courier will have to travel at least three hundred miles before reaching Polrenek."

"You and your investigative team!" sneered Adam. "We're not paid enough to post a letter, never mind hire couriers to speed across the country. And I need to track Gideon to his *rendezvous* with Gabby, and then follow her to Rufus."

"OK. OK. The *Hawk* has flown in. I'll take it to Gideon now. Go skulk on the Prom, if you really intend to monitor him."

Nadine would have relished her opportunity to send provincial reporters running around in futile circles, and the situation was suddenly absurd, bearing no resemblance to Charlotte's *Clarion* world of planning disputes and Council kafuffles. Whatever Nadine's reason for revenge, Charlotte was ashamed to find herself caught up in the plot against Rufus Olsen. If he were a charlatan, Gabrielle deserved him. And Daniel Henver ought to be fleeced. Ought to face bankruptcy.

"It's here!" Gideon said jubilantly, as Charlotte approached his office doorway, *Hawk* envelope in hand. "You've checked that everything's present and correct?"

"Naturally," agreed Charlotte, giving him the envelope. "I knew my source was unreliable, and that's been proved yet again. Nobody's got a clue what it's all about. The accounts seem entirely above suspicion, and I can't think why they were passed to me. Or why someone would bash your lock to get at them."

"A coincidence. Random events, Char, with time the sole link. It's how conspiracy theories start," Gideon declared, but his mind was elsewhere. "Gabby must have been well-liked at Farfield Manor. And she's had boyfriends by the dozen, I expect."

Did Gideon hope to be told that Gabrielle was a sensitive soul, who yearned only for her one true love? Or would he prefer to hear that she had chosen him from a wide selection of candidates? Charlotte was undecided. "I didn't really know Gabrielle at school. She went around with two close friends, Nadine Napier and Fenella Beckett."

"Gabby's never mentioned them to me, Char. Though the name Nadine does ring a bell, but I can't place her."

"She was that fatal-mugging victim on the Trevail site last week. There's still a police appeal for dash-cam footage. Adam's watching the story for developments."

"That was Gabby's friend?" Gideon stared at Charlotte in disbelief, and then shook his head. "No, obviously it's a different Nadine. Gabby would have told me. And she'd be anguished."

"Some things are too painful to discuss," said Charlotte, her words awkwardly trite, but Gabrielle was playing a part for Gideon, which presumably meant that her real self shut down when they were together. Unless the grief, so plentiful in Charlotte's flat, was the performance? After all, Nadine had apparently betrayed Gabrielle by bringing Rufus Olsen to *Clarion* attention.

"But Gabby's never uttered a syllable about this Nadine," protested Gideon, ready to convict Charlotte on fake-news charges "You've made a mistake. You must have."

"No. The victim was definitely Nadine. Gabrielle emailed me."

"But Gabby will assume you'd tell me her best friend was dead. Why didn't you?" Gideon looked accusingly at Charlotte, and his expression told her to prioritize a new-job hunt. "Staff members ought to keep me in the picture at all times. Gabby might imagine I'm totally callous."

"She'll think you don't want to distress her. She'll think you're being tactfully silent." A lame suggestion, even to Charlotte's ears, and again Gideon shook his head.

"I should have been fully informed from the start."

"But when Nadine died, I didn't realize you'd met Gabrielle."

"I hadn't then."

Of course not. Gabrielle would have had no cause to beguile Gideon before the unproductive *Clarion* breaking and entering, yet Charlotte was somehow still held responsible for not alerting her boss to a death in Gabrielle's social circle. Nadine would have loved to know she was having such malign sway over Charlotte's life.

Pointless to reason with him. Gideon would do as he chose, and Charlotte had never won against Nadine. "I'll get back to work then. Quite a reader reaction to the traffic-calming measure in Fore Street."

Gideon nodded a curt dismissal, Charlotte's editor-calming measure as out of favour as the Council scheme, and she returned to her newsroom desk, feeling oddly untroubled to have hit a *Clarion* rock-bottom. Even if Charlotte's journalist career were over, nobody in the town need be unemployed for long with continual superstore and cleaning vacancies. Charlotte Paxton would survive, maybe not with an enhanced CV, but she would survive.

Gideon strode by, refusing to acknowledge her presence, and as he was in his coat with the brown envelope under one arm, Charlotte reckoned he was *en route* to Gabrielle. A quick text *Gid leaving now* was answered by Adam's *Hope no taxi*, but a spectacular car chase of toppling bins and screeching tyres seemed unlikely. Gabrielle would be waiting for Gideon in the town centre, eager to protect Rufus from whatever his *Hawk* could reveal.

"Where's Gideon?" asked Rosalind. "Conrad's on the phone. And the warpath."

"Why?" Charlotte tried to sound nonchalant, but had a childish fear that her text to Adam might have been intercepted and read by Penry *père*. "Is there a crisis?"

"Yep. Gabrielle Henver."

"That's unfortunate, as Gideon's just left to meet her. What's she done?"

"Kiboshed Conrad's chance to acquire the old cricket-club land. Daniel Henver put in a last-minute bid, which will be accepted. So the indictment against Gideon is that of blabbing Penry financial secrets to a *femme fatale*. How else could Daniel have known the amount to offer?"

"And how do you know his bid will succeed? You ought to be the reporter, not me. You're wasted in advertising," declared Charlotte. "Have you got a spy in the Planning Department?"

"A schoolfriend, but don't ask me her name. I never divulge my sources. Oh well, I'll get back to Conrad and his bad temper." Rosalind sighed in mock timidity, although Polrenek rumour held that she would have the upper hand in any dealings with Conrad Penry, and had done for years. "Gideon's switched off his mobile. A sure sign of guilt in his father's view."

"Conrad could be right," said Charlotte. Gleaning insider information would be a secondary prize for Gabrielle, but she needed to please her finance-providing Dad. At least Gideon would be unable to blame Conrad's thwarted get-richer scheme on *Clarion* staff.

"Does Gideon know he's a Henver stooge?" asked Rosalind.

"If not, he'll soon find out," Charlotte predicted.

*

"Where's Ad?" Gideon was back, soothed and bumptious after three hours in Gabrielle's company. The brown envelope had gone, along with his hostility to Charlotte. Gabrielle must have been very accommodating indeed.

"Adam? Oh, he went to interview somebody about something. Not sure what exactly. I was on the phone when he left." Safer to be vague than give details that Adam might later contradict. Let him invent his own story Adam was quite capable of concocting plausible rigmarole.

"Gideon, your father left a message asking you to phone him," Rosalind called, speeding from her room at the sound of Gideon's voice. "Apparently your mobile's switched off."

"I'll go ring him now." The attempt at breeziness did not convince. Should Conrad Penry phone his son, it was to complain, not chat, and Gideon knew it.

"Shame we can't print the real local news," Rosalind said, after their dejected editor slunk into his office. "According to the *Clarion*, all families are happy, everyone's hard-working, the dead were saints, and Councillors are incomparable. Even our MP's principled."

"That's the *Clarion* world," Charlotte agreed. "And if any reader comment doesn't belong in our cloud-cuckoo universe, we edit or delete, losing the spiciest morsels unfortunately."

"Adam read out one message that made me wonder why the sender hasn't been sectioned years ago. Where is Adam, by the way? He's another absconder not answering his mobile. I want to remind him that the School Harvest Festival happens this afternoon. They actually shelled out to advertise it: a trend I wish to encourage. Adam wasn't keen on putting in an appearance there, so I reckon he's deliberately gone dark to avoid the jollifications."

"No problem. I'll go," said Charlotte, as her own avoidance strategy was to keep Gideon at a distance until he recovered from Conrad's phone call. "The Council Meeting's scheduled for a three o'clock start, but they're never on time."

"Adam won't last at the *Clarion*, if he doesn't alter his attitude," declared Rosalind. "OK, so local trivia bores him. It bores me too. But what else can a Polrenek reporter work on?"

The crimes of Rufus Olsen. No Harvest Festival could compete.

*

Charlotte knew she had made a prudent decision to file her copy from home, when Gideon sent email after email demanding rewrites and yet more rewrites. Conrad must have been at his most acerbic, and Charlotte did another job search in-between drafts, until a fist began pounding on the front door. Adam had arrived for a consultation.

"Gabrielle didn't take the *Hawk* stuff to Rufus," Adam announced, producing a notebook to underline his diligence. "If her car hadn't got delayed by traffic lights stuck on red in Fore Street, I'd never have kept up. She went straight to Estuary Avenue. You know that area: turrets and battlements, presumably in case the occupants need to pour flaming oil down on unruly peasants. Anyhow, a woman about Gabrielle's age opened the door, and an hour or so later, Gabby left without the envelope. Rufus could have been inside, but it's not his shack. He lives along Wharf Road. Becketts inhabit the swanky abode: Luke, Beatrice and —"

"Fenella," said Charlotte. "There'll be a Vanessa too."

"You know them?" Adam demanded, head jerking up from his notes.

"I knew Fenella Beckett and her sister at school." Charlotte had certainly known ginger-haired Fenella, small and slight and as phony as saccharine. Fenella the hanger-on, ready to agree with anything Nadine or Gabrielle said and did, eager to follow their lead, desperate for attention, the eternal disciple. Fenella had barely existed without them.

"So this Fenella's yet one more Farfield-Manor heiress," Adam concluded. "I wish you'd introduce me to your trust-fund pals."

"They're not my pals, and I haven't a clue why Gabrielle took the *Hawk* to Estuary Avenue. Perhaps Fenella's been involved with Rufus, though it's a mystery why Gabrielle would run around on somebody else's behalf."

"Maybe Fenella had a manicure appointment, or another equally vital engagement, but now regrets betraying philanderer Rufus. I bet she was the *Hawk* source. I'm right, aren't I?"

"No. You're way off-target," Charlotte replied, smiling at the tortuous route Adam's mind had followed, but in a direction that might take him closer to the truth than he knew.

"Could Fenella be the Rufus go-between?" Adam wondered over-casually. "If he's mad at Gabby for giving you the *Hawk* stuff —"

"Nice try," said Charlotte. "But Gabrielle isn't a source either. Incidentally, don't aggravate Gideon. Daniel Henver put in a higher bid for some development land that Conrad regarded as his personal property, and Gabrielle's probably the temptress who got insider info from Gideon."

"So if his Dad's fuming, Gabby might be dumped."

Adam's tone was calculating, and it amused Charlotte. "Aiming to nab her on the rebound? Would it be tactless to point out that you already have a girlfriend?"

"Well, she's the one who decided to reassess our relationship, so only fair that I do a little reassessment myself. And wowing Gabrielle Henver is in the line of duty."

"Lucky Gabrielle."

"I seem to detect a slight sarcasm in your voice, but journalists often go undercover to investigate major crime stories."

"Assuming there has been a major or even minor crime. Tax fiddles happen every day." And so did quarrels. Nadine could have offended both Gabrielle and Fenella over Rufus: a gate-crasher clearly in demand.

"The headlines are practically written. I know there's something big here. I can sense it." Adam should be less derisory of ouija boards, when the future was so plainly divulged unto him. He and Gabrielle might have more in common than non-psychic Charlotte had realized.

"Whatever will or won't happen, Conrad would be euphoric if you dig up dirt on Rufus and then link the Henvers to him."

"Arrange to see Gabby," ordered Adam. "I'll turn up too. Or would Fenella be a wiser choice? She doesn't know we're onto her."

"But might get suspicious, if I materialize out the blue after avoiding her for years."

"Fenella's reaction could tell us a lot," mused Adam. "She might panic, or go running off to Rufus, or —"

"Or slam her Estuary-Avenue door in my face."

"That'll tell us we're on the right track."

Adam was so sure of himself, and so confident, that he would never understand her reluctance to meet either Fenella or Gabrielle again. They belonged in Charlotte's past, but a past still able to affect the present, even though school bullies were a minor glitch by the standards of human cruelty. Charlotte ought to have scorned them, because she had won the right to an education at Farfield Manor, while money needed to change hands before Gabrielle, Fenella and Nadine could cross the overpriced threshold. It was high time Charlotte began to liberate herself: high time she became a hardened journalist.

"The *What's-On-Next-Week* page can wait. I'll doorstep Fenella in the morning, while you track down Rufus," Charlotte said, trying to feel strong and decisive. "I've got a diamond anniversary in the afternoon, but dealing with Fenella won't take all day."

Charlotte could get a foot in the door by saying she had to gather data for Nadine's obituary, and tag-along Fenella would crumble on her own. She had been a mere echo of whoever led the pack, and Charlotte could shrivel her with an icy gaze, if Fenella denied all knowledge of Rufus and his *Hawk*. Charlotte would then claim that Nadine had spoken freely, and the visit was just a courtesy call before *Clarion* headlines triggered police raids on Mr Olsen's house. Fenella would collapse, spill every bean in her possession to the new and improved Charlotte Paxton, tenacious reporter.

It was unlikely to be that simple, but Fenella would not be prepared, and the surprise element might help Charlotte glean something useful. As Adam insisted, there had to be a story. There had to be.

And probably was. An hour or so later, when Charlotte checked her emails, she was taken aback to find one from Fenella Beckett. *Hi, Charlotte. Gabby says the two of you are in touch. Come see me at home tomorrow morning at 10. It's important.*

Fenella saw no reason to specify her address. Of course everyone in town must know exactly where the Beckett family resided, and Charlotte felt distinctly cross that Fenella's assumption was correct.

*

A visit to the Beckett house, plus an imminent diamond-wedding celebration, demanded more than Charlotte's *Clarion* attire of jeans and fleece jacket. Besides, she might feel self-assured sauntering around Estuary Avenue in her best clothes, and Charlotte required all the assistance available. Hair and makeup scrupulously dapper, she caught a bus to the posh end of Polrenek Promenade, where even a boisterous Atlantic wind was subdued in deference to wealth.

"I was born to live in this area," Melanie had proclaimed one Sunday afternoon stroll down the Prom, Charlotte carrying sandwiches, her mother a thermos flask. There had been earlier mentions of ice-cream as well, but no van would ever dare tout for trade near those haughty Victorian mansions with their circular driveways and wrought-iron gates. Melanie had been stylishly petite in a pale-green dress, fair curls restrained by matching ribbon, while her cuckoo-child was visibly growing out of the blue frock still classed as Sunday wear. A random memory, at least fifteen years in the past, and yet so vivid, that for a split-second Charlotte could almost believe that spirals of time did exist simultaneously.

"If the clock does turn back, I'll refuse point blank to go to Farfield Manor," she promised herself. Yet it was a present-day advantage to understand Fenella Beckett, although deceit and overbearing tactics ought to shame the sedate child who had walked along a promenade with her mother.

"Rubbish! Your career comes first. You need to earn money, and anyone living in Estuary Avenue has all the dosh they'll ever require," declared Melanie's voice.

Her mother would have got on well with Adam, Charlotte reckoned.

They had sat on a bench to eat sandwiches and admire the horseshoe bay, glittering blue and silver. Equally glittering were the gates of a house behind them: gates that Charlotte had been convinced were made of genuine gold, the absolute last word in riches, a fairytale come true. No wonder her mother yearned to live in Estuary Avenue's enchanted realm. Years later, and the gates were still there, still gleaming in October sunshine, but the gold was merely paint, and Charlotte no longer had faith in those magical three wishes. She perched on the same bench, and knew that turning into a second Nadine Napier might be necessary to intimidate Fenella. But was the job worth it? Was any job worth acting like Nadine?

"Charlotte?"

Edric Lambert was getting out of a gold-coloured car opposite the fake-gold gates, sunlight adding golden glints to his brown hair. He crossed the road, and then flopped down in apparent exhaustion beside Charlotte on Melanie's bench. "Surely you weren't given orders to cover the story? Even Gideon Penry ought to have a modicum of empathy."

"What story?" asked Charlotte, sounding much too bland.

"You don't know." Edric slumped further back, surprising Charlotte who had thought a man so poised would never feel helpless.

"What don't I know?" Edric shook his head at the discomfit of having to explain, yet knew he was lumbered with the task. "There's no way to break this gently. She died — Fenella died last night."

"Fenella?" echoed Charlotte. "Fenella Beckett?"

"I'm sorry." Edric clutched Charlotte's hand in sympathy, but it was disbelief, not sorrow, that stunned her. "Being at school together, you'll have known Fenella better than I did."

"You're certain it was the same Fenella Beckett? I mean, her first name's unusual, but —"

"Charlotte, it was definitely Fenella. Her mother's my aunt."

Of course she was. Of course the Lambert and Beckett families were related. Edric's father was probably cousin to Daniel Henver, and the Napiers as well. Money married money, and Polrenek was a small town.

"I've just driven back from London," Edric was saying. "My mother phoned. She spent the night with Beatrice, and I'm here to take Mum home. Sorry. You don't want to hear me rambling on."

"Was Fenella sick? Did she have an accident?" ventured Charlotte, unable to equate Edric's dead cousin with an alive Fenella dispatching emails to the *Clarion*.

"She was found on the beach late yesterday evening. Drowned or a head injury or both, it seems. No, not here," Edric added hastily, as Charlotte swung around to look at the shoreline's deceptively placid water. "By our lifeboat station. *Life*boat! It sounds horribly ironic. Some drunken teenagers stumbled on her. I guess that rapidly sobered them up."

"Fenella couldn't swim."

"So I gather."

Nadine had ruled that chlorine would totally wreck skin and hair, which meant she plus followers had pretended to concentrate on tennis instead, parading the Farfield grounds like Wimbledon champions in expensive outfits with expensive rackets. Charlotte had chosen an athletics option to avoid them.

"Fenella might have fallen down those granite steps leading to the beach. It would have been quick. She probably didn't know a thing."

Edric was actually attempting to comfort her, Charlotte realized. He had no idea that she was a fraud who would never shed one tear for Fenella. Or Nadine either. Fenella and Nadine. Both connected to Rufus Olsen. Both now dead.

"Do you need a lift anywhere, Charlotte?" asked Edric, uneasy with silence. "Mum won't mind waiting. It's no problem."

"Thanks, but I'm OK." Perhaps. Perhaps not. Charlotte had to think. The *Hawk* documents might go hand-in-hand with danger. Was she in danger too? Was Adam? And yet her mother's voice fixed on an entirely different aspect of the situation.

"You're refusing lifts from a man with aunts rich enough to live in Estuary Avenue? And I thought you were clever!" Had Melanie forgotten that Edric might be in cahoots with Gabrielle Henver? Or even Daniel Henver? But how could Melanie know anything? The imaginary voice came from a wish to hear it, not an omniscient spirit kingdom, Charlotte reminded herself.

"I can't leave you here alone." Edric sounded anxious, still misinterpreting her reaction to Fenella's death.

"I've got to attend a diamond-wedding anniversary, and interview the family. A walk should clear my head." After emailing Charlotte, had Fenella gone to meet Rufus and return his paperwork? Had he killed her? Had he also killed

Nadine? Charlotte's mobile began ringing, and she switched it off, incapable of speaking to Adam while Edric was with her. "Your mother will have had such a stressful night. You ought to pick her up as soon as possible."

"I want an excuse to put off seeing Fenella's parents," admitted Edric. "Awful to be thinking of myself, not them, but there's nothing I can say or do to help. Can we meet up after that diamond wedding? I'd like to be certain you're OK."

"I hadn't run into Fenella since school." The words seemed to be an apology, but it was preferable to announcing she had loathed Fenella Beckett. And only taken notice of her email because *Clarion* copy might have been garnered.

"I spoke to Fenella a few days ago. She called me, though I hadn't seen her in ages. We all have regrets." A nicely vague response, all-encompassing but noncommittal. Yet Edric might have inadvertently revealed that Fenella had sent him to Charlotte's front door with his bouquet and questions concerning an investigative team.

*

Charlotte retreated along the Promenade, only reaching for her phone when she was certain Edric would be out of sight. There were five messages from an increasingly imperious Adam. *Ring me. Phone now. Where are you? We have to meet. It's urgent.*

Adam was too eager, almost salaciously so, but their current job involved newsgathering, and Fenella's death would make front-page headlines in Polrenek. Charlotte had no right to pretend sensitivity while she accepted *Clarion* wages.

"Why weren't you answering your phone?" Adam demanded, fielding the call on its first buzz. "You won't believe this, but Rufus Olsen has agreed to an interview. He thinks I want to amass the particulars of his amazing success story. It's arranged for tomorrow."

"When did you meet him?" asked Charlotte, suspecting a trap. Rufus might be the Polrenek killer, not an inoffensive businessman hoping for local-paper obsequiousness. "Where did you see him?"

"At his place half an hour ago. He'd just arrived back from a meeting in London, and I hope you applaud my tenacity of purpose. I hung around an empty house all night to see if Fenella or Gabrielle would turn up. I'm shattered. Can you cover that steam-engine rally for me this morning? I couldn't take the noise or enthusiasm after a sleepless night. Have you talked to Fenella yet, by the way?"

"She's dead." The statement was too abrupt, following Adam's excited babble. And the bay's glossy reflection of a cobalt sky was inappropriate as well. Yet it had been sunny the afternoon Melanie died, although she never saw that summer day. Why should the skies mourn Fenella?

"What did you say?" queried Adam, assuming he had misheard. "Fenella's what?"

"She's dead."

"You're thinking of Nadine," decided Adam.

"No. Fenella's cousin told me. A possible drowning."

"You don't mean that woman found near the lifeboat station?" queried Adam, although dubiously. "I saw a police report, but they didn't give her name. You're certain it was Fenella Beckett?"

"According to her cousin, and he seemed very sure."

"Did she have the *Hawk* stuff with her? No, presumably not, as Rufus was in London last night."

Edric too. A coincidence? Obviously a coincidence. People went to London every day of the week, even Polrenekers. Charlotte wondered if she could be developing paranoia.

"Mind you, I've got no proof that Rufus *was* in London." Adam remarked, sounding hopeful. "He didn't take a suitcase from his car, or any luggage. I bet Rufus needs to establish an alibi for last night. What time did Fenella die? And why weren't you following her?"

Dereliction of duty, Adam's tone implied, and Charlotte went into automatic-apology mode. "Sorry, but Fenella emailed me about meeting her today. I reckoned she'd head straight to Rufus last night, and you'd be on guard at his house."

"We can't assume a thing in this case. Rufus will be unpredictable. And cunning. Even psychopathic for all we know. He chose a good place to dump Fenella's body. No CCTV, as long as you avoid the lifeboat's slipway. Rufus knew he could make her death look accidental there." A scenario so lucidly clear to Adam, no supporting evidence was necessary.

If Rufus had killed Nadine, Fenella's death might appear predictable, but random muggings happened, so did accidental falls and drownings. Adam's hypothesis was simply too over-the-top for an autumnal morning by calm waters, and commonsense nudged Charlotte. "We never get histrionic stories like that in the *Clarion*."

Adam sighed, impatient with Charlotte's hesitancy. "Why did Fenella want to meet you? What exactly did her email say?"

"Just that it was important, but she didn't explain why. I could see Gabrielle," Charlotte conceded. "Ask her outright what's going on."

"Yeah, she'll be thoroughly rattled by Fenella's death," said Adam, cheerful again. "Text me time and place you're seeing Gabby, but let her stew until this afternoon. I need to sleep, and you've got that steam-engine shindig now. Don't forget to send your copy to my computer, so I can file it myself, or Gideon will get suspicious."

"OK. I'm at a diamond wedding straight after the steam rally, so I'll try and contact Gabrielle this evening." An excuse to put off the unpleasant chore, and working would be a welcome distraction from Fenella's fate.

*

"I thought Adam was supposed to cover that steam rally." Jethro Kern remarked. He had been the *Clarion* photographer for decades, and copies of his masterpieces could be seen in many frames on many mantelpieces throughout the area. Jethro emphasized his artistic talent by dressing in colourful shapeless clothes, while pale hair flowed irrepressibly around a thin face. However, the bohemian image was somewhat belied by his fondness for expensive cars, and Charlotte was glad to accept a lift to their next job.

"Adam's on another story," she replied, as they drove away from the raucous gusto of a steam-powered carousel belting out *The Emperor Waltz*.

"That woman found near the lifeboat station?" said Jethro, but it was hardly psychic intuition. Adam would already have something online, and the story was going to be front-page news. "Gideon sent me to photograph police activity, but the tide had come in. Though Gideon will love my shot of crimson roses tied to the Prom railings. He goes for kitsch."

Roses left by Gabrielle, Charlotte guessed. Surely better to throw flowers into the sea that might have claimed Fenella's life, rather than leaving them on Polrenek Promenade to rot.

"I gather she was local," continued Jethro, "but the police wouldn't give me a name."

"Fenella Beckett. I met her cousin earlier, and he told me what had happened." Turning the details into just another *Clarion* piece was sensible. Also mean-spirited, but pretending to mourn Fenella would be worse.

"You know the Becketts?" queried Jethro, never having imagined that Charlotte Paxton might move in such exalted social circles. "I take photos for their happy-family cards. Poor Luke. Oh well, Christmas is fantasy time."

"I went to the same school as Fenella and her sister."

"Farfield Manor? Are you a secret millionairess?" Jethro was even more surprised, but he was busily making connections. "So you'll have known the mugging victim as well?"

"I knew her, but we weren't friends."

"The police called it a mugging when I was there, yet that doesn't really add up. I mean, why would she leave her car to visit a building site? And in stiletto heels? Bag apparently untouched, phone present, and no jewellery missing, though her attacker might have thought she was decked out in fake stuff. After all, this is Polrenek. But what do I know? I only take pictures of police officers on their knees doing fingertip searches. Daniel Henver's the guy who might have to come up with a few answers."

"Henver?" queried Charlotte, his name an instantaneous trigger.

"He owns the Trevail site. Have you forgotten your poignant prose last April about the Inn's granite doorstep having been worn down by long-gone generations and their many footfalls? I supplied an emotive picture of that very same concave doorstep."

Charlotte had tried to rabble-rouse *Clarion* readers, while pretending her copy was impartial, in an effort to persuade Polrenek's Town Council not to sell the sixteenth-century Trevail Inn. She was unsuccessful, and Daniel Henver bought it at auction. He had then demolished the building without permission, and a row over whether or not Daniel should be forced to rebuild the Inn was still rumbling on. "You're right, Jeth. It puzzles me too. Why would Nadine go there?"

"Ask Daniel Henver, who might have a job flogging any of his future *luxurious yet affordable* apartments. We cling to superstition around here, and local legend will soon claim the area's haunted."

Nadine would enjoy wielding such power, her place in town history secure. "I expected Gideon to object to my partisanship, when I wrote about the Inn being at risk in Henver hands," Charlotte admitted.

"Gideon knew it would please his father. Rosalind maintains that the sole reason Conrad acquired a newspaper was to stymie the Henver attempt to become an MP. We owe our jobs to their warfare." Jethro was amused that they should benefit from a small-town feud, and Charlotte smiled too.

"Did you know that Gideon's currently transgressing with Gabrielle Henver?"

"Yeah. Rosalind told me he'd fallen for the glamorous spy." Jethro shook his head at Gideon's gullibility, but no *Clarion* staff member had a high opinion of their editor's commonsense.

"I've heard gossip about Gabrielle and a Rufus Olsen," Charlotte remarked, trying to sound casual. "Is he one of Henver's mob?"

"Don't recognize the name. Olsen can't be local. There isn't a family in Polrenek I haven't photographed at one time or another. Is Gabrielle Henver a friend of yours?"

"Absolutely not."

"Keep it that way," Jethro advised, grinning at Charlotte's emphatic reply. "Especially if you hope to continue being paid by Conrad Penry."

5

Diamond-wedding celebrations were copy without effort. The entire family would unite in a pretence of harmony, enabling Charlotte to garner cheery anecdotes and enough reminiscences to fill several *Clarion* pages. The assignment even left Fenella outside, a neglected ghost.

*

Got a Gab meet yet?

As she hurried home, the message from Adam's phone brought Charlotte back to reality with a sickening lurch, and she ignored his text. Reaching Gabrielle would be tricky anyhow, as Charlotte had erased all Henver contact details, but the problem could be put off until *Clarion* tasks were done. She translated her diamond-anniversary notes into grammatical English, and sent the result to Gideon for him to criticize or post online. He would doubtless demand a rewrite, still peeved at her failure to enlighten him about Gabrielle's link to Nadine. Well, Charlotte could avoid repeating the same offence, and she dispatched an email to tell Gideon that the beach victim's name was Fenella Beckett, another of Gabrielle's schoolfriends.

Gideon now had a choice. He could ingratiate himself with his father by abandoning Gabrielle, or he could speed to her side. She might ultimately ditch him, but at least Gideon had a shot at standing up to Conrad.

Duty message in the ether, Charlotte churned out a summary of steam engines and their activities, aware that Adam would condemn any reference to history as boring. She had almost finished the précis when her mobile rang. Adam, thought Charlotte. She was wrong.

"*Another* friend of Gabby's, Char? *Another* death?" queried Gideon, ready to reprimand Charlotte for spreading fake news. "A name hasn't been released. Are you certain?"

"Completely. Fenella's cousin told me. Adam's gone to the scene, and he'll be able to confirm, if you don't believe me."

"Of course I trust you, Char." Yet Gideon's response was automatic, his concentration elsewhere. "Does Gabby know? Have you told her?"

"I can't. I've lost her phone number."

Gideon paused. His instinct might urge him to rush to a vulnerable Gabby, but the awkwardness of breaking bad news could be delegated. Gideon must have learnt Gabrielle's number by heart, so swiftly was it said, although his tone remained hesitant. "Let me know how Gabby is. Were she and Fenella close friends?"

"Inseparable at school."

Far too emotional a prospect for Gideon, even if he did consider himself a latter-day Romeo preparing to defy his father. Mercifully, decisions can be postponed. "Well, get back to me after you've spoken to her. I'll send flowers in the meantime."

Charlotte gazed at Gabrielle's mobile number, and then slid the note into a book. She would think of an appropriate message while finishing Adam's steam-engine chore. Condolences obviously. But how to suggest meeting

Gabrielle? Impossible! Charlotte was on strike. Gideon could sort out his own difficulties. Charlotte emailed the rally paragraphs to Adam's computer, and followed them up with a text stating that she had been unable to contact Gabrielle so far. Victory in Charlotte's personal liberation war: a conflict fated to be rather short-lived.

Somebody was knocking on her front door. Charlotte gave a cautious glance at the frosted glass, and saw a haze of coal-black shoulder-length hair above a sage-green jacket. Journalism prevailed, compelling Charlotte to send Adam a second text: *GH MY PLACE NOW.*

"I can't believe it," Gabrielle was saying, even as Charlotte opened the door. "It can't be Fenella. Just can't be her."

Because the heavens ought to oblige Gabrielle Henver? Charlotte said nothing, and was pushed aside as her visitor ran into the front room. Gabrielle knew that Fenella was dead, the crimson roses Jethro had seen tied to Promenade railings proved it, and no infantile outburst could alter facts. Charlotte looked up and down the road, as if expecting Adam to appear in response to her text sent less than a minute earlier, but handling Gabrielle might be simpler without Adam's directness.

Gulping down tears, Gabrielle sat by Charlotte's open computer and studied the screen as though desperate for anything to distract her. Had she hoped to read about Fenella? "Why are you bothering with that stupid steam rally?"

"Because I work for a local paper, and the *Clarion* is very local," said Charlotte, embarrassed at having done her job that day. Yet what had been the alternative?

"Fenella had an accident, didn't she? That's right, isn't it?" Gabrielle was seeking reassurance. She hoped to be told that Nadine's death had no link to Fenella's: the timing a piteous fluke.

"Gabrielle, are you in danger?"

"Why should you think that?" The words were jumpy, and Gabrielle began crying in earnest, perhaps to avoid further questions, even though she would realize Charlotte was still going to ask them.

Paper tissues and a glass of water helped reduce the tears, but a mirror from Gabrielle's handbag was the more effective restorative. "My makeup's a mess," she wailed, foundation cream and wet-wipes joining the mirror to facilitate repairs.

"Why come here, Gabrielle, if you're unwilling to talk?"

"I thought you could tell me how Fenella died."

"I'm not sure, but it must have been quick. I gather she hit her head."

"How?" snapped Gabrielle.

"That won't be established yet."

"But you're a journalist. You must be in touch with the police. What are they saying?" Gabrielle was nervous. Did she really want an answer? Maybe, for the first time, a Henver surname offered her no security.

"I haven't spoken to the police. Gideon sent me to report a diamond-wedding anniversary."

"A wedding anniversary?" Gabrielle was disorientated. The world should grind to a halt when she was in distress. "Can't your investigative team ask the police what's going on?"

"Why don't you tell me?" suggested Charlotte. "Or talk to the police yourself?"

"And say what?" A casual tone, but Gabrielle was speaking too quickly. "I've seen enough films to know that journalists pick up loads of info they don't print."

"And I haven't printed a word about Nadine giving me the *Hawk* accounts you retrieved via Gideon. I'm guessing that Fenella was somehow mixed up in it."

"I hadn't seen her for ages until yesterday," Gabrielle stated, makeup again in peril as she fought back more tears.

"Yesterday! Only a few hours ago, and Fenella was Ok then. And almost happy in her way. Life can't just end without warning."

Indeed it could. Death even had the temerity to snatch a Beckett.

"Happy in her way?" echoed Charlotte. "Aren't people either happy or they're not?"

"Fenella didn't know what she felt," replied Gabrielle, hovering between nostalgia and disparagement. "You remember her. She always needed a cue. Somebody else had to laugh before Fenella realized that a joke was funny. So when I told her things would be OK, she was OK."

"Because you'd return the *Hawk* stuff?" Charlotte made her words a question, but Gabrielle avoided answering while she fine-tuned her makeup. No denial though, and Charlotte added, "Why did Nadine want me to look at those accounts? Was she aiming to help Fenella or bully her?"

"Nadine never bullied anyone ever." Gabrielle's listener could contradict that statement, but journalists have no place in the stories they uncover, and Charlotte allowed Gabrielle to bluster. "Think how kind Nadine was to Fenella at school, although we both knew she wasn't exactly the sky's brightest star. Fenella wouldn't have had any friends at all, but for Nadine letting her trail around after us."

Us? In Charlotte's judgment, Gabrielle had been a second shadow. Nadine required followers, not friends, but that was irrelevant and Gabrielle seemed too busy rewriting the past for caution. A chance to gain info. "So Nadine tried to help Fenella by contacting me, but you disagreed with her?"

"Disagreed with Nadine? Never! She was right; of course Nadine was right. Fenella turned chicken." Indignant that Charlotte should doubt the Nadine supremacy, Gabrielle glared, defying a gate-crasher to challenge her.

"Then why did you reclaim the *Hawk* accounts by casting your seductive spell over Gideon Penry?"

"Him!" Gabrielle forgot her rancour, and simpered in dismissive amusement. Gideon might wistfully recall Gabrielle Henver one day, but she was unlikely to think of him again. "Fenella got in a panic and phoned, begging me to grab the *Hawk* stuff back. I told her Nadine's plan would be spot on, but Fenella kept nagging. She shouldn't have involved us in the first place. It might be all her fault Nadine was killed."

If so, Fenella had certainly faced dire retribution, whether accidental or malign. "Rufus Olsen," said Charlotte, expecting Gabrielle to be warily defensive, even unnerved, and the lack of concern was surprising.

"What about him?"

"*Hawk Enterprise* is Rufus Olsen's firm, isn't it?"

"Guess so, but I don't have a business-type brain." Gabrielle seemed to be boasting: a façade if she had, on Daniel Henver's behalf, inveigled Gideon to reveal Conrad's bid for ex-cricket-club land.

"Did Fenella work in the Olsen headquarters?" asked Charlotte, although Fenella Beckett as industrial whistleblower was hard to imagine. "Did she photocopy his accounts?"

"Fenella!" Again an unmistakeable hint of scorn in Gabrielle's voice, despite her endeavour to mask it by a would-be affectionate smile. "Can you picture anyone employing Fenella? Lucky she had a rich father."

Gabrielle was also describing herself, but Charlotte maintained a poker face. "Then how did *Hawk* papers end up with Fenella? I'm assuming Nadine got them from her. Is that right? And if Fenella wanted the *Clarion* to have a story, why not give me the documents in person?"

"Fenella! Do something herself, when she could get a go-between!" Gabrielle smiled again, contempt now blatant.

"How did Fenella acquire the accounts?"

"Not a clue. Nadine asked her, but she wouldn't say. We thought Fenella must have been crazy over Rufus Olsen, and he dumped her, so she was hoping for a spot of revenge. Journalists at his door would worry him, and might lead to the tax people taking an interest. Nadine laughed, and said it was such a typically Fenella crime of passion: get the brute audited." Gabrielle was grinning, but then flinched. She would never share a joke with Nadine again.

"So the whole kafuffle was just Fenella yearning to spite her ex-boyfriend." Naturally. It had been a Polrenek scoop. Charlotte worked for the town's paper, not a metropolitan daily, and Polrenek experienced petty crime with petty motives. Nadine was killed by a mugger, while Fenella's death had been an accident.

"We thought it was funny, but now Nadine's dead and so is Fenella," whimpered Gabrielle. "I can't think straight. You haven't mentioned me to your investigative team, have you?"

"Journalists never name their sources. Even Gideon doesn't know about Nadine's connection to the *Hawk* paperwork, unless you've told him. Incidentally, what's Rufus Olsen like? Are you worried that he might have hurt Fenella?"

"I've never met him, but I reckon my Dad would be in an absolute frenzy if his paperwork went AWOL. Nadine said Rufus Olsen was an over-ambitious nonentity, trying to gate-crash his way to the top, and he deserved a comeuppance."

Precisely her opinion of Charlotte Paxton. Nadine had belonged in a previous century, before the peasants got uppity, which meant Rufus Olsen might be guilty of nothing more than a refusal to accept the insignificant place that Nadine Napier had ruled was his. Adam would be inconsolable to lose a passport to London, and presumably he was behind the fist now battering Charlotte's front door.

"Who's that?" Gabrielle demanded, clutching the table edge as if it had enough protective solidity to save her from an earthquake.

"Probably a *Clarion* colleague. He's due here to help me compile the next *Clarion* quiz page."

Gabrielle nodded, gulping down air in an attempt to calm herself. "Does he know about me?"

"Only that you're Gideon Penry's girlfriend. Staff members are baffled why you'd even glance in his direction."

Gabrielle managed a chuckle as Charlotte went to the front door, angry that she should feel uncomfortable because Gabrielle appeared to trust her. Yet the Henvers warranted every lie they were told.

"Hi, Adam," Charlotte announced, adding in a whisper, "You know nothing except Gideon's loopy about her."

Adam glared at the idea of being forbidden to rush inside Charlotte's flat and start an instantaneous grilling. "But if I catch her unawares, she'll give the entire game away."

"There's no story," murmured Charlotte, reverting to normal volume for Gabrielle's benefit, "I think a street-name quiz would work next week."

"Well, you can dream up the questions yourself," declared Adam, a smile replacing his scowl as he walked into the front room and saw Gabrielle.

"Hi. A new *Clarion* recruit? I hope you're less dictatorial than Charlotte. Street names would be the yawn of all yawns, wouldn't they?"

"I'm not a journalist," said Gabrielle, seemingly gratified by Adam's suggestion that she might be. "I'm just a friend of Charlotte's."

"More Gideon's," added Charlotte, recoiling from her unexpected promotion in the camaraderie stakes. "Adam, meet the famous Gabrielle."

"I'm not falling for that joke. Gideon could never attract someone so fantastic." Awe was in every syllable Adam uttered, providing Gabrielle with a welcome return to the world she understood. Adam's accent was pure Polrenek, his appearance unkempt, but the show of admiration had been suitably fawning, and Gabrielle's eyes twinkled.

"Gideon's not in my life now," she said.

"Good news for every other man in town," Adam stated.

"Guess I'm in the way here." Gabrielle fiddled with her bag, although it was plain she never felt in the way anywhere. "You and Charlotte have to work, and I left my car parked on yellow lines."

"Are you OK to drive?" asked Charlotte. "Should I call a taxi?"

"Is something wrong, Gabrielle?" Adam demanded. "Could I help? Do you need a chauffeur? No car of my own right now, but I can drive, unlike Charlotte. And it'd be a pleasure to escape her dreary quiz questions."

"I feel safer when I'm not alone," Gabrielle admitted, apparently seeking permission to be human.

"Of course you're tense," agreed Charlotte. "Anyone would be. I'll go with you to the car. Lock yourself inside, and drive straight home. You'll be there almost immediately."

"Is Gabrielle in some sort of danger?" Adam's wide-eyed shot at guilelessness was laudable, despite scarcely camouflaging his impatience to cross-examine Gabrielle. However, she only heard sympathy: solace to her shocked bewilderment. And that would reinforce Adam's faith in his precious scoop.

"I'll take Gabrielle home," he announced. "She's not in any state to drive."

The domineering tone succeeded. Gabrielle was a follower in search of another leader. "I'd be so pleased not to have to drive home. My hands just can't stop shaking and my legs are total jelly. You'll phone and let me know what's happening, won't you, Charlotte? You will keep me in the picture? It's horrible: an absolute nightmare. I keep thinking I must wake up; I've got to wake up."

"The present moment is all we have. Neither past nor future exist," Adam said, as if quoting from a personal philosophy that guided his life. He would soon urge his target to unburden herself by confiding in him, and she might even fail to remember that Adam was a journalist.

Big mistake, Gabrielle Henver, thought Charlotte.

*

Which jubilee gave Jubilee Parade its name? What was the former station between Whistle Lane and Railway Cottages known as locally? Cornelius Crescent recalls which nineteenth-century landowner? Who first lived in the eighteenth-century mansion that once stood opposite Octavia Road? Which war does Victory Hall commemorate? Who funded Polrenek's first public library?

Even as she typed questions into her laptop, Charlotte knew that Gideon would hate the quiz. Far too classroom and blackboard chalk, she could hear him say. No vim or vigour. Charlotte might argue that *Clarion* readership was largely middle-aged, and therefore distant enough from school to have become nostalgic, but it would be a waste of breath. Gideon wanted trendy trivia, despite Polrenek's steadfast refusal to show interest in fleeting pop or screen idols.

"I always said you ought to be a teacher." Melanie again, of course.

"Too late, Mum." Charlotte leaned back, frowning at her computer. Films? TV? Neither seemed likely to reach Gideon's vim-and-vigour approval rating, while any mention of sport would encroach on Kay Lytton's territory. But Kay might be persuaded to set the next quiz. And then Gerald Tate could supply kitchen-based questions. Had to be Gideon's idea, naturally, but Charlotte would lament her own ignorance of superstar footballers and celebrity chefs. That should activate Gideon's brain.

The knock on her front door would be Adam, keen to discuss Gabrielle or his theories à-propos Rufus Olsen: gatecrasher and possible assassin. A quiz about local murders? Insensitive even to think of the topic at such a time. Perhaps local mysteries? Were there any?

Charlotte was taken aback to find Edric Lambert on her threshold. He looked weary, which was not surprising after the day he must have had, and Charlotte felt awkward to re-offer standard condolences for someone she had loathed.

"I'm so sorry about Fenella. I should have said more earlier, but I couldn't grasp what had happened."

"No one can. Her father wants to know precise details, but the police aren't exactly forthcoming."

And Luke Beckett would be unaccustomed to waiting. He was also unaccustomed to situations beyond his control. The rich had no belief in accidents. Their children were not meant to die by chance.

"I'm afraid I can't tell you much," said Charlotte. "Another reporter is gathering details."

"That's OK. I promised Fenella's Dad I'd see a local journalist, but it was my excuse to escape for an hour or so. Am I disturbing you?"

"Not at all."

Edric took her words as permission to enter the flat. He might be thrown awry by Fenella's death, yet his overconfidence was unshaken. Edric assumed he would be a welcome visitor anywhere. Just as Gabrielle did. Just as

Nadine had done. Charlotte could detect Farfield Manor, even in people who never attended the school.

"Don't be daft," ordered Melanie. "With him, you wouldn't have to worry about electricity bills or council tax ever again."

"You're busy." Edric stopped abruptly, as he caught sight of Charlotte's open computer on the table.

"It's OK. I'm not working on an exposé of Council schemes to turn Fore Street into one colossal cycle lane. Give me material for next week's *Clarion* quiz, and you'll be a godsend. I can't cook up anything beyond street-name questions, and Gideon Penry will hate them."

"Why would he? Sounds the ideal quiz for a local paper." Edric sat down without glancing at the laptop screen. He had little interest in the *Clarion* or Gideon: therefore none in her except as a source. Charlotte took note, and wondered what Luke Beckett thought she might know.

"Gideon claims that historical stuff is a total bore, even though there are usually more comments each week about our heritage section than any other piece. Gideon puts it down to lacklustre reporting of councillor gobbledygook."

"No one could enliven those interminable meetings." Edric had picked up a biro, and was trying to balance it vertically despite repeated failure. He was either putting off a specific query, or wanted to share gen. Charlotte could recognize the signals an informant sent out. Polrenek Town Council leaked like a sieve.

"Every item in the *Clarion* has history behind it." An inane remark to relax her visitor. "That's my argument, but Gideon's not convinced."

"I guess you'll aim at the London newspapers eventually." Edric was still in a dither, still fiddling with the biro, but his message would soon be delivered. He might have more *Hawk* documents, or evidence of a Rufus-Fenella relationship. Whichever, Adam would be happy.

"London was my original goal," admitted Charlotte, to continue the pretence that Edric's visit was merely social. "I'm not so sure now. Polrenek's home, but if I lose the *Clarion* job, there won't be a similar one around here."

"Why would you lose your job?" asked Edric, flatteringly mystified. "Unless the papers going bankrupt?"

"I don't think so, but Conrad Penry isn't in the habit of discussing his finances with me." Charlotte was amused by Edric's sudden alert curiosity. Insider information concerning money spoke his language, and could detour him even when he was preoccupied with other matters. "Lack of funds won't be why Gideon sacks me. The *Clarion* was first printed in 1861, and that's the era where Gideon maintains I belong. He's right, in a way. My mother used to get the paper each and every Saturday, so it represents my childhood as well as the best day of any week. I resist all changes to the *Clarion*, while Gideon yearns to alter everything."

"No call to fix what isn't broken," Edric commented. Again he was no longer focusing on her, and Charlotte knew that Melanie would be disappointed if she did have awareness of her daughter's life. Edric Lambert might hear Charlotte's voice, but what she said about herself was plainly of negligible importance to him.

Sorry, Mum, but there's no future house in Estuary Avenue for me, thought Charlotte. Maybe if she stopped babbling, silence might force Edric to speak. After all, he was British.

A few minutes, and the tactic had defeated Edric. "There's rather an impasse — well, that is, the Becketts can't accept what they're being told by police officers. And my mother says they've got a point: the Becketts, not police. Sorry, I'm waffling hopelessly."

Edric waved both hands in frustration, an awkwardness he might previously not have known, and Charlotte moved him on with a question. "What are the Becketts being told?"

"Suicide, but Fenella wasn't depressed, according to her parents. Well, she'd been upset over a friend's death, but who wouldn't be? Yet the police liaison officer was talking about agoraphobia, but Fenella simply didn't go out much, and she hated parties. That was just Fenella, and she'd been like that since birth. The internet was made for her, and it's fairly common these days to work from home. Not that Fenella had a formal job, but she helped her Dad with business correspondence and so on. She was close to him, but girls often are to their fathers, aren't they?"

"No idea," said Charlotte. "My father died before I was born."

"Oh, sorry. I didn't know." Edric winced again at being caught off-guard, and added hastily, "Anyhow, the police are on about Fenella's mental frailty. OK, so she was unusual, but not ill. Merely a bit quieter than most."

"Fenella seemed happy enough at school when she was with her crowd," said Charlotte, trying to sound neutral.

"Before her Dad went to the golf club yesterday, Fenella told him that a schoolfriend would be visiting her."

Gabrielle, Charlotte reckoned: Gabrielle plus *Hawk*.

"Her mother was at home all evening, but Beatrice had the telly on, and didn't hear a guest arrive or Fenella leave the house. In fact, no one realized Fenella wasn't there, until police officers were at the front door."

"So Fenella went out with, or because of, her friend."

"Presumably. Oh no! Forgot to say 'off the record' before I began talking." Edric was disconcerted at having spilled Beckett gossip so heedlessly to a reporter, but Charlotte could reassure him.

"Anything said to a *Clarion* staff member is off the record, unless we're told it's official. The paper can't risk alienating locals."

"That's a relief." And it was, Edric's expression affirmed. A boss's son ought to be more circumspect. "The hitch is, Fenella's parents don't know who was with her yesterday night, but you were at Farfield Manor as well, so I figure you could hazard a guess."

"She had two friends at school: Nadine Napier, the woman who died, and Gabrielle Henver." Facts that many ex-Farfield pupils could supply, not betrayal of a source, but still Charlotte felt uneasy. And yet she might have done Gabrielle a favour, if Edric persevered with his assignment. He was exactly the sort of man Gabrielle would expect to meet and then marry. Correct accent. Correct background. Correct money.

"You mean Daniel Henver's daughter?" Surely a needless question in golf-club circles.

"You ought to check with Vanessa. She was still lower school when we were in the sixth form, but a sister's bound to know more about Fenella's pals than I do."

"Vanessa's been at college in London for over a year. Besides, they were never chummy. Too big an age gap. Had you met Fenella recently?"

"No. I avoided the school reunion. But I gather she didn't go either."

"A journalist will pick up rumours though. I bet you're constantly hearing stuff that never gets into the *Clarion*, but might still be important." Edric obviously believed that Charlotte could give him comprehensive and accurate replies, if she chose. Should his enquiries concentrate on Fenella's time at Farfield Manor, Edric would be right.

"A reporter is the last person anybody confides in," Charlotte pointed out. "And if someone did, it'd be off the record anyway. I couldn't tell you."

Edric paused for a moment, sensing that Charlotte would decline to budge. Different strategies were required, and he became less vague. "Have you ever met a Rufus Olsen?"

"No. Why?"

"There was an envelope addressed to him in Fenella's room. Her father opened it, and found pages of accounts from an Olsen company. It was Fenella's handwriting on the envelope, but how she got her hands on his paperwork is a mystery. Luke didn't realize Fenella knew Olsen."

"What does Olsen say?" Charlotte had imagined that Fenella went out to return the *Hawk* documentation. A film featuring midnight trysts with Rufus by the lifeboat station had run through Charlotte's head, but now her movie would need editing.

"I haven't approached Olsen." That would be an eyebrow-raising breach of etiquette, Edric's tone intimated, and Charlotte fought back a smile.

"Quite impossible, if one hasn't been introduced to the gentleman."

"Well, yes, that's an insurmountable barrier," conceded Edric, grinning. "But actually, it's trickier. How did Fenella acquire the accounts? She might have hacked into his files."

"Doesn't sound much like her. Fenella had no interest in computer studies." Or anything else taught in a classroom. Nadine had decreed that schoolwork was time-wasting drivel for nerds. "What do the police think?"

"They haven't been told. I suggested burning the *Hawk* stuff, but that would destroy proof of an Olsen link to Fenella. Yet her Dad isn't keen on alerting police to illegal activity. Not that Fenella would try to hack anyone, but mud sticks."

"Could she have dated Rufus Olsen?"

"Nobody can remember her mentioning the name, but she must have known him. Why else would Fenella zoom in on his company?"

"You said she did some work for her father," Charlotte recalled. "Do his interests overlap what Rufus Olsen does?"

"Not in any way," Edric replied, with a touch of disdain. "The Becketts were already building boats long before income tax was invented, but you'll know their history better than I do. Olsen's a fly-by-night who doubtless styles himself an entrepreneur. Whatever he does, it'll be dodgy, and Olsen might have twigged that Fenella could blow his cover."

And consequently disposed of Fenella Beckett, the woman least likely to be astute enough to spot or foil a tax scam. Gabrielle was probably right. Fenella had wanted vengeance on a fickle ex (an ex kept under wraps as he was far below Beckett expectations for their daughter) and she lost her nerve after Nadine's death. "Sorry, but I can't explain any of it to you. I never knew Fenella that well. Or her friends."

"There's one thing you could do, Charlotte, if it's not against journalistic ethics or suchlike." Edric made his words sound diffident and he hesitated, but only for show. "Yes, you might really help Fenella's parents by arranging to interview Rufus Olsen. A business profile in the *Clarion*, or similar twaddle, and he'd be too full of himself to suspect a hidden motive. You could mention Fenella halfway through the chat, as if his connection to her was no secret in Polrenek, and see how Olsen reacts."

"OK," said Charlotte.

"You will?" Edric must have assumed he would have to switch on overwhelming charm to persuade her, and Charlotte's instant compliance took him by surprise. And maybe worried Edric too. "You won't tell Olsen about the accounts Fenella managed to acquire, of course."

"Naturally not. We're off the record," Charlotte reminded him.

*

Either Daniel Henver or Conrad Penry had thrown up the oblong house Rufus Olsen called home. Sparklingly modern in contrast to a grim granite terrace opposite, it would be too flimsy to outlast the storms and centuries neighbouring properties had already endured, but Rufus was unlikely to brood on that. No doubt he aimed at riches, and a more imposing future address, perhaps even Estuary Avenue. Charlotte stood by the bus stop further down Wharf Road, and waited for Adam. Still unable to prevent herself from overreacting to a childhood of Melanie's late entrances, Charlotte was fifteen minutes early, which made Adam seem behind schedule when he arrived on time.

"Got Gabrielle to talk yet?" asked Charlotte, trying not to be snappy. Her own fault that she was chilled by an east wind.

"Gabby's upset," Adam said, as reprovingly as if Charlotte had denounced Gabrielle as phony. "I took her for a drink, and she bleated on about some pitiless ex-fiancé and the only real friends she ever had, now both dead. Not the cheeriest companion. And then Gabby interrogated me concerning the police. Did they believe Fenella had an accident, or is there a crazed murderer running around Polrenek? Gabby's frantic to know. I said I'd make enquiries, and meet her for dinner this evening. I'll have to borrow the money from my girlfriend though, unless you can assist a good cause. I told Gabby to choose our *rendezvous*, and she selected the Hotel Penloweth."

"Doesn't your girlfriend object to funding dates with other women?"

"With a source. That's who I'll be meeting," Adam retorted. "Journalists have to coddle sources, and this could be the turning point in my career. Gabby will talk. She said I was a sensitive listener."

Adam was smugly sure of himself, and Charlotte speculated how far he would go in persuading Gabrielle to reveal all. The Penloweth had rooms that could be booked, and his source was vulnerable. "Gabrielle will be on her guard the instant you mention Rufus Olsen."

"I won't have to. She'll tell me about him," predicted Adam. "And Gideon will sack you, if he thinks you're a rival for Gabrielle's affection."

"I don't care. The *Clarion*'s practically in my past."

Perhaps. Perhaps not. They began walking to the Olsen house, but Charlotte had exonerated a fellow gate-crasher of being villainous. No matter how Fenella got her hands on the *Hawk* accounts, no matter why she died, her plan had been to return his paperwork by post. So if not intending to see Rufus, Fenella might have left Estuary Avenue to visit her latest clandestine love: info possibly shared with an envious Gabrielle, who could not bear to admit that insipid Fenella had outdone her in the romance sweepstake. Typical Henver egoism. "Was Fenella murdered? What do the police say?"

"They're banking on suicide, but that doesn't acquit Olsen. If he threatened Fenella, she'd be under immense pressure. Or Olsen could have demanded the *Hawk* stuff back, and when they met, decided she knew too much, so he attacked her. Fenella had a head wound, similar to the injury that killed Nadine. Clearly his favoured MO, but a man like him is capable of anything."

"A man like what?" Charlotte enquired, immediately identifying with a belittled outsider, even though Adam's interpretation of events might have been correct. "For all we know, Olsen's computer was hacked by a business rival. He could be more victim than master criminal."

"You reckon Fenella's Dad is behind all this? Or Gabby's?" Adam did an elaborate eye-roll, pitying Charlotte's naïvety. "Olsen's nowhere near the same league as either Luke Beckett or Daniel Henver. A mere wannabe, that's our Rufus, while the others have family riches that date back at least a century or two. Any hacking would be by Rufus. But whoever our hacker is, I still reckon Gabby's caught up in the middle, if only through Fenella."

Or Nadine, who had made her unilateral decision to contact Charlotte, a choice Fenella and Gabrielle then regretted, yet none of them had had the slightest hacking skill. In their view, a minion dealt with intricacies, so the hacker must have been a person they would deem trustworthy. Charlotte tried to pin down a suitable candidate, as Adam began thumping on Rufus's front door. No one could hide from the *Clarion*, Adam's broadside proclaimed, and his forceful insistence could make Olsen defensive, even if he had nothing to conceal. Subtlety was not Adam's strong point.

The door opened, and Charlotte's already positive attitude toward Rufus Olsen was boosted by his affable smile. He was in his mid-thirties, moderately handsome, but would have melted unseen into any Polrenek crowd. Medium height, medium build, medium facial features, medium brown hair: a description that could fit multiple men in the area. There was nothing aggressive or sinister about Rufus Olsen, which must have sorely disappointed Adam.

"*Two* reporters?" said Rufus, shaking his head in wonder. "Didn't realize I was that enthralling. I'm flattered."

"You should have had three of us, but our photographer's a part-timer, and he isn't available today," Charlotte replied, to dilute the belligerence Adam was ready to unleash. "We'd like a picture to accompany the profile, if you've no objection. Our readers will be interested in your background, future ambitions, and so on. Guidance for students as well: which qualifications are useful, the best advice you were given. That sort of thing."

"But I don't run a local business."

"You live here," Charlotte pointed out. "Good enough for the *Clarion*."

"OK," said Rufus. "But why target me?"

"Because our editor told us to," claimed Charlotte.

"He thinks *Hawk Enterprise* sounds intriguing." Adam did his utmost to appear neutral, and seemed to fool Rufus.

"Your editor? You mean Gideon Penry? I didn't know he'd ever heard of me." Rufus opened his front door wider, as though the Penry surname could automatically grant access to any building.

Adam might have hoped to spot clues concerning a suspect, but Rufus Olsen's house kept his secrets. No memorabilia, photos, or everyday clutter detracted from the sense of being in a hotel room, which suggested he was either obsessively neat or beginning life anew.

"Why *Hawk*?" asked Adam, even before he sat down on a sofa that might have left the shop only hours earlier. "Why name your company after a bird of prey?"

"Why not? Had to pick something memorable, and I must have chosen well as you've remembered it," said Rufus, and his serenity made Charlotte think of Edric Lambert. Self-belief was central to both men.

"You're from the film world?" Adam's query was more accusatory than polite, and Charlotte intervened.

"Our readers would love insider showbiz gossip. Do you have any sizzlingly hot anecdotes?" As Charlotte spoke, Adam gave an irritable grunt. They were there to trap a killer, not chitchat like movie fans.

"Spill embarrassing beans, and you don't get jobs. But as I haven't met any household names, I can't supply gossip, even off the record. I've worked on three films so far, and all were low-budget. Nobody's ever heard of them, and I bet nobody ever will. You'll find the details on my website, if required." Rufus was smiling at his dearth of accomplishments: a placid man for whom muddling through would be sufficient.

"Why live here?" Adam frowned, deducing subterfuge. "Surely the main opportunities will be in London."

"Everything's online these days," Rufus replied. "It doesn't matter where I am. Besides, I can drive to London in a few hours."

"Your job must be fascinating," commented Charlotte.

"Beats unloading boxes in a warehouse," said Rufus. "That was my Saturday job before I left school."

"Do your parents work in films as well?" asked Charlotte, to divert the scepticism emanating from Adam.

"My parents? Definitely not!" Rufus laughed, but with warmth rather than ridicule. "Mum's a school secretary in Rotherhithe, while Dad's the superstore manager. They're very supportive of my career choices, as well as very baffled by them."

"Rotherhithe?" demanded Adam, pouncing on what he apparently deemed a crafty attempt to cloak the surreptitious past of Rufus Olsen. "You went to school in *Rotherhithe*?"

"At a local comp. Not quite as prestigious as Farfield Manor." Rufus glanced at Charlotte, beaming as though they were accomplices. "Now, that's a school worth having on your CV."

"I didn't tell you Charlotte would be here today," Adam stated, leaping on further proof of Rufus's Machiavellian nature.

"I've learnt to gravitate toward wealth. It's now instinctive," Rufus admitted. "That's the film world. Money first, and only then inspiration."

"A waste, gravitating in my direction," said Charlotte. "Alas, I was a penniless scholarship girl."

"Did you research all the *Clarion* staff?" Adam was startled by such diligence, even in a desperate killer.

"I never need memorize stuff. Details just stay in my head. I was talking about this profile to someone or other, who told me that a *Clarion* journalist named Charlotte Paxton had gone to Farfield Manor."

"And was Gabrielle that edifying someone or other? It seemed more probable than not. "A bad time for ex-Farfielders. Two girls I knew there have recently died."

"One very recent." Adam saw his chance, and grabbed it. "I'm covering the story, and spent yesterday at our lifeboat station, talking to witnesses and police officers."

"Witnesses?" queried Rufus. "She wasn't alone? The online reports don't mention witnesses. Did they try to save her?"

"Precise details are yet to be established," said Adam, reverting to the safety of police statements.

"I hear suicide hasn't been ruled out. So tragic, when she had her whole life ahead," Rufus sighed, gazing at Charlotte with unmerited sympathy. "Was she a close friend?"

"No. We were just in the same year."

"Fenella," stated Adam. "Fenella Beckett."

"Yes, the Beckett daughter." Rufus bowed his head, as if he saw a funeral cortège pass by. "Dreadful for her mother. For both her parents."

"You're a family friend?" Yet more words Adam managed to turn into an accusation.

"I know Luke Beckett by name. And reputation. He'll be distraught." Rufus's head again bowed at the malice of fate. An act, Adam would maintain, but it appeared genuine sadness to Charlotte.

"Do you have relatives in the area?" Adam persisted.

"Such a Polrenek question," sighed Rufus, although his tone began to recapture its cheerfulness. "Everybody asks me that. I know the town because of a girlfriend, and your relaxed lifestyle suits me. If I stay here sixty years or so, maybe by then I'll qualify as local."

"Not a chance. It'd take at least five generations," said Charlotte, her chattiness annoying Adam.

"Who's your girlfriend?" he demanded.

"Couple her name in the *Clarion* with an outsider's? Never!" Rufus was chuckling, unaware that gossip might be able to supply the info.

"She'll value your discretion," Charlotte remarked. Fenella? Gabrielle? Nadine? Possibly none of them. Possibly sidetracks leading nowhere. "How did you start in movies?"

"Through a college friend. His Dad was with the Farrenton Film Company, and I did an unpaid work-experience stint there."

"So you've never had money problems?" Adam was enquiring. "Taxes aren't a worry? Do you employ an accountant to handle your finances?"

"No, but life would be pleasanter if the Inland Revenue exempted our film industry. Still, I manage to get by. And with good broadband access, Polrenek's business future is rosy, you can assure *Clarion* readers."

"We will," Charlotte agreed hastily, before Adam could expand his prosecution. "You haven't any trouble at all, being Polrenek-based?"

"Not so far." Rufus stood to indicate time was up. "I'll have to cut short this interview, I'm afraid. Sorry, but I've an online conference looming, but we can reschedule if you need extra gen."

"Thanks for speaking to us," Charlotte said, to stifle the objection Adam was opening his mouth to bellow. "We really appreciate our opportunity to meet you. A few follow-up questions might occur to us, but we can return with our photographer."

"Press attention is always welcome," Rufus declared.

*

"Olsen won't confess to murder," Charlotte said, as she and a grumbling Adam walked back to the *Clarion* office.

"We should have gone in vigorously, not chatted like at a party, giving him time to think. And as soon as I mention tax, he boots us out. Why did you keep shutting me up?"

"Because it was simply reconnaissance," Charlotte replied. "We need proof before he can be challenged, and there are some useful leads to chase. Find the girlfriend, and check a Rotherhithe past. Look for County Court Judgments too. And if you get Gabrielle to talk, then we do an Olsen follow-up interview."

"You reckon Gabby might be the girlfriend?"

"She's a possibility." So was Fenella. Or Nadine.

"Gabby would have told me," Adam insisted. "We got quite friendly, and I asked her outright if she'd met Olsen. She said no."

"A Henver denial? Worthless! How much did you tell her?"

"Not much." Yet Adam was suddenly defensive. Had he been pumping Gabrielle for info, or she him? Did it matter? Gabrielle was no mastermind.

"Tell her you've met Olsen, and watch the reaction."

"I'm a journalist," snapped Adam. "I know how to do my job. And I know how to interrogate suspects. You were the one soft on Olsen."

"We couldn't go in forcefully without evidence." And now Charlotte was sounding too defensive.

"Olsen doesn't know we're onto him. He was expecting your type of easy questions: local-paper questions. A brisk cross-examination would have taken him completely by surprise. He'd be too dumbfounded to act innocent. You've lost us our advantage."

"But he'll agree to another interview," argued Charlotte. "And we should know more about him by then."

"So what?" Adam retorted. "Olsen's not a fool. Why would any newspaper want to profile a self-styled businessman nobody's heard of? Even the *Clarion* isn't that desperate for copy. We'll never be given another chance to confront him. You just don't understand journalism, Charlotte."

Adam was probably right.

*

Would she ever again find a decent job, after the *Clarion*? Charlotte weighed up options, as adrift as she had felt when Melanie died. A fresh start could be auspicious, but might only seem so in retrospect.

Gideon peered around the newsroom door, saw Adam, and then said, "Char, a word in my office."

The end, thought Charlotte as Adam imitated cutting his throat with one hand while waving her goodbye with the other.

"Who cares?" scoffed Melanie's voice. "The *Clarion*'s loss. You'll get a million job offers with your qualifications. Maybe in freight transport?"

It was precisely what Melanie would have said, and Charlotte relaxed as she went into Gideon's sanctuary, where he sat behind an extensive desk devoid of the clutter elsewhere on *Clarion* workspaces. Future reference in mind, Charlotte stood, pandering to Gideon's self-importance, and prepared to accept her dismissal with impressive grace.

"Char, have you talked to Gabby since — well, since Fenella?" Attempting nonchalance, Gideon opened and then shut a laptop, uncertain how to appear casual.

"Gabrielle visited my flat yesterday."

"Why didn't you phone me?" Gideon demanded. "I'd have got to your place within seconds."

"We were remembering Fenella." Therefore Gideon would have been an intruder, Charlotte was implying. Big blunder. Gideon might take offence.

"I've heard Gabby was in a pub last night. Were you there too?"

So Adam had been spotted with Gabrielle. A Polrenek inevitability. "That must have been later. No, I wasn't there." Thus abandoning the defenceless Gabrielle to a dastardly predator. Gideon's frown was an indictment. Charlotte ought to have chaperoned Gabrielle right up to the Henver front door. "Did you introduce her to Adam Rigg?"

"He turned up at my flat before Gabrielle left."

"And then took her straight to a pub? Right after they'd met?" Gideon was bewildered. Presumably he had never had such an immediate impact on any woman.

"I don't drive, so Adam volunteered to take Gabrielle home."

"Via a pub?"

"Adam was meeting his girlfriend there," decided Charlotte, wishing she had the nerve to say that Gabrielle was free to choose her own companion. "I guess Adam didn't want his girlfriend to worry about an accident, if he got delayed, and Gabrielle just went into the pub with him."

"I see." Gideon saw what? That Charlotte was spinning yarn after yarn?

"She's a medical student, Adam's girlfriend," added Charlotte, which was true, but felt like a lie. "He's devoted to her."

And that was definitely a lie.

*

"What did he say?" demanded Adam. "Are you a goner?"

"Not yet," replied Charlotte.

"He lost his nerve? Don't worry. Gideon will never get around to sacking anyone. He's a loud-mouthed coward."

Yet if Adam took Gabrielle on another pub crawl, he too might be doing a job search. "You were observed escorting the beloved Gabby into dens of iniquity."

"Gideon can't possibly imagine he ever had a chance with her," jeered Adam. "Even he's not that dim."

Adam was underestimating Gideon's imagination.

6

A reprieve for Charlotte? Gideon might have postponed sacking her because he believed she was Gabrielle's friend, but Charlotte knew she ought to regard the *Clarion* as a temporary career path that would soon reach its end. Polrenek too might be a distant memory one day, if work necessitated a move.

Charlotte found herself glancing nostalgically around the streets she passed on her bus ride home, and memories jostled each other for primacy, as if saying goodbye to the town were imminent. Even after going inside her flat, Charlotte needed several seconds to readjust when the phone rang.

"Could I ask a favour?" Uncharacteristically awkward, Edric Lambert was reluctant to continue, obliging Charlotte to take over.

"You can certainly ask, although it might rather depend on what the favour is."

"One of the more unpleasant, as favours go, considering you were at school with Fenella. Her parents want to know more than they're being told." The words came out in a rush, surprising Charlotte who had assumed nothing would faze Edric.

"I haven't worked the story, so can't tell anyone much." An excuse, and he would realize it.

"But you must talk to colleagues, and journalists spot pointers."

"A family liaison officer is the person to ask." Even though he or she still might not know about a possible hacking of Rufus Olsen's computer.

"Luke's spoken to the police. They're fudging, so now he's set on speaking to you."

"I can't enlighten him," maintained Charlotte.

"I gather you've done that interview with Rufus Olsen. We live in a gossipy town, and the guy likes to brag."

"About a mention in the local paper?" Charlotte queried. "Olsen's not difficult to please."

"We understand you can't name sources and so on, but a few minutes could really help Fenella's parents. You've no idea how much." Edric might have been promoting a charity appeal, and he seemed to imply that Charlotte had exhaustive knowledge that sheer meanness of spirit made her loath to share.

"Well, OK, although —"

"Thanks a million. You're at home? I'll pick you up in fifteen minutes." Edric was his confident self again, lordly primed to bestow rewards on an acquiescent menial. "My chauffeur service includes a restaurant meal after."

Charlotte's acceptance taken for granted, Edric ended the call, and wishing she had never written a Lambert puff-piece, Charlotte rang Adam. "What's the Beckett latest?"

"Why are you asking?" Adam enquired, suspicious that she might be trying to steal his thunder.

"Fenella's parents want to talk to me."

"The old-school network," Adam commented, angry at the ease with which Charlotte could access people who would rebuff any approach from him. "Are you interviewing them for a sob story?"

"Of course not. They aim to pump me for gen."

"And you're pumping me to supply it. OK, you can tell them the police favour a suicide theory."

"That can't be right," declared Charlotte. "Fenella thought she'd be alive the next day. I was meant to see her then. She arranged it."

"Yeah, I agree with you. That's proof Fenella was murdered, but the police say suicide isn't necessarily planned, and could follow a single moment of extreme depression. Their conclusion seems carved in stone. Fenella didn't socialize much, *ergo* mental problems. A neat deduction that closes the case, and minimizes paperwork. Anyway, if she did kill herself, Rufus Olsen drove Fenella to it. Be fun, when our front page presents the police with inconvenient evidence they've overlooked. Butter up those parents, and get whatever they know about Olsen. And don't be too forthcoming. This is our scoop."

"Assuming there is one."

Adam huffed scornfully at Charlotte's caution.

*

"Sorry to put this on you, but Mum's totally convinced that the Becketts should meet you." Edric sighed in mock resignation at being a nagged son, but he was using family pressure as an excuse. If his mother did recollect a Charlotte Paxton and her *Clarion* job, it would be because Edric had reminded his parents of freight-transport blarney.

"What are they hoping I'll say?" asked Charlotte. "Fenella's death is awful, no matter what the explanation. There's no comfort I can give."

Edric was silent, his expensive car almost equally soundless. Melanie would have adored being driven around in such opulence, and the thought gave her voice an excellent opportunity to hassle Charlotte again. "The guy's loaded. What's wrong with him?"

Nothing much. In fact Edric was perfect, but too perfect for Charlotte. She would never belong in his car or his world, just as she had never belonged at Farfield Manor. And he was using her as a source. Any reporter could spot the signs.

"I think they just want to quiz you about Rufus Olsen," Edric finally acknowledged. "You'll have gen on him, and he hadn't crossed the Beckett radar before. They can't figure out why Fenella would have a copy of his business accounts."

"That's something I can't figure out either."

"Have you garnered any hint of a connection between Olsen and Fenella?" The question was tentative. A chancer like Rufus had no place in either Beckett or Lambert realms. "What's the dirt on him? You can tell me."

"I work for the *Clarion*," said Charlotte, with exaggerated primness. "We're very respectable, and don't delve into people's private lives."

"Handier if you had a scandal-sheet job," lamented Edric, smiling. "I'd love a précis of Olsen's grubby little secrets."

It was what Adam trusted Charlotte would glean during her visit. And if Rufus Olsen had been in any way responsible for Fenella's death, or Nadine's, he deserved retribution, yet talking to the Becketts still felt like betrayal of a fellow gate-crasher. However, passing through Estuary Avenue's golden gates was a childhood fantasy come true, and Charlotte wished Melanie were with her to admire the massive oak front door that might have been looted from a castle. The jeans-and-jersey clad girl opening it was in the wrong century.

"Hello, Charlotte. You won't remember me. I was lower school when you were sixth form." At nineteen, plain ginger-haired Vanessa Beckett could string words into a coherent sentence, and no longer stared downward when she spoke.

"Actually, I do remember you," said Charlotte. "I remember you hiding in the library one sports day."

"And you didn't report me. I nearly cried with gratitude."

"I couldn't report you. I was hiding in the library myself."

A negligible episode for Vanessa to recall, but not so in Charlotte's case. She had worried that Fenella would hear of it, because Nadine specialized in making sure gate-crasher contraventions reached staff ears. Bizarre that Charlotte now found herself inside the Beckett family home, and even weirder that Fenella's sister seemingly considered them old friends.

The house was a series of showrooms, all stylishly furnished, all flawlessly decorated, and as pristine as if no one lived there. Rufus would certainly approve, and Melanie love the set-up. It was film-star territory, a film star's palace seen in the magazines she had read so avidly, and yet situated slap-bang in Polrenek. Vanessa led them through the ideal-home exhibition to a verandah overlooking the back garden. Flowerbeds and bushes surrounded a velvet lawn, presumably artificial turf as raggedy autumnal disarray could not be permitted to tarnish a luxuriant patina of wealth.

The ginger hair and slight stature inherited by both daughters came via Luke Beckett, yet the girls would have been wiser to resemble their mother. Beatrice had a delicate fair-haired beauty, defying both age and grief, that reminded Charlotte poignantly of Melanie. For the first time since Fenella's death, Charlotte's condolences were genuine.

"What do you know about Rufus Olsen?" Luke's voice was peevish, possibly to end the commiserations he had heard too many times. Or because he was accustomed to instant answers.

"So good meeting you at last, Charlotte," said Beatrice, to modify her husband's tetchiness. "Would you and Edric like something to drink?"

"Thanks, but I'm fine." Charlotte sat on a wooden bench, its back and armrest carved in vine patterns. No cheap deckchair for a Beckett. Vanessa positioned herself beside Charlotte, as if an ex-sixth-former might retain the power to deflect questions. She knows more about Fenella that her parents do, thought Charlotte.

"You must have something to drink," urged Beatrice, clearly in need of a distraction, and Charlotte found it odd to think that the diabolical Fenella could have been a loved child.

Luke was increasingly impatient with the formalities, but Edric came to Beatrice's rescue. "I'd like coffee, but Charlotte prefers tea, as do all journalists. Well, in films anyhow. Shall I forage around the kitchen and start boiling water?"

"No. Stay here, and don't let Luke bellow at Charlotte." Beatrice jumped up, glad to be busy, glad to avoid a discussion of potential reasons why her daughter was dead. Moving closer to Charlotte, Vanessa seemed to be aiming at invisibility: the nervous child she had once been suddenly reappearing.

"Well?" Luke asked, expecting Charlotte to mind-read his question.

"I don't know much about Rufus Olsen yet. *Hawk Enterprise* doesn't have a distinguished past behind it, just location management on three very low-budget films." So far, so good. Nothing Charlotte had said came as a bombshell to Luke, who would have done his own internet research. No embryonic scoop was being compromised. Adam could relax.

"Sugar? Milk?" called Beatrice from the kitchen. So she could hear them, but preferred to stay unseen: maybe fearing emotion on display.

"How could Olsen possibly work in films down here?" scoffed Luke.

"It's all online these days, I gather. And Olsen must be making some money to need tax records." Should she mention Nadine? Suggest Luke speak to Gabrielle? Adam would be furious at such a lack of discretion.

"Why did Olsen turn up here in the first place?" demanded Luke, as if they were dealing with a trespasser. "He's got no relatives in Polrenek."

"Followed a girlfriend to the area. I don't know who she is yet."

"Fenella?" Luke grimaced, doubtless picturing a fortune-hunter, although Rufus could meet far wealthier prey than Fenella in the film world.

"But you'd know of a relationship between them, wouldn't you?" However, frankness had never been a priority for Fenella or any Nadine ally, and Charlotte moved on. "She might have held the documents on behalf of a friend who planned to shop Olsen to the tax people. Revenge after being dumped by him or —"

Charlotte's voice tailed off under Luke's withering gaze, but Vanessa was accustomed to her father's irritability and she had learnt to redirect his grumpiness. "Fenella's best friend at school was Nadine Napier."

The name silenced Luke. A correlation between the two deaths was evident, and might be why Luke wanted to find out what a local journalist knew. Would it help him if he were told that the *Hawk* accounts had been given to Charlotte by Nadine? But that meant citing Gabrielle's involvement, and she was Adam's source, if only a potential one. He would insist they could help Fenella's parents more by uncovering the truth, and Charlotte dithered, but her decision was put on a backburner when Edric began speaking.

"Olsen's film job might be genuine. He contacted Dad to ask if we had a few 1950s trucks or motorbikes lying around, because of some prospective blockbuster. Olsen apparently assumes we're so transport-obsessed, no one can bear to ditch any machine on wheels."

"You've met him?" Luke demanded.

"It was just an email. We couldn't oblige Olsen, so the Lambert surname won't be glorified in screen credits."

"How's business faring, Edric?" Beatrice called from the kitchen. "Petrol prices must be a headache. Unless your vehicles are electric now?"

"What have you heard about Nadine Napier?" Luke asked Charlotte, ignoring his wife's contribution. "Is a mugger in custody yet? What clues are the police chasing?"

"There hasn't been much progress so far," Charlotte acknowledged. "Your liaison officer will have the latest update."

"She maintains the two cases aren't connected, but you know something. What is it?" Luke was bluffing, but he made Charlotte doubly ill-at-ease. Guesses would be too harsh, and she had little else.

"Dad, Charlotte's an experienced journalist," said Vanessa. "She works alongside investigators, and can't discuss any leads they're checking. When Charlotte's got watertight facts, she'll tell us."

Another person mightily impressed by the *Clarion* investigative team. *Ergo*, another person unfamiliar with her local paper. However, Charlotte had been given an excuse to appear enigmatically clued-up. "Vanessa's right. I'm sorry, but I can't quote details at present, but when there's something solid, I'll let you know before a word gets printed."

"You'll be discreet, won't you, Charlotte?" Beatrice was back on the verandah, her face piteously beseeching: an expression Melanie had often employed to get her own way, and it made Charlotte curb a smile. Odd to see your mother replicated in someone else, yet Beatrice was skilfully utilizing the exact same artifice.

"Charlotte won't print a thing bad about us," declared Vanessa. "She never told the staff when I skipped games, and once explained how to do my French prep, although she was in the library to study for her own exam. We all trusted Charlotte, which definitely wasn't the case with any other sixth-former. They'd report us like a shot."

There was warmth in Vanessa's voice, surprising Charlotte, who had assumed that all Farfield pupils held her in the same contempt as Nadine and cronies had done. However, Beatrice started to relax, certain she had won. Melanie would have felt equally safe.

"The *Clarion* is always discreet." Charlotte could speak for Gideon on that point, if not for Adam, and she continued even more graciously, "We're not in the business of embarrassing our readers."

His family's intervention had subdued Luke, a blusterer who could be deactivated either by wife or daughter. Charlotte had once thought the Beckett parents would be cold-hearted autocrats, which seemed to her the only explanation of Fenella. Yet a young daughter had just reined in Luke, and Beatrice was Melanie's twin. Despite their wealth, the Becketts were closer to being average Polrenek than ogres.

"Charlotte was discretion itself when she wrote about us Lamberts," Edric declared. "And everyone in town knows my Granddad should have been prosecuted on a regular basis. You can trust Charlotte."

"I'm positive we can. Thank you, Charlotte." Beatrice again smiled Melanie's smile, secure in her power of persuasion, and she made Charlotte wonder what the Becketts feared could be learnt concerning Fenella.

Objective achieved, Estuary Avenue and its golden gates were free to dismiss Charlotte, and she followed Edric back to his car.

"Does your mother look like Beatrice?" asked Charlotte.

"No, and she's spent her life regretting it."

Charlotte could sympathize. From earliest youth, she had regretted not taking after Melanie.

*

A little research in the *Clarion* archive tossed up a wedding photograph of seventeen-year-old Beatrice Fennel, in disguise as a fluffy meringue, while her late-twenties bridegroom Luke Beckett was a facsimile undertaker. Beatrice worked as a model, according to the write-up, and Luke was eminent in their local business community: the sort of fawning piffle that Charlotte herself had often produced.

"What did you get out the Becketts?" asked Adam, rushing into the newsroom as though ready to make a monumental announcement.

"They know less than we do," replied Charlotte. "I learnt zilch. Have the police said anything definite yet?"

"They're still shilly-shallying over Fenella. Head injury that might be the result of an attack, or bashing herself against rocks after a fall, but Gabby's frightened the murderer will be stalking her next. She's jumpy, and no wonder. I mean, her two buddies dead within days of each other. It'd be enough to give anyone the shakes."

"What's Gabrielle told you?"

"That remains a work in progress." However, Adam was brashly sure of himself, and he stated, "Won't be long before she confides her darkest secret to me. I'm now Gabby's best pal. We're practically soul-mates."

"Well, don't let Gideon know, or you might join a dole queue even quicker than me."

"I refuse to quake at the prospect, despite his email ordering me into the office today." And Adam was plainly untroubled. He had supreme faith in a dazzling future beyond Gideon's reach.

"I got the same email." Charlotte was also untroubled, but for a different reason. She had become accustomed to the idea of her *Clarion* career ending.

"Gideon's the past. We'll both be living and working in London before New Year's Day," predicted Adam.

Charlotte felt less optimistic, but life would be what happened to her, rather than a choice she made, and the next stage was approaching fast. They could hear Gideon puffing up the stairs, and even he seemed closer to a memory than Charlotte's present-day Lord High Executioner.

"Nice to see at least two staff members condescending to adorn the premises," Gideon remarked. "Where are the rest?"

"Avoiding a waste-of-time commute," said Adam, already installed at a national daily in his mind. "More hours to write copy and chase leads, when you work from home."

Gideon frowned at a specious argument, but he had to believe that his ideas and input greatly benefited the *Clarion*. Thinking otherwise would be to doubt himself, and no true Penry could ever do that. "A word in my office, Char. Now."

Adam did a gruesome imitation of being hanged, but Charlotte was almost glad that the blow would finally fall. She was sick of tiptoeing around Gideon, careful not to offend him, although keeping in with an ex-boss would be just as essential. After all, whatever her future held, Charlotte needed a fulsome reference.

"Close the door, Char," Gideon instructed her, failing to notice she already had. "There are going to be changes around here, but time and tide flow on regardless."

"Indeed they do." Resigning would look better than the sack on future CVs, and she might get a more effusive reference from Gideon by making the situation easier for him. "I'll be sorry to leave, obviously. I've enjoyed working at the *Clarion*, but no job lasts forever. Would a month's notice be OK? Or maybe two weeks?"

Gideon was staring at her in bemusement, and his expression told Charlotte that he had anticipated an immediate departure. References were vital, and had to say how cooperative and agreeable Charlotte Paxton was. "Straightaway will be fine. No problem."

"You can't leave, Char. Gabby would think you'd been unhappy here," Gideon protested, adding as an afterthought, "You belong at the *Clarion*, Char. It's virtually your home."

Had she backed gutless Gideon into a corner? Or had Gabrielle Henver become an extremely well-disguised blessing? Either way, it was a reprieve.

"You're the one staff member I can rely on, Char," Gideon was saying, possibly in the hope that his benevolent words would reach Gabrielle. "There will be changes. Well, change is inevitable in any workplace, as you'll appreciate. And I was wondering if you'd take on a new challenge."

"I relish challenges," said Charlotte, quoting Gideon's favourite adage. No mention of a pay rise though, she noted.

"Could you handle Adam Rigg's work as well as your own? It won't make much difference, as you've been covering for him all year. His heart just isn't in the *Clarion*."

And perhaps that same heart was showing more interest in Gabrielle Henver than Gideon could tolerate. Adam ought to have been ultra-discreet in so gossip-rampant a town.

"He's forever chasing copy," said Charlotte. "Adam's no loafer."

"He wasn't at the steam-engine rally, but you were. Adam Rigg isn't pulling his weight, and the *Clarion* doesn't carry passengers. He disobeys my orders, and has also been pestering Gabby about her friends, and that's unforgivable at such a tragic time."

Charlotte had previously seen the targeting of Gabrielle through Adam's eyes alone, but too many questions would make his quarry nervous. Adam was evidently drawing near whatever Gabrielle wanted to remain clandestine, and therefore he had to be neutralized via Gideon. Not the most sensible manoeuvre. Adam would regard the *Clarion* door slamming behind him as confirmation that his enquiries were headed in the right direction.

"Tell him to see me now," said Gideon, the steadfast hero prepared to tackle any task in his mission to shield Gabrielle.

"Isn't it going a tad overboard to sack Adam?" ventured Charlotte. "I mean, a warning might be adequate."

"No," stated Gideon.

Survivor guilt. Charlotte wished she could run straight home and never face Adam again. But there he sat in the newsroom, totally convinced that his next month's wage was secure.

"Gideon wants a word with you. I'm afraid it's not good."

"He's getting rid of us both!" Adam shook his head in wonder at Gideon's ruthlessness. "Unbelievable! Why didn't you inform him we're about to shake Polrenek to its foundations?"

"Gideon won't listen. Gabrielle's gone whinging to him, spooked by whatever you've been asking her. I guess you're on track, but she's from a rich family, and the rich are used to dominating people." Charlotte paused, building up courage for her other revelation, while Adam assessed his contact with Gabrielle.

"I just said it was an odd coincidence, her schoolfriends being killed, and shouldn't she worry about her own safety. I wasn't graphically blunt, or went into minute detail. Simple friendly concern for Gabby's welfare, when a murderer's on the warpath. She overreacted, and it proves I'm close to the truth. Gideon should congratulate me, not boot us out."

"I think Gideon sees you as his rival for Gabrielle, and that's the actual problem."

"Then why sack you as well?"

"He didn't," admitted Charlotte.

"So you're threatening to leave, if he sacks me." Adam grinned, certain that workforce solidarity would bring Gideon to his senses. "Teach him to mix personal matters with business."

"Well — in fact, I — well —"

"You didn't threaten to quit?" demanded Adam. "Why not?"

"Because I never thought of it," confessed Charlotte.

"So much for staff unity and the fight to defend press freedom," sighed Adam.

"You wouldn't flounce out, if Gideon had fired me instead."

"We're not discussing what I might or mightn't do," objected Adam. "Still, at least I'll be able to borrow money off you, while I discover exactly what's going on in this town. Must be front-page stuff, if Gabby's panicking after a mere hint."

As Adam could hint with sledgehammer force, Gabrielle's response could be deemed predictable. No Henver would take kindly to the prospect of newspaper limelight turned on family members.

"Gideon thinks he can end my career," scoffed Adam. "And Gabby needn't imagine she's won. I'm onto something big. This story's got it all: corruption, murder, fraud —"

"Or none of the above," warned Charlotte. "*Hawk Enterprise* appears to be legit, and Fenella might have died accidentally."

"Then why was Gabby so desperate to get her hands on those *Hawk* accounts?" Adam retorted. "She's got to have been the burglar who smashed Gideon's lock. Or her Dad was. Who else? You know I'm right."

A valedictorian's statement, before Adam strutted across the newsroom as though he would sack Gideon, rather than the other way round. Gabrielle thought Adam could be dismissed like a presumptuous servant, but she was miscalculating. And if the Becketts imagined that Charlotte had become their trusty representative, they were also mistaken.

*

"So Adam's been sacked. I didn't reckon he'd last here much longer," commented Rosalind. "Not when Daniel Henver's daughter was two-timing Gideon. Bad idea to dally with the boss's girlfriend. Is Adam very upset?"

"Yeah, but he never planned on staying permanently at the *Clarion*. London was always his eventual goal." And Charlotte would help Adam reach those gold-glistering pavements, if she could. "Incidentally, have you ever met Daniel Henver?"

"Beneath his dignity to deal with underlings. I contact an agent if the place needs a patch-up repair, which is the best this building gets. Conrad will be livid, but Gideon might ask you to do a Henver puff-piece next."

"I'd refuse," cried Charlotte. "I'd refuse outright. Better the sack than give that charlatan any praise."

"And Conrad would applaud you. But I fear Gideon will then attempt to write a grovelling article himself, in the belief that he could end up as son-in-law to devious Daniel. After all, look at the effect your Lambert flimflam has had on Edric. Gideon will hope *Clarion* history gets a repeat performance."

So the Polrenek rumour mill was already linking Charlotte Paxton to Edric Lambert. Melanie would have been ecstatic. "Gideon can do as he chooses, but I'm on strike if ordered to sweet-talk Daniel Henver. Although, by coincidence, Adam and I were exploring an idea for local-business profiles. We approached a Rufus Olsen, whose company does film-location catering or some such thing. Do you know him?"

"Olsen? He doesn't advertise with us." And that was that. Unless the guy began shelling out on adverts, he held no interest for Rosalind, despite how exotic his job might seem in their minimum-wage town.

Glancing sternly around him, as if eager to flush wildfowl from each corner, Gideon bustled into the newsroom. "Where's everyone else? I told them to be here today."

"Adam was, as you know," said Rosalind, pointedly acrid. "Now only Charlotte remains. Why panic? It's too early in the week to fuss over copy."

"But I insisted that *all* staff had to come in this morning," Gideon complained, indignant that his word was not a command.

"Oh, they'll turn up," said Rosalind. "Too busy right now, I expect."

"Pandemic restrictions are long gone. No more working from home, I told them," carped Gideon, taken aback by the latter-day Peasants' Revolt. "Staff members have to be at their desks in future. I sent multiple emails. And I was very clear what the penalty for non-compliance will be."

"You didn't threaten to fire them?" Rosalind sighed, shaking her head at Gideon's rashness. "Oh well, let's hope Charlotte knows all about agriculture, gardens and sport, in addition to being an expert cook who's a skilled photographer."

"Sorry, but I dodged games throughout my school years, never had a garden or bothered with cameras, and my knowledge of cookery is limited to wielding a tin-opener or defrosting a packet."

"Then the *Clarion*'s next edition will be somewhat slender," Rosalind foresaw. "There's only one way out, Gideon. Claim your computer was hacked, and you know nothing whatsoever about those emails."

"That'd be giving in." The mere notion of surrender made Gideon scowl. He was the boss, and subordinates ought to leap to attention when he issued a diktat. "I'll replace any slackers with new staff."

"By this weekend? That might be a little optimistic." Rosalind's scepticism was blatant, and Charlotte nodded in agreement. She had zilch to lose, having resigned herself to unemployment.

"Nobody's slacking. Copy always gets here on time," said Charlotte, hoping reason would modify Gideon's obstinacy, but he had reached his dogmatic worst.

"Char, advertise the job vacancies online at once, and I'll start interviewing candidates tomorrow."

"Tell them to bring sample articles about sport, gardening and cookery," advised Rosalind. "We won't fill Saturday's *Clarion* otherwise."

"It'll work," decreed Gideon. "I'll make it work. This is a challenge, and I relish challenges, as you know."

"Oh yes, we all know that," said Rosalind, exchanging glances with Charlotte. "But I'll do some phoning, and try to persuade your affronted ex-employees to revise their decision."

"No! I never back down. Never! I've made my decision, and I stand firm," Gideon proclaimed, hurrying toward the safety of his office before Rosalind could persuade him to see sense.

"He'll recant," Rosalind stated. "He'll have to. And soon."

"Maybe the others are on strike in sympathy with Adam," Charlotte suggested, uneasy at not having taken her own stand to support a wronged colleague.

"This isn't about Adam. Gideon's in a showdown with people even more stubborn than him." Rosalind grinned at the foreseeable result of an ultimatum to staff members who had been working at the *Clarion* when Gideon was still behind a school desk. "Never threaten anyone close to retirement with the sack. We've usually paid off mortgages or bank loans, and are gleefully near our pension. At last we can afford to be in a huff and prance off to freedom."

"It won't seem like the *Clarion* without its regular staff," lamented Charlotte. "But will there be a *Clarion* at all, if Gideon won't budge?"

"I'll have a word with Conrad," Rosalind decided. "We can't continue this way. Gideon doesn't have a clue."

"Surely Conrad won't let you rubbish his son. My mother never stopped criticizing me, but she wouldn't have listened to a word anybody else said. She'd slam the phone down before you got started."

"There's a vast difference between your mother's allegiance to her daughter and Conrad's to his son. Conrad told me to call him, if Gideon messed up. Actually, I remember Conrad saying *when* Gideon messed up. Not exactly a trusting Papa."

Charlotte had heard the gossip about haughty Conrad and proud Rosalind. They were rumoured once to have been Polrenek's very own star-crossed lovers, with vengeful fate separating them until a middle-aged *rapprochement*. Town hearsay might be more accurate than usual, if Rosalind had instructions to phone Conrad with a report of Gideon's latest and silliest misdemeanour. Yet no matter how smitten with the source, Melanie would still have been furious at any disparagement of her daughter. She held sole rights to rebuking Charlotte.

"Don't waste time like Rosalind did," ordered Melanie's voice on cue. "You should be engaged to Edric by now. What's wrong with a whirlwind romance?"

The fact that Melanie's frequent whirlwinds had resulted in disaster zones. And traits were hereditary.

"But he's rich and docile." That would be Melanie's rejoinder. "Do you want to spend the rest of your life alone?"

Preferable to being conned. Edric was kind, tolerant and attractive, so naturally there would be a snag. Melanie's multiple disillusionments had taught Charlotte the lesson her mother never learnt.

"I've already had a job application, Char," announced Gideon, racing into the newsroom. His voice might have sounded less exultant, had he known who Rosalind was phoning. "Well done, Char, getting adverts online so quickly. Or did you email her about the vacancies? Is she a friend of Gabby's as well?"

"I haven't sent any emails yet," replied Charlotte, aware that no vacancies might exist, if Conrad intervened. "Who do you mean?"

"Vanessa Beckett," Gideon said impatiently, expecting Charlotte to be a mind-reader. "She's made an enquiry about working here, and given you and the Farfield headmistress as her references. Is she Gabby's friend?"

"Her sister was," offered Charlotte, wondering where else the Beckett plan would veer. "Fenella died. Adam's found-by-lifeboat-station story."

"Oh." Gideon paused, the awkwardness of having to mumble condolences at a job interview curbing his enthusiasm. But Vanessa was still Gabrielle's friend's sister, and she might help him smarm his way further into the Henver world. Gideon rallied. "Well, Char, as you're recommending Vanessa, I'm positive she'll be invaluable here."

"But I don't really know her. She's around six years younger than me, and I've only seen Vanessa once since Farfield. Anyhow, I thought she was attending college in London or somewhere."

"Vanessa couldn't leave her parents at such a tragic time." Gideon's tone reproached Charlotte for heartlessness. Naturally, Gabrielle's friend's sister would be an altruistic paragon, devoted to family. "Vanessa will need to rethink her future, and start earning money close to home."

"She's Luke Beckett's daughter. I doubt money will be a problem."

"Oh, *those* Becketts. I'd forgotten that." Yet another point in Vanessa's favour. No additional reference would be necessary, and Charlotte marvelled that she had been able to gate-crash the *Clarion* without backing from any high-rank relative whatsoever.

"I must phone Gabby, and tell her Vanessa's got a job here," said Gideon, certain that all his wishes were now reality. He had purged the *Clarion* of unsatisfactory staff members, and could forge ahead into a blissful future, hand-in-hand with Gabrielle. Charlotte was tempted to remind him that fairytales never came true.

"I'll arrange to see Vanessa as soon as possible," Gideon was saying. "She might be able to take over the sport pages. Or gardening. Not that it really matters. There could be other candidate applications already. I'll check my inbox straightaway."

Gideon scurried off, believing he would single-handedly save the *Clarion*'s next edition. Such confidence should have been inspiring, but nobody would ever see Gideon as he saw himself, and Charlotte tried to concentrate on work instead, hoping her copy might actually appear in print that week. Yet the Beckett manoeuvre would not be set aside. Luke presumably wanted Vanessa to infiltrate the *Clarion* because he doubted Charlotte's loyalty. A wise conclusion on his part.

*

"I've spoken to Kay and Gerald," Rosalind told Charlotte, after closing all newsroom doors for greater security. "They've been sent a second ultimatum: either come into the office immediately or it's instant dismissal. The sack's fine by them, they both say."

"What was Conrad's reaction?"

"A few words of discontent escaped his lips."

Would Conrad simply shut down the *Clarion*? Sell it? There were other jobs, Charlotte assured herself for maybe the hundredth time. She was going to survive, whatever happened. "Will the paper live on?"

"Down to advertising revenue: its lifeblood. Conrad's a businessman." Yet Rosalind was unworried. Their discussion must have been reassuring, and Charlotte could breathe again.

"Any chance Adam might be reinstated?"

"I didn't mention him to Conrad. It would have meant a Henver recap." Rosalind grimaced at the idea, before asking, "Is flighty Gabrielle pursuing Adam or vice versa?"

"Very much vice versa. She got him sacked."

"Why did Adam risk his job for a *Henver*?"

"I guess Adam didn't see any risk."

"Young men assume they're indestructible," sighed Rosalind. "They also think they're irresistible. Adam's never appreciated Katlyn."

"Who's she?"

"His girlfriend, Katlyn Kyle," said Rosalind, surprised by Charlotte's question. "Hasn't he ever mentioned her?"

"Oh yes, often. But not by name." To Adam, Katlyn was a shadow following him around, and Charlotte hoped that the future Dr Katlyn Kyle would find a partner who valued her rather more than Adam did. So easy to sort out another's life, yet so difficult to weather your own.

Rosalind scuttled back into her office, in case Gideon should appear in the newsroom suspecting a plot against him, and Charlotte began to check emails. A school bring-and-buy sale, the Rotary Club fundraising quiz, a waltz night in the

Victory Hall: each event a useful column filler, and Charlotte was dutifully taking notes when Gabrielle's email jumped into the computer.

After Adam's copy-hunting expedition, Charlotte had imagined she would never again hear from Gabrielle, but apparently he alone was deemed a *Clarion* culprit. *Service for Nadine tomorrow 2:00. Meet me outside church. Open to all.*

Even lowly beings like Charlotte Paxton, it seemed. Luckily, she could be unavailable when it came to mixing in Napier social circles, and Charlotte ensured that her diary would be too full by arranging to interview Polrenek's Council Leader at 1:00pm, an ex-mayor at 2:00pm, and members of the local operatic society at 3:00pm. *Sorry,* Charlotte informed Gabrielle. *Interviews all tomorrow afternoon, but will see what I can do.*

With an additional appointment at 4:00pm, if necessary.

Gabrielle's response arrived in minutes, and was the whine of a spoilt child not getting her own way. *Can't cope by myself. I'll tell Gideon you have to be there with me. I'm counting on you.*

Charlotte trusted that Gideon had more to worry him than obeying Gabrielle, but presumably Conrad was still to contact his son. The newsroom door opened and Gideon began demanding, "Surely you can spare an hour for Gabby, can't you, Char? We must help her through this tragedy. She's devastated."

"I've got interviews the whole afternoon," said Charlotte, hoping she sounded regretful. "And there's no one to cover for me now."

Because Adam had been sacked. An oversight Gideon chose to ignore. "What about sending Vanessa to do your interviews, Char? I'm seeing her in ten minutes or so, and she might be able to start immediately."

"Facing Town Councillors and a mayor on her very first day? She's raw, and only nineteen." Charlotte had no need to speak. Gideon's solution was impossible, and he knew it. "Couldn't you spare the time to accompany Gabrielle? I know how busy you always are, Gideon. Incredibly busy. But doesn't this count as an emergency?"

Gideon dithered, unable to regard a funeral as the ideal date, but there was Gabrielle's gratitude to take into account, and escorting her would be a formal announcement that they were a couple. Gideon hesitated no longer. "I'll make time. Gabby can't go alone, when she's under such stress. Some things have priority."

Decision made, Gideon could pride himself on his ability to grasp resolute control of a problematic situation. He had no idea how rapidly his next problematic situation was approaching.

"Your father's on the line, Gideon," Rosalind called from her quarters. "Shall I switch the call through to your office?"

"OK," replied Gideon, pompousness already in retreat as he hurried to retrace his steps. Thankful never to have been afraid of a parent, Charlotte sat back to await repercussions. No point working if both her future and the *Clarion*'s were in flux.

"There's a job applicant outside, Charlotte," whispered Rosalind, almost tiptoeing into the newsroom, her hushed voice more appropriate to the event that Gideon might find himself attending with Gabrielle. "I guess either you or I should interview her, as she's here. Our emergency might be over, by the way. Perhaps. I acclaimed Kay and Gerald, swearing that advertisers love their stuff, but I'm not sure Conrad was still listening."

"Could Adam be rehired too?"

"Don't know. Anyhow, someone's got to see the girl, and Gideon won't be feeling very polite right now."

"You'll have to be the interviewer," said Charlotte. "Conflict of interest for me. I gather Vanessa gave my name as a reference. I was in the same school year as her sister."

"The memory doesn't appear to enthuse you," remarked Rosalind.

"We're not meant to speak ill of the dead, but Vanessa's sister, Fenella, was no friend of mine."

"Lifeboat-station Fenella? Oh, that's awful! Terrible!" Rosalind wailed, her face contorting in distress. "I won't know whether to ignore the death, or offer condolences and risk Vanessa dissolving in a flood of tears. Why did the girl apply to work here? Doesn't she realize a local paper will be reporting the story? Does her family hope to manipulate what gets printed?"

"Possibly. The father's Luke Beckett."

"I'd better talk to Conrad when he's finished with Gideon," said Rosalind, hurrying back into her office. "He might owe Beckett a favour."

"I want to steer clear of Vanessa, so I'll leave you to deal with the ramifications," called Charlotte.

"Oh, before I forget." Rosalind put her rush to seek the boss's edict on hold, and asked, "Would you recommend Vanessa for a job?"

"I don't really know her. All I recall is that she dodged games."

"Didn't you admit to an identical transgression?"

"Yeah," agreed Charlotte. "But I never got caught. Vanessa doesn't appear to have a talent for deception."

"Not journalist material then," Rosalind concluded, restarting her dash to the phone.

Too right, thought Charlotte. Glad that a Beckett endeavour to infiltrate the *Clarion* would be dealt with by Conrad, she went to retrieve her jacket from a walk-in cupboard grandly styled the cloakroom, which would serve as an expedient hiding-place until Vanessa was inside Rosalind's office. No wonder Adam despised Charlotte's lack of gumption. He would leap at any chance to meet, befriend and cross-examine a Beckett.

Sheer hard-headed determination might eventually result in Adam working at a London daily, while Charlotte continued to report Council spats for the *Clarion* or another provincial weekly. Ambition was meant to be laudable, but after the Farfield experience, a niche in her own community ought to rank higher. Timidity or commonsense? Charlotte knew what Adam would think.

7

A new day. Was it paired with a new régime? Or the *Clarion*'s demise? A Gideon insurrection? Unlikely. An exasperated Conrad selling the newspaper? Possible. Charlotte travelled into work, speculating why no message had updated her overnight. A sign that things were the same? But normally when Charlotte arrived, Gideon would be in his office or prowling the newsroom, and yet no Gideon anywhere. The paper advertised itself as an incomparable source of local information, but that morning its sole reporter had no idea whether or not her job still existed.

Then the door swung open, and Rosalind was there. Any tidings were preferable to uncertainty, and Charlotte demanded, "What's happening?"

Rosalind shrugged, another *Clarion* crisis behind her. "The Conrad verdict is that staff can work wherever they choose, as long as all copy is in on time and up to scratch. Everybody's reinstated, but not Adam, I'm afraid. Gideon got his pennyworth in first, and denounced Adam for consorting with Daniel Henver's daughter in pubs. I did my best to maintain she was just a source, but Conrad decided he'd heard enough about the *Clarion* by then. Gideon's still in situ as editor, but Conrad's got the last word from now on."

"Gideon agreed to that?" Charlotte said in surprise.

"If he stomped out, who'd headhunt our Gideon? We're stuck with him, but at least he shouldn't throw his weight around so much."

Bad news for Gideon's ego, and for Adam as well, but Charlotte could apparently count on having a job, unless Conrad grew bored with overseeing Gideon's ineptness. "But there's no plan to sell the paper?"

"Not while it remains in profit," replied Rosalind, frowning at the thought of how meagre that profit could sometimes be. "Conrad's the total businessman, but he also likes to have local influence. And à-propos local influence, Conrad told me to hire the Beckett girl. She can shadow you, and we'll see if it pans out. I wasn't impressed with her, but she might have had interview nerves."

"I reckon Vanessa applied to work here on a whim. She didn't mention any journalistic ambition when I last saw her."

Yet Conrad's decree was final, and Charlotte began checking the police website for overnight posts, but Rosalind paused in her office doorway. "Was Adam chasing a Henver story?"

She sounded casual, but might be asking on Conrad's behalf, and Adam would need some good copy to kick-start his career. If the London dream came to nothing, he could sell a tale of Henver misconduct to the *Clarion*, and maybe rejoin its staff. "Yeah, Adam's been looking in Henver's direction. That was the rationale behind sweet-talking Gabrielle in pubs."

"Well, if he does find any dirt clinging to Daniel Henver, Conrad would be thrilled. Pass that on to Adam."

"OK." Perhaps Vanessa could be useful after all. Her parents were likely to know the Henvers, and Luke might share Conrad's prejudice. Adam ought to meet Vanessa. A chance encounter would be best, and easily arranged by texting him. *Lunch? Prom café? Possible source.*

Adam's response hit Charlotte's phone within seconds. *OK. Who?* But before a reply could be sent, Rosalind had hurried back. "Vanessa Beckett's toiling up the stairs. I'd give her an entrance code, but I'm not that trusting. Besides, Gideon might blame me for a security breach if he starts claiming even more desperados have smashed their way through his lock. Oh well, whatever the Beckett motive, I suppose one of us should act as a genial host and treat this girl to lunch on her first day."

Rosalind's tone was so apathetic that Charlotte laughed. "I'll take Vanessa to the Prom Café, and tell her all reporters eat in places like that. She might reconsider being a journalist. But why are you against Vanessa? Know of Beckett transgressions that I don't?"

"I'm not keen on how she pushed herself in here, as though the *Clarion* doesn't have any discretion," Rosalind grumbled. "We wouldn't print a nasty word about her sister, no matter the reason Fenella killed herself."

"Suicide hasn't been officially established, and accidents happen," said Charlotte. "Who was your source?"

"We in advertising never reveal our sources. But that's unimportant." Unimportant because the newsroom door was opening, and Vanessa peered tentatively into her impending workplace.

"Hi," said Charlotte. "Welcome to the *Clarion*."

"Welcome," echoed Rosalind, overdoing her graciousness. "Welcome indeed. You'll soon pick up our routine, and we've got an empty desk just waiting for you."

Adam's desk, but Vanessa would not think to ask why there should be a vacant seat. And Adam had sacked himself by crossing Gideon.

"You'll get a handle on things in no time," Charlotte made herself say. "It's all pretty straightforward."

"I'll do my absolute best." Vanessa was tense but excited, maybe picturing herself on a fast track to Fleet Street, judging by the brand-new business suit. She had much to learn, and not only about local reportage, because the Beckett surname would have assured her from birth that wanting was a mere prelude to getting.

*

"Lunch," announced Charlotte, interrupting Vanessa's acquiescent scrutiny of the latest planning applications. "I'll treat you to a sandwich in the Prom Café, before we hurtle to that fundraiser thing. Well, perhaps treat isn't the right word, as you might be put off food for life, but it's where local reporters hang out. The owner's a prime source, and he'll already know what should be in next Saturday's *Clarion*."

"The fundraiser's an auction," said Vanessa, eager to impress with her efficiency. "A Red Cross auction. Will you interview people there?"

"As many as I can. If their names get printed, they often buy several *Clarion*s that week. More, when they're in a picture too," Charlotte explained, wondering if the novice would disapprove of schemes to fleece their readers. "But you'll find almost everyone has a good story to tell, if you dig."

Vanessa absorbed each syllable with rapt attention, under the delusion that Charlotte was an ultimate authority on all matters journalistic, which felt more unnerving than complimentary. However, the myth would soon end, along with Charlotte's job, should Gideon learn that Adam's Henver pursuit was being facilitated by *Clarion* staff.

Pleasant to be out in a brisk wind after their cooped-up morning, and Charlotte began to relax, until a sickening recollection hit her with punch-like force. She and Vanessa were beside the very shore where Fenella had died. Sea spray was crashing across the Promenade in wide arcs, and Vanessa seemed intent on defending her suit from tidal surges, but she would be conscious of the location, and Charlotte wished she had chosen another café, any other café, for the *rendezvous* with Adam. But too late, much too late, and Charlotte condemned herself as an obtuse fool.

"Do we have to tell a photographer which pictures to take at the auction?" asked Vanessa.

"No need. Jeth's been with the *Clarion* for decades. You'll meet him this afternoon. Jethro Kern."

"Oh, I already know Mr Kern," said Vanessa, relieved that she would spot a familiar figure among strangers. "He does the photo every year for our Christmas card."

Fantasy time, according to Jethro. However, there would no longer be a Fenella to complete the family portrait, and presumably no Beckett photo on Christmas cards again. Cursing her thoughtless mention of Jethro, Charlotte attempted to distract Vanessa with a word flurry. "We're approaching the caff in all its glory. You'll never see Gideon Penry here, which is an advantage, because it means staff members can unwind. Or am I slighting your dearest friend?"

"I don't know him," replied Vanessa, gladly allowing trivia to take over. "Is he very bad-tempered or something?"

"No. Gideon's OK. You get used to him and his ideas. Luckily they're often ancient history by evening."

Charlotte pushed open the café door, and led Vanessa into a gloomy olive-green cavern that only came to life during holiday seasons. Then there were outside tables, protected by stripy sunshades to foil marauding gulls with a taste for pasties and ice-cream cornets, but bright colours were packed away in autumn while summer workers went back to college. Locals could reclaim their town, and appreciate lowered prices in tranquillity, free from irascible interlopers who seemingly hated their children, their companions and the entire West Country.

"Hi, Hector," Charlotte said to the morosely angular man wiping down a counter as though insulted by his lowly task. "Meet Vanessa, the *Clarion*'s newest recruit."

Hector Quennell grunted an acknowledgement of the introduction, signifying that Vanessa had been accepted. She might prefer to circumvent the area in future, but her status as a local was granted.

"Any good stories for us today, Hector?" added Charlotte.

Horace's sallow face revived like a weed given water, and even his drab hair appeared to shine. "Laurel Sutton down Harbour Way got Florence Cobb to rid her cottage of a scratching bowgle."

"Did the spell work?" A haunting was invaluable copy. The legend of Polrenek's latest spook might fill two whole pages, enhanced with photographs parading sixteenth-century granite fireplaces and beamed ceilings. Yet despite her mother's refusal to rest in peace, Charlotte would have been more inclined to consult a vermin expert, rather than the town's resident white witch, to sort out any sounds emanating from woodwork.

"No luck so far, but Florence says she'll persuade the bowgle to leave," Hector reported, although he plainly had his doubts. "You should interview Laurel. And Florence too."

"What's a bowgle?" enquired Vanessa.

Only then did Charlotte recall the Beckett bereavement, which made discussion of ghosts taboo, and she hastily spoke over Vanessa's query. "Thanks for the tip, Hector. It's a real scoop. Are your cheese-and-tomato sandwiches on the menu today?"

"What scoop?" Adam asked, presenting himself in the doorway as if in response to a cue.

"You're too late," said Charlotte. "It's my exclusive."

"But I'm the *Clarion*'s freelance roving reporter," protested Adam. "Therefore we should have no secrets."

"Ideally," replied Charlotte. "Vanessa, this is Adam Rigg, and the less said about him the better. Adam, meet Vanessa Beckett on her first day at the *Clarion*. We're off to a charity auction after lunch."

Adam registered the surname, but he was too canny for a reaction that might alert Vanessa, and Charlotte felt ashamed of how callously she was behaving. Yet the Becketts were due no allegiance from her, and a reporter's job entailed ruthlessness when chasing copy. That would be Adam's contention anyhow, as he guided his quarry to a corner table, leaving Charlotte to order (and pay for) sandwiches. At least his girlfriend might save a little cash that day, assuming she still subsidized Adam.

"Beckett? Is she Luke Beckett's daughter?" Hector frowned at Adam, the overambitious libertine out to worm his way into Polrenek's highest society. "Last I heard, he was romancing Daniel Henver's girl."

"Fake news. Adam cares solely for Katlyn Kyle, his one true love," said Charlotte, to end the sidetrack. "Actually, could I interview you sometime? We're doing a series about local businesses and their problems in the current economic crisis."

"VAT," stated Hector. "And transport costs. That was a good advert you did for the Lamberts. Rumour says you're now engaged to Edric."

"More fake news," declared Charlotte. "When can we schedule your interview? Adam and I have already begun talking to people who run businesses here. We started the other day with a Rufus Olsen and his *Hawk Enterprise*. Do you know him?"

"He's not a local," said Hector, condemnation in each syllable.

"No, he isn't," conceded Charlotte. "Olsen works mostly online, I gather, but he's based here, so *Hawk* counts as local."

An excuse that failed to impress Hector. His café had been in the Quennell family for three generations, and that automatically downgraded an outsider playing around on computers. "Why did you bother with Olsen?"

"The editor thinks it might encourage school leavers to create their own online businesses," claimed Charlotte, strategically blaming Gideon who had never patronized the Prom Café. "So many kids have to move away from Polrenek to get a job, but you can live anywhere working online. It could bring extra revenue to the town. After all, Rufus Olsen will be spending his money here."

Cash spoke directly to Hector's heart, and he was forced to nod in grudging agreement, yet with certain reservations. "Where's he from? Why doesn't anybody know him? What's his secret?"

"Keep reading the *Clarion*, and perhaps you'll find out." Or perhaps not. Yet Adam and Vanessa were already deep in conversation, their heads close together over a tabletop. "When would be the best time for your interview?"

"After our breakfast rush," Hector replied, to foster his image as the dynamic businessman who rarely had a free minute. "I get to sit down then. Tomorrow morning? Ten o'clock?"

Charlotte wrote down the appointment in her notebook, paid for lunch, and crossed the room with sandwiches on a tray to join the couple now apparently whispering confidences.

"No coffee or tea?" carped Adam, transferring his attention to the fodder provided. "And I'm simply chacking for a drink."

"I can but apologize. These trays aren't large enough to carry everything at once," said Charlotte, amused by Adam's sense of entitlement. "Terribly sorry. I'll fetch your coffee without further delay."

"No problem," Vanessa assured her, forgetting that the waitress might outrank a *Clarion* newcomer. Evidently Adam alone existed for Vanessa, and he was intent on charming her. Gabrielle had discerned his phoniness, but Vanessa would be less wary.

"I'm interviewing Hector tomorrow," said Charlotte. "You know: the series about local businesses."

Adam nodded, but neither he nor Vanessa could even pretend interest in whatever Charlotte was telling them. She had brought the pair together, and was now superfluous.

*

If Vanessa had expected working for the *Clarion* to add zest to her life, she must have been disillusioned by the day's end.

"Plans for tonight?" remarked Charlotte, having noted the many text messages sent and received by Vanessa throughout that afternoon.

"Just Adam helping me get the hang of journalism." But Vanessa sounded self-conscious. There was clearly more in those texts than she wanted Charlotte to know, and doubtless none made reference to Adam's girlfriend. However, Charlotte had offered up Vanessa as a sacrificial source, and could hardly criticize Adam's convenient absent-mindedness. The whole world operated on pretence from Becketts to Henvers to Edric Lambert, and therefore Charlotte was merely adding her own contribution to the norm.

"You've decided to leave college?"

"It was an absolute non-stop bore," declared Vanessa. "I'd complete a load of essays and stuff, then another pile would instantly drop on me. It never ended."

"Exactly like being a *Clarion* reporter," commented Charlotte.

"That's different."

Why? Because Vanessa saw herself as a secret agent protecting the family reputation? Because Luke Beckett could put pressure on Gideon to suppress any bothersome facts concerning Fenella's death?

"Will you see Edric tonight?" Vanessa queried, attempting casualness.

"Only if he turns up at the Council barney about a pedestrian crossing in Fore Street. We *Clarion* reporters live the high life."

"Should I be there as well? Are Council Meetings part of my job too?" Vanessa looked distinctly unenthusiastic at the prospect. Perhaps a get-together with Adam was already coordinated. He would be impatient to glean whatever gen she might have.

"You've done enough for a first day," said Charlotte. "And it's essential to build up your boredom threshold to astronomical heights, before tackling a Councillor in full bellow."

Vanessa giggled, but she was glad to hurry away and start her evening, whether with parents or Adam. She gave no sign of being grief-stricken over Fenella, but few sisters seemed storybook close, and might often grow up resenting each other. The Beckett family was not a Hollywood myth.

"You and Edric could be," Melanie's voice insisted. "He's perfect."

And yet Melanie ought to know that perfect men were the phoniest myth of all. Her daughter's existence proved it.

*

"A terrible time for trade. Yes, terrible," sighed Hector Quennell, sipping coffee that made plain why only low prices kept his café in business. "I was thinking the other day, it's like we've reached a full stop and there's little point going on. Everybody's in the same boat. Sid Tyrrel gave me an estimate for new windows and doors, but said he'd need half the money upfront, not just a ten-percent deposit. Sure sign that firms are in trouble when established ones can't get their materials on credit. If they face suchlike hitches, we're definitely spiralling downward. Sid put too much faith in that Henver contract."

"What Henver contract?" asked Charlotte, journalistic instinct alert. Indeed, every instinct alerted by the Henver surname.

"Future flats on Old Mother Trevail's land. You know, where the Nadine woman was found. Sid figured he'd get months of work, with all that double-glazing to be installed. And Henver ought to have the decency to employ local tradespeople, if he expects Polrenekers to buy his so-called *luxurious yet affordable apartments*."

Would any town resident buy a home on the site where a woman was killed? Nadine's ghost would be resentfully malicious, feared even by those who had never met her. Sid Tyrrel might be lucky not to have his name associated with Daniel Henver. "I could ask Sid for an interview," Charlotte suggested. "Some free advertising might help him out a bit."

"Talk to Alfie Quayle as well. He's the best carpenter around here, but you'd think nobody wants a gate or garage door these days." Hector almost smiled, enjoying his fairy-godfather ability to boost the area's economy. "And there's Nolly Luxon as well. The last chandler in Polrenek: perhaps in Britain. A real piece of times gone by. His great-grandfather opened the shop."

"That'll make good copy," said Charlotte, scribbling down names. Apparently local-firm interviews would be a popular feature, if only amongst the interviewees. "Thanks for your help. Would it be OK for Jeth Kern to take a few photos to go with the article about you?"

Horace's family was large enough to hike up *Clarion* sales the following week, and Charlotte felt she had done a useful hour's work. However, back in the newsroom, Vanessa was half-defensive half-contrite.

"You didn't say to meet you at the Prom Café. I was going to rush straight there, but Rosalind said not to bother as you'd have finished the interview before I got downstairs."

"It doesn't matter." Used to working alone, Charlotte had forgotten her apprentice, and guiltily attempted reassurance. "You haven't lost a unique opportunity. We'll be covering the Methodist Chapel's Concert for Ukraine this afternoon. Is Gideon in his office?"

"He hasn't shown up yet. Rosalind said she'd phone him to check what's going on." Vanessa looked apprehensive, as if Gideon's absence might somehow be her fault.

"Don't panic over him. Just say you've known Gabrielle Henver for years, and Gideon will be your docile lackey, afraid you'll badmouth him to her." Charlotte sat down to email Jethro about photographing the Prom Café, but Vanessa was still anxious.

"I don't really know Gabrielle. She never spoke to me at school."

Lucky you, thought Charlotte. "No need to burden an editor with trifling detail."

"Adam says Gideon won't be in charge here much longer," added Vanessa, starting to relax as nobody appeared angry with her.

Was Adam just talking, or had his father overheard golf-club rumour? Gideon had never previously taken a day off, or even arrived late for work. Was he already *Clarion* history? That would mean learning to handle a new editor's whims, if the paper continued, but Charlotte told herself that she had coped before and could cope again. On the plus side, Vanessa had yet to enquire about their investigative team.

"Adam's so clever." Additional praise that Vanessa was unable to resist airing. She had been enchanted by Adam, but his mask might soon slip, exposing his true features: the huntsman who had spooked Gabrielle.

"Adam's a born reporter. He'll say or do anything in pursuit of copy." Charlotte tried to make her statement a somewhat belated warning, but Vanessa thought Adam's dedication to journalism was being acclaimed.

"He'll end up famous."

"It's certainly Adam's goal." Idle chat, Charlotte assumed, but Vanessa was bracing herself to ask the question that might explain why she had applied for a *Clarion* job.

"What will be in Saturday's paper? About Fenella, I mean. You haven't altered the website yet."

"I won't, until there's a police update," Charlotte said, hoping her reply was soothing. "But I'll tell your parents in advance."

"Have the police linked Fenella with *Hawk Enterprise*?"

"Don't think so. I'd have heard. And what I do know is mostly from your family, so it's off the record for me." But not for newshound Adam Rigg, who might wheedle Vanessa to disclose further details.

"The police won't find a thing on Fenella's laptop. She had trouble retrieving her own files, and couldn't hack a wall clock," Vanessa declared.

Only no-hopers need fiddle with stupid machines, Nadine had ruled. The rich and successful could pay accountants or similar gofers to do boring stuff. For her, ignorance had been an ultimate hallmark of distinction.

"Dad sent Fenella on computer courses after she left school," Vanessa was saying. "But Fenella's mind never functioned like that."

Did Vanessa's? She was the sole person Fenella would be able to boss around, and Vanessa abruptly turned away as though guessing what had passed through Charlotte's head. Another Adam-alert was only fair.

"I'm adequate online, but Katlyn Kyle is brilliant with a computer. Do you know her? She's Adam's girlfriend. A medical student."

"Yes, he told me about Katlyn."

And how she fails to understand him, Charlotte reckoned. And how the relationship was at an end anyway. Adam would have covered all bases to foil any gossip reaching his targeted source.

"It's so sad, so totally sad," Vanessa sighed, her voice softening with pity. "Poor Adam. Such a horrible situation. I feel dreadful for him."

"Don't worry about Adam," said Rosalind, hurrying into the newsroom. "He'll always land on his feet. Copy appeal, Charlotte. Could you file your stuff early this week? Jeth and I need to be extra careful with the layout and mock-up, as we can't blame mistakes on Gideon. He's stomped off."

"Permanently?" Charlotte had foreseen a possible showdown between father and son, but figured Gideon would backpedal.

"He had the row with his Dad that should have happened when Gideon was an adolescent. I hope this Gabrielle Henver is worth it."

"I don't think she's as keen on Gideon as he is on her," Charlotte ventured, unsure how Vanessa would regard criticism of her sister's friend.

"My Dad says Daniel Henver's a crook," Vanessa commented.

"Produce evidence, and Conrad will adore you. Oh well, Gideon's chosen his side, and that's that." Yet Rosalind merely shrugged. She had chosen her side too: Conrad's.

"Who'll be editor now?" asked Vanessa.

"We can survive without one for the time being." Rosalind shrugged again. Gideon was no loss in her opinion, and none in Charlotte's either. "We might have to find new premises for the *Clarion* though. Fat chance of a lease renewal now. Henver will evict us, unless Gideon endears himself to Daniel, and then makes peace with Conrad."

To Charlotte, it seemed unlikely that Gideon could endear himself to anyone, including Gabrielle, but he might be comforted by having left boats and bridges smouldering in his wake. Gideon could believe he was akin to those heroes of yore, sacrificing all for a fair lady, and Charlotte felt mortifyingly practical. She would never give up her journalist foothold for an illusory dream of romance. Too often, much too often, Charlotte had witnessed her mother squandering life's limited duration on fly-by-night eternal love.

"That series profiling local business people," Charlotte said, expelling the ultra-perfect Edric from her mind. "Is it OK by you, Rosalind?"

"Yes, indeed! When their names are in print and mates start to comment on what you've written, they might decide *Clarion* advertising will pay for itself." Rosalind smiled at the prospect to channel additional profit in Conrad's direction: a fail-safe method of ensuring the paper had a future. "Remember that Polrenek's filled with hard-working entrepreneurs: doughty fighters who honour our hometown. The usual guff."

"Nothing but," agreed Charlotte.

"And don't neglect that would-be movie mogul you once mentioned. Olsen, wasn't he? Butter him up. If a film of his ever gets shown around here, he might fork out on a few adverts."

"I can't talk to Olsen," declared Vanessa. "I'm sorry, but I just can't."

"Why not?" queried Rosalind, a *Clarion* uprising unprecedented.

"I'll do the talking. Not a crisis," said Charlotte. Observing Rufus's reaction to the Beckett surname would be enough to help steer questions. "You'll get used to interviewing people. Hector Quennell suggested we speak to Alfie Quayle as well, Rosalind. And Sid Tyrrel, Nolly Luxon —"

"I can't see Mr Tyrrel either," Vanessa stated. "I simply can't. It'd be awful, having to meet him. He was supposed to replace our windows, but then Fenella got Dad to cancel the whole thing."

"Have you upset every businessman in Polrenek? I must note down the firms our reporters are currently boycotting." As she returned to her office, Rosalind's voice was frosty censure of Vanessa's rebellion. Employees were meant to put the *Clarion* first, not their own preferences.

Rosalind had a point, and although the office door was not slammed behind her, it did close decisively. Their jobs were paramount, and demanded more commitment than breezing through the easiest option, but Charlotte suspected that a rich man's daughter might never be able to understand that.

"Your family should have employed Sid Tyrrel. His double-glazing stands the test of time," Charlotte remarked as a distraction, before asking outright, "Did you hack Rufus Olsen's computer? Is he your victim?"

"Mine!" Attempted laughter, but Vanessa was suddenly on edge. "Do you imagine I'm a hi-tech genius?"

"Guess I do," replied Charlotte. "Who else could Fenella trust? She and her friends barely learnt how to switch on a laptop."

Vanessa was uncertain whether to accept a compliment or resort to stout denial, but she believed Charlotte was her ally. "Off the record?"

"Naturally." Of course illegal activity had to remain confidential. The alternative would be too unfair on Vanessa, and Charlotte added, "But never ever tell anyone else what you did."

"Not even Adam?"

Especially not Adam, thought Charlotte.

"Don't overburden him. He's already got enough troubles."

"Oh yes, you're so right, Charlotte. Adam's had to deal with one dreadful thing after another lately." Vanessa sighed again, her own fears diminishing as she recalled the multiple misfortunes of hapless Adam. "No, I mustn't add to his problems."

"Not even off the record," Charlotte stressed. "No matter what your excuse, hacking's a risky pastime. Why did you chance it?"

"Fenella told me to." All the explanation Vanessa deemed necessary. She had been younger, therefore obedient. Sixth form versus lower school.

"Were you angry with Rufus as well?"

"Why should I be? Never met him, but Fenella wanted to know if he fiddles his tax or whatever. She was the person mad at him." Vanessa faltered, reluctant to ask, and yet compelled to, "Did he kill Fenella?"

"I don't think so."

"Though it's possible?"

More than possible, given Fenella's determination to settle a score, but Charlotte hurried on. "He seems benign. Why was she mad at him?"

"I guess he dumped her or something. She didn't say." And it would have been futile to enquire, Vanessa's tone implied. She had had a subservient place in Fenella's world, and

Charlotte's sentimental only-child belief in sibling devotion needed drastic revision. "Rufus Olsen didn't strike me as violent or abhorrent. A braggart, maybe, but nothing worse than that." Tepid recommendation, but it was the best Charlotte could do.

"You'll go back and ask him more questions though, won't you?" urged Vanessa. "You're not just stopping now, are you?"

"The *Clarion* is hot on his trail," declared Charlotte, making Vanessa giggle. "With your computer skills, you could do some useful research into the Olsen background. But no hacking, please, or we could find ourselves hauled up before the press regulators. Rufus wasn't very forthcoming about his early years, although he did mention Rotherhithe so dig a little. And remember that showbiz types often change their original name for something more harmonious."

"I never thought of that," gasped Vanessa, ready to beat herself up for rank stupidity. "It's like Olsen appeared out the blue in his twenties. Yeah, he must have changed his name along the way. Nobody's that invisible."

The chore should keep Vanessa busy, and might produce an interesting result, whether or not it made *Clarion* copy. Charlotte expanded her notes from the Quennell interview until she had a passable first-draft article, and then found the business card Rufus Olsen had given her as if bestowing an honour. He plainly saw himself having much future contact with reporters, and the request for an additional interview should seem routine. A phone call would allow him less time to invent excuses than an email, and Charlotte dialled his mobile number.

"Sorry to disturb you, Mr Olsen, but I'd like to schedule the follow-up *Clarion* interview. If you can spare a few minutes," Charlotte said, forcing herself to sound meek. Rufus hesitated, permitting the sound of gulls and waves to distract her. Was he near the Prom? A headland? Maybe in London by the Thames? An expedition that would delight Charlotte, but might be a run-of-the-mill commute in Rufus's opinion.

"After lunch," he replied at last. "Yes, this afternoon after lunch. I'll be home then."

"I'll bring our photographer with me. If that's OK? We'd like a picture to accompany the feature." Jethro Kern's presence would diffuse Rufus's attention, and perhaps make him less guarded when answering questions. It was close to an Adam strategy, but he had the innate drive to become a rising journalist, and Charlotte ought to mimic him.

"Yes, yes, the photographer," agreed Rufus, lordly aping a Hollywood magnate. "It'll save time if you're both there."

"Thanks so much," Charlotte said, despising the humble gratitude in her voice as she ended the call.

"He's really going to talk?" Vanessa glanced up from the computer that had been Adam's, seemingly in no doubt that Charlotte would excavate each and every secret Rufus had kept since that suspiciously incognito childhood.

*

Jethro parked his car with rakish unconcern for any other driver, and began unloading superfluous paraphernalia in a heap across the pavement. He liked to impress with vast arrays of photographic equipment that would never` actually be used, and Charlotte was smiling as she headed down the street to join him.

"Hoping your versatility will amaze Rufus Olsen, and launch you on a new career as his cinematographer?"

"You've got to trust to luck now and then," Jethro pointed out. "Is this Olsen guy the genuine article or a small-town bigmouth?"

"I'm not sure, but probably the latter. Need any help?" Charlotte hung two bags over an arm, and then hoisted a tripod onto her shoulder. "Jeth, you once said something about the Beckett Christmas card being a fantasy. What did you mean?"

"Vanessa not up to *Clarion* standards," Jethro concluded.

"It's only her second day in the job. Too soon to tell how it'll turn out," said Charlotte, noting Jethro's disdain of a family that would be described as 'prominent' in the *Clarion*. "But Vanessa's got better computer skills than I'll ever have, and they might come in useful."

"And just as useful that her Dad chances to be pally with Conrad," Jethro remarked.

"Most jobs are the who-we-know type in Polrenek. What makes you think Vanessa won't be OK?"

"Sheer prejudice. Rich kids imagine that success is an entitlement, instead of something you have to work towards. Childhood teaches them they're special, and so obviously they can't be at fault if life goes haywire. But Vanessa might become more realistic after her sister's fate," Jethro conceded.

"Inevitable, I guess. How long have you known the Becketts?" asked Charlotte, as she and Jethro began walking toward Rufus Olsen's house.

"I've spent twenty-six years overcharging Luke Beckett for family photos, described as portraits to up my bill." Jethro laughed at his scheme, acknowledging, "I'm as phony as they are."

"Don't all families put on a show for outsiders? The Becketts won't be any different."

"No, but that marriage was a sham from the start. Beatrice would never have chosen Luke if he hadn't been loaded. She was set on surpassing her sister, a girl Beatrice wrote off as plain in childhood, and yet who had married into the wealthy

Lambert pack. It was a challenge, in Beatrice's view. She was determined to nab someone even richer."

Even so, the marriage had apparently worked out, thought Charlotte. Perhaps cold-blooded calculation was more sensible than being dazzled by a will-o-the-wisp. Her own mother's head-in-clouds attitude had been no advertisement for happy-ever-after endings.

"As a teenager, Beatrice assumed she'd be a world-famous model or film star, and she talked her Dad into paying me for numerous glossy photos," Jethro continued. "They were sent to modelling agencies, and although the camera loved Beatrice, in that scene all the girls are beautiful. She was just another wannabe, and no one got in touch. Her daughters were lucky to take after the Beckett side. Less heartache that way."

Then Charlotte had had an overabundance of good fortune not to inherit Melanie's stunning features. Maybe Jethro was correct, but Charlotte would always feel inadequate when confronted by mirrors. In a different school, in a different time, in a different world, she and Fenella might have jointly commiserated.

"Why does Beatrice's failure to be a model mean that the Becketts are phony?" asked Charlotte. "She must enjoy being rich."

"Yeah, but Beatrice took a second-best option, and blames Luke for pulling the plug on her dreams, although he didn't. She made the choice to give up and marry him, but now thinks Luke trapped her. That's my guess, anyhow." But a shrewd deduction, going by Jethro's confident tone, and his hypotheses were often fairly accurate.

"Off the record?" Charlotte suggested.

"Strictly off the record. Not that our dear *Clarion* would print an unfavourable word concerning the Beckett family, but Beatrice isn't perchance the faithfullest spouse in Polrenek.

She needs attention and admiration the way lesser humans need air."

Melanie's ambition had never gone beyond her hometown's perimeter, and she would have been astounded that any woman could require more from life than a husband rich enough to live in Estuary Avenue. Yet Polrenek might seem close to imprisonment for somebody who grew up deeming stardom her rightful destiny, and Beatrice had reacted like a spoilt child who finally realizes that the universe will decline to revolve around her. If she were found dead, the police's prime suspect would almost certainly be Luke, but nothing should have happened to Fenella, even after a Rufus liaison, and there was no evidence of an affair between them. Charlotte's mind raced on. Beatrice and Rufus? Could she be the girlfriend he followed to Polrenek? Rufus was younger than her, but age gaps were no deterrent to romance, and he did have a showbiz link that would appeal to Beatrice. Fenella had somehow discovered their secret, which was as good a scenario as any, although offering no reason why Rufus should kill Nadine along with Fenella. Charlotte gave up, and allowed commonsense to replace melodrama.

"Collected any chitchat à-propos Rufus Olsen?" Charlotte asked Jethro, as they stood outside their target's house. "He's not a local, so discretion isn't first and foremost. I could add intriguing hints to my copy."

"The guy remains a mystery," replied Jethro, sighing at the rumour void, unusual in Polrenek. "You must have a notion or two though, arranging his re-interrogation. Tell all."

"Nothing specific to report so far."

Jethro knew that Charlotte could amplify her statement, if she chose, and his grin was quizzical, but before he could seek extra detail, they were interrupted by a wheezy shout.

"Stop! Wait! Wait a mo!" panted Adam, running down the street to catch them up. Hair skew-whiff, face pink with exertion, hands on knees, he bent forward to recover his breath and demanded, "Why didn't you tell me? Why keep this a secret? Why no text, Charlotte?"

"I heard you'd left the *Clarion*," said Jethro.

"A technicality," Adam informed his knees. "If Vanessa hadn't rung me, I might never have known. You don't play fair, Charlotte."

"But nothing fresh has come up." A lame excuse, and Charlotte knew it, yet she tried not to seem apologetic. "I thought Rufus would go for an appointment next week, but he stipulated this afternoon. It was all last minute."

"You should have sent a text even so," snapped Adam, endeavouring to stand upright again. "Plain sneaky to cut me out."

"What's the big deal with Rufus Olsen?" asked Jethro.

"That's what I'm attempting to learn," retorted Adam. "You can't trust anyone. Charlotte had no right to see the guy behind my back."

"You talk to him then. I don't mind." Charlotte's belief in herself, rarely strong, waned at Adam's onslaught. She was unlikely to outwit Rufus Olsen, whatever he might or might not have done. Police officers were investigating Fenella's death, Nadine's too, and perhaps a connection to Rufus would eventually emerge, but Charlotte was no detective. She worked for a provincial newspaper, and its headlines were usually the particulars of traffic-speed violations or a controversial planning decision, not rampant homicides.

"I'm definitely the person to tackle Olsen," snarled Adam. "You were hopeless, Charlotte, with your feeble questions. He won't be given wriggle room this time."

"Fine by me." Charlotte handed Jethro's bags to Adam, and thrust the tripod at him. She knew he was manipulating her in order to secure a story that might be unique in the town, but Adam needed to restart his career, while she was still employed.

"Should I be here, if it isn't a *Clarion* interview?" queried Jethro, glancing at Charlotte for guidance.

"Stay," Adam commanded. "You'll be a good distraction. Keep telling Olsen to look left or right or straight ahead."

"But I get paid by the *Clarion*," Jethro pointed out. "Who'll foot my bill today? You?"

"Yeah, yeah. OK, Jeth, I will," Adam said too hastily, doubtless confident that his girlfriend would subsidize the impending conquest of London.

"Grab a few pictures for the *Clarion*," Charlotte told Jethro, wondering when Katlyn Kyle would regain her financial senses. "I told Rufus he was part of a local-business series, and I can cobble something together from my original notes."

"What were you going to ask Olsen?" demanded Adam, still suspicious. "And why the sudden rush to make a second appointment? What have you got?"

"Jeth knows as much about Rufus Olsen as I do," Charlotte replied. "Try interrogating him."

"But as a loyal *Clarion* employee, my lips are sealed when it comes to Charlotte's incomparably sensational scoop," said Jethro. "A matter of ethics, Adam, never mind the photographer's moral code. I'm sure you understand."

Adam most certainly did, and blasted an irate scowl in Jethro's direction. Only Adam Rigg was allowed to mock people, while he remained sacrosanct. A goodbye wave, and then Charlotte began strolling back to the *Clarion* office, content that an interview she herself had arranged could be somebody else's assignment. It was clear that investigative journalism and Charlotte Paxton were not destined to become a successful partnership. She and the *Clarion* deserved each other.

*

"Did Adam get there in time?" asked Vanessa, looking up from her computer screen as Charlotte opened the newsroom door. "He was very eager to question Rufus Olsen."

"Adam's wish has been granted. I left him there. He's a better cross-examiner than I'll ever be."

"Adam will get the truth out of Olsen," declared Vanessa. "He's so clever. He's brilliant."

And liable to go further in journalism than Charlotte, but she could live with that if the *Clarion* kept paying her wages. "Found any alluring scraps in the Rufus background?"

"Just a school he might have attended, assuming I'm on the right track. Facial recognition's not bad, but it isn't a hundred percent accurate." Vanessa frowned at the possible false lead in her research, and then added, "Oh, Sidney Tyrrel left you a message. I'm so glad Rosalind took the call, not me. If you interview him, don't mention I'm here. He'll still be livid because our replacement windows were cancelled."

"Your presence at the *Clarion* will be classified information," said Charlotte. "What was Sid's message?"

"You can see him at his place this afternoon, if that's convenient. He'll be there doing paperwork."

"Then I'll go now, as I'm unexpectedly free."

And glad to visit somebody for a chat, rather than monitor an Adam grilling. Charlotte was at ease when she did the typical *Clarion* interview that Adam despised. He had no time to fritter away on cosying up to potential advertisers, Adam would maintain derisively. He sought hot news: hard news: real news. Was his voice going to haunt her, in addition to Melanie's? Unendurable! Charlotte left the *Clarion* office, hoping to leave Adam behind as well.

She had first met Sidney Tyrrel twelve years earlier, when his double-glazing replaced draughtily rattling sash-windows in her mother's flat: the flat now Charlotte's, along with those very same windows. To get conversation off to a pleasant start, she would congratulate Sidney on his excellent workmanship, and say how fortunate Polrenek was to have trustworthy businesses.

"Yeah, waste your days as a smarmy creep," Adam's voice sneered. "Isn't that Rosalind's job?"

Being haunted by a dead parent would seem inevitable, but listening to the *Clarion*'s ex-employee was excruciating, chiefly because Adam's assessment of her felt spot-on accurate. At Farfield Manor, Charlotte had aimed at beating all competition, but now she wanted to relax and be herself again. Adam was a needless reminder of the driven person she had hoped to discard.

Sidney Tyrrel ran the double-glazing company from a cluttered office at the side of his house in a street near the Promenade. It had been a prosperous district throughout the Edwardian era, but former glories were gone, and only decaying shabbiness remained. Yet Sidney clung with tenacious resolve to an area he had known from birth.

"My Dad started the business close on seventy years ago," he told Charlotte, leading her into a miniscule room almost filled by one overcrowded tabletop. "I was hoping my cousin's son might take charge when I retire, but Warren's a bit doubtful. Oh, but you know Warren, of course. I was forgetting you were at primary school together. He's Warren Sutton. Remember him?"

"Yes, him I definitely remember. He once tied my plaits to the playground railings, and I only just managed to untangle myself before the bell went."

"Always a live wire, our Warren." Sidney chuckled, his amusement compelling Charlotte to join in. Yet tiresome joker Warren had later redeemed himself by punching a ten-year-old entrepreneur, whose protection racket fleeced younger children of their pocket money. The scrawny and dark-haired Warren might have grown up to resemble Sidney, as both had plain faces that were transformed by a smile.

"You went to that posh school next," remarked Sidney. "I guess you hang out with Henvers and their sort these days."

"You guess wrong. I was better off imprisoned by my plaits."

Charlotte had said the passwords that proved she was still a true Polreneker, and Sidney's grin became conspiratorial. "I should have known you wouldn't be taken in by them. I remember your Mum."

So did every man who had seen Melanie. "She was very pleased with those replacement windows you put in her flat ages ago. I still live there, and the place is completely draught-free even now."

"My work's always good." Sidney was contradicting an invisible someone: indeed, forcefully contradicting that person. The loss of a Henver contract had left deep wounds, which was no revelation. Supplying the doors and windows for a construction project would boost any small business, and late-lamented Old Mother Trevail's Inn was likely to be the largest building site in an area where well-paid jobs were scarce.

"I can give your double-glazing an unsolicited recommendation," said Charlotte, to inform Sidney that she and the *Clarion* were his steadfast allies.

"I took full responsibility, and replaced those windows cost-free within the week. No argument. No hesitation. No excuses. Not a single word. Not one," Sidney complained, his voice rising in frustration. "OK, so Warren needed more experience as a surveyor. But that's all. And if I can get over his mistake, why should anybody else carp? Warren learnt a valuable lesson, and a lesson certain to stay in his mind. It's how we improve. No reason to blame me. I did my bit."

Sidney had forgotten he was talking to a journalist, but *Clarion* readers knew the paper would back born-and-bred tradesfolk, however unacceptable their windows. The *Clarion* was Sidney's friend.

"I gather you won't be voting for Daniel Henver, if he attempts to storm Parliament again," Charlotte commented.

"Henver doesn't care about Polrenek," declared Sidney, the bitter recollection of his wrongs continuing to anger him. "Any job can hit a snag. That's why honouring your guarantee is vitally important."

"What could be more important? Honoured guarantees mean a dependable firm."

"And the first windows were perfect. Not a thing wrong with them. If Warren had just taken a ladder, he'd have seen that the gutters would stop those bedroom ones opening properly. It was too windy for a ladder, Warren said, as though he couldn't have returned the next calm day to finish his survey. But that's water under bridges now. Family is family, and he's my cousin Laurel's son. We've since moved on."

But not very far away, to judge by Sidney's tone.

"Will insurance policies kick in to give you a hand?"

"Not a chance," grieved Sidney, shaking his head. "I'm sorry Andrew Napier's girl died, but she was a vindictive bitch, telling Daniel Henver and Luke Beckett not to employ me."

"*Nadine* Napier?" demanded Charlotte. "They were her windows?"

"And I replaced them as soon as I could. She had no call to try and destroy my business."

Yet Nadine would have regarded denying Sidney work as suitable retribution after making her wait before she could display a superlative house to envious acquaintances. Nadine would order Gabrielle and Fenella to ensure that any parental contracts with Sidney Tyrrel were cancelled, and that spitefulness meant he lost two lucrative jobs. More than one Polreneker might have had cause to hate Nadine Napier.

"You helped renovate the Old Schoolhouse, didn't you?" Charlotte said, not liking the suspicions that had formed in her mind. "Those new windows look marvellous. I'll ask Jethro Kern to get a picture of the place to accompany your *Clarion* article."

"I did Mevyn Hall as well. Warren's girlfriend lives in the village, and she got us that job," Sidney disclosed, brightening at his chance of a free advertisement.

"Jeth can take some photos in Mevyn too." Charlotte decided she would push for a double-page spread to celebrate Sidney Tyrrel's work. As the *Clarion* still lacked an official editor, all decisions were liable to be Rosalind's, and she would envisage cascades of advertising payments snatched from a grateful Sid.

Yet Charlotte's motive for bolstering the Tyrrel business was based on a desire to thwart Nadine's attempt to harm it, whatever the rights or wrongs behind a double-glazing saga. Charlotte had been born into Sidney's world, with Farfield Manor a preposterous aberration. Unthinkable to doubt the Tyrrel version of any event.

Adam could concentrate on Rufus Olsen. Charlotte had no intention of suggesting there might be an alternative suspect with reason to hate Nadine, even a third as Warren Sutton was no meek pushover either. Charlotte herself could testify to that, although she never would. Polrenek solidarity held fast.

8

"Good idea," declared Rosalind, eyes gleaming at her opportunity to increase *Clarion* revenue via a susceptible target. "Yeah, double-page spreads will demonstrate how important publicity can be. Sid's bound to cough up for adverts after that."

Not if he or Warren were in the dock on a murder charge, thought Charlotte. "Jeth could take photos of the Old Schoolhouse, and Mevyn Village Hall as well, to showcase Sid's work."

"He'll love that." And a latent advertiser's gratification ranked far above what might interest other *Clarion* readers, in Rosalind's view. "Try the same approach with as many businesses as you can."

"OK," said Charlotte, turning around as Vanessa hurried in from the newsroom.

"Charlotte, Olsen's on the phone," whispered Vanessa, apparently fearing Rufus might have a hidden microphone in Rosalind's office. "He wanted to speak to the editor, but I told him Gideon wasn't here, so now Olsen insists on talking to you, and he sounds livid."

"Shall I tackle him, Charlotte?" asked Rosalind.

"No, I'll face the music, whatever tune he screeches." If Adam had accused Rufus of being a murderer, Charlotte was better equipped to deal with the situation. After all, she could truthfully disown Adam, and avert possible *Clarion* lawsuits. Even so, it was a struggle to keep her voice calm.

"Mr Olsen? Charlotte Paxton speaking. How can I help you?"

"That Rigg liar is going to find himself in court," fumed Rufus. "And so will the *Clarion*, if it prints a word of his allegation."

"I'm sorry if Adam Rigg has overstepped the —"

"Overstepped! I'll be consulting my solicitor. As if I'd harm Beatrice's daughter — Beatrice Beckett's daughter — the Beckett girl." Rufus was shouting, and also telling Charlotte more than he realized. To him, Fenella's sole identity had been as Beatrice's daughter. "Rigg should be sacked."

"I agree, Mr Olsen. Adam Rigg is no longer on the *Clarion* staff," announced Charlotte, imitating Farfield's headmistress. "We're a reputable paper, and never make false accusations. Thank you for reporting Rigg's disgraceful conduct, and please accept my apologies. Such behaviour is deplorable, and Adam Rigg is dismissed with immediate effect."

"You can do that?" queried Rufus, taken aback.

"I'm senior reporter in the newsroom, and assure you that Adam Rigg is fired. If you care to check the *Clarion* website, you'll see I've already removed his name from our staff roster. I hope this ends the matter, but naturally that's for you to decide." Did she seem authoritative enough? Certainly Vanessa was gazing at her in wide-eyed astonishment, and Rosalind, at the doorway of her office, was grinning.

"Did you know Rigg had come here to accuse me of murder?" Rufus demanded, mustering his anger for a final rant.

"Mr Olsen, no *Clarion* journalist would ever be dispatched to insult anyone," Charlotte stated, permitting a distinct frostiness to enter her voice at so base a slur on the paper's proud standing. Farfield's redoubtable Miss Polnan had specialized in icy rebukes that could shrivel her victim quicker than a winter hailstorm blasted lingering autumnal plants. "The *Clarion* is not a scandal sheet."

"No, of course it isn't," said Rufus, instantly humbled. "Well, thank you for fixing things with such speed."

"Thank *you* for bringing this to my attention. Rest assured that Adam Rigg has lost his job here. We will never tolerate contemptible actions at the *Clarion*."

Rufus was more stunned than grateful at so satisfactory a conclusion to his grievance. Mumbling further thanks, he ended the call, and Charlotte felt a surge of triumph that she had never before experienced. No surprise that people queued up to become MPs, or even Town Councillors. Wielding power made you feel immortal.

"You sounded just like Miss Polnan," Vanessa said in awe.

"More masterful than Gideon could ever manage," laughed Rosalind. "What's Adam done now?"

"Been himself. Gone in feet-first, accusations blazing without backup evidence. Olsen was a bit incoherent, so actual details are vague, yet crisis deflected, I hope." Impossible to explain properly while Fenella's sister was there, but Rosalind appeared content with a hazy report, and went back into her office, still chortling.

"What did Adam say?" asked Vanessa.

"Olsen didn't itemize his complaints," said Charlotte, forcing a smile. "But when Adam starts hurling questions at people, he rapidly turns into a hurricane, which isn't precisely the staid *Clarion* method. Adam will be much happier if his Fleet-Street dreams come true."

"He thinks Olsen killed Fenella, and so do you. That's why I'm researching him, isn't it? His *Hawk Enterprise* is shady, and Olsen believes he can quash Adam's story by threatening court cases. But that won't happen, will it?" Vanessa's matter-of-fact tone was more disturbing than Adam's palaver. She might be disguising grief but, if so, Vanessa's camouflage was remarkably effective.

"I'm not sure Adam's on the right path when it comes to Rufus Olsen," said Charlotte, doubting that Vanessa would listen. "But Adam will get you answers, sooner or later. Best leave the story in his hands. We've got another *Clarion* to fill by next weekend. Look at our emails, and see what comments people have made."

Hopefully nothing about a Rufus-Olsen-Beatrice-Beckett affair, thought Charlotte.

*

The Tyrrel windows were glowing crimson in a glorious reflection of the twilight sky, as Charlotte approached her flat. Surely replacement double-glazing could not trigger two deaths, no matter how bitter Sidney or Warren had felt regarding work lost through Nadine's malice. A ridiculous reason for homicide, despite the post-pandemic cost-of-living crisis. Unrequited love, catastrophic affairs, jealousy and rejection were established murder forerunners. But double-glazing? No opera or play would feature a villainous window-replacement firm, and Charlotte feared her commonsense had taken flight on *Hawk* wings for even weighing up the likelihood.

Then a man hurried across the road, calling Charlotte's name, and she turned around, glad of a distraction, although one that made her awkward. "Hi, Gideon. How are you? Coming back to the *Clarion* soon?"

Gideon waved an impatient hand to dismiss futile questions, and demanded, "Have you spoken to Gabby? What did she tell you, Char?"

"I haven't heard from her in a while. Is something wrong?"

Very wrong, according to Gideon's face, and he sighed querulously. "When did you last check your phone or emails? Gabby must have told you I asked her to marry me, and yet she hasn't replied to my text. Any of them."

"Maybe Gabrielle's waiting at home for you to turn up in person with red roses, prior to a bended-knee proposal." The *Clarion* could run a new feature: *Aunt Charlotte Advises*. Not that Aunt Charlotte had high hopes of Gabrielle returning Gideon's affection, whether or not he bore roses. Indeed, Aunt Charlotte was unable to imagine anyone willing to marry Gideon.

"Where's the nearest place to get a bouquet?" asked Gideon, lurching from gloom to optimism in a split-second.

"Superstore on Polowther Road." As Charlotte spoke, Gideon rushed off, believing he could control his future with whatever flowers remained after a day's trading. She ought to have kept quiet, Charlotte informed herself, and been a mere sympathetic listener, instead of spouting starry-eyed tosh. Yet, if Gabrielle did reject him, Gideon might become realistic enough to make peace with his father: surely a better prospect than marriage with Gabrielle Henver. Even Gideon would never deserve that fate.

"You're too cynical," Melanie's voice scolded. "I was open to all of life's potential."

"And look how calamitous that plan was," Charlotte muttered. "No wonder I'm cynical."

As she opened the front door, her phone began to ring: a convenient break from Melanie's nagging. For one uncomfortable moment, Charlotte feared the caller might be Gabrielle, garrulous ouija board having told her that a romantic Gideon had been dispatched. But, more predictably, the number shown was Adam's.

"Olsen threw me out," Adam declared, boasting of an achievement. "He's got stuff to hide all right."

"Doesn't everybody? At the first accusation, I'd throw you out too." Charlotte closed her front door, and went into the streetlamp-lit flat. Car headlights were swirling brightness around walls, as though she had entered a lighthouse guiding ships toward safer waters, and it would be easy to go along with Adam's histrionics when a familiar room could appear so alien. However, he must not be allowed to switch his attention to Sidney Tyrrel. Information concerning the Napier windows was classified.

"Olsen isn't his real name, that's certain," continued Adam, intent on proving a point. "Vanessa's convinced the guy's using an alias. Why do that, if you're so squeaky-clean above board? Olsen's got to be distancing himself from a crooked past."

"They change their names all the time in showbiz."

"Yeah," Adam conceded reluctantly. "But —"

"But nothing. You need more than a guy hating the name his parents lumbered him with." If she were encouraging, Adam might become suspicious, and figure out that Charlotte was hoping to nudge him in the direction of a dead-end sidetrack. Yet excessive discouragement could make Adam seek other options that eventually led him to Sidney and Warren. It was a difficult balancing act.

"Olsen killed Fenella because she knew too much. That's totally straightforward."

"Fenella might have had an accident," Charlotte reminded Adam while doubting her own words, and he could sense it.

"Did Nadine Napier have an accident as well? And I've another question. Was Edric Lambert the source who gave you those *Hawk* documents? Lambert's a Beckett cousin, and rumour says you're practically engaged to him. Don't deny it. I've got my sources too." Adam was smug, but Vanessa would have been his informant, and Charlotte laughed.

"Faulty detective work. I didn't meet Edric until after getting my hands on the *Hawk*. He isn't a source about anything, not even the cutthroat world of freight transport."

"Whatever's going on, it's all around you." Adam was thinking aloud, his voice a murmur, before inspiration jerked him into prosecutorial mode. "You've known those Becketts and Napiers for years. The *Hawk* stuff was passed to you, and Edric Lambert's constantly at your side. Vanessa told me her Dad's got the Olsen accounts now, and I reckon that's why she was sent to spy on you. You're right at the centre. What do you know? Or what do they imagine you know? What aren't you telling me?"

A significant amount, Charlotte realized, but Sidney and Warren could be bystanders who deserved protection from Adam running riot through their lives. "Sorry, but I'm as baffled as you are."

"No, you're not," said Adam, stubbornly sure of himself. "It's a rally-round-the-dear-old-school conspiracy against Rufus Olsen."

"I hated the dear old school and its entire populace. Anyhow, Rufus didn't get his paperwork back by killing Fenella, and Luke Beckett merely has your doctored replacements. Olsen might still be unaware that his *Hawk* has flown."

"Does Vanessa know about those fakes?" Adam demanded, fearing the possible alienation of a useful contact. "Did you tell her I altered them?"

"Course not. And should Vanessa be a spy in our midst, she's not an astute one. According to her, you're brilliant."

"An extremely perceptive girl, I'd say, but stop trying to distract me. I need info on Nadine Napier. Olsen killed her for sure. Who else would have done it? And don't cite a passing mugger. Too coincidental."

"The second husband?" suggested Charlotte. "Nadine was divorcing him, and now her chance to raid his bank account is over. Though a building site would be an unlikely *rendezvous* for estranged partners."

"But the Trevail Inn is yet another connection to you," Adam argued, only half-joking. "Until your article claimed the hovel was a sacred relic from Polrenek history, nobody had given that derelict dump a thought for years. I mean, everyone else was amazed to hear Daniel Henver bothered to hire a demolition team. I'd have simply waited for the next brisk wind to whirl through town. I reckon Olsen selected his crime scene after reading your mawkish hyperbole about vandalism of a sacrosanct monument. Only then did he realize the site was perfect for hiding a body. Nadine could be shoved underneath builder débris within minutes. But something made Olsen panic and he fled."

There had been no attempt to hide the body, which would indicate an unpremeditated attack, or an effort to look like one. Yet why had Nadine left her car at the roadside to scramble in stiletto heels over rubble toward a bulldozed Inn? After spotting the person she yearned to berate once again? Sidney Tyrrel? Warren Sutton? Her soon-to-be second ex? Or Rufus Olsen?

Could Nadine have told Rufus that she had just handed his accounts to a journalist? But why would Olsen be prowling around construction sites? Work had stopped until the planning dispute was resolved, but small firms might go there to price a job for Daniel Henver, and that brought Charlotte straight back to Sidney and Warren.

"I still think Nadine was killed in a mugging," said Charlotte.

"Yeah, yeah, and Fenella had an accident," jeered Adam. "What's spooking you?"

The idea that she hoped a murderer might escape justice. Charlotte had had good reason to hate Nadine while at school, but that was no excuse. "I'm being realistic."

"You're ignoring the facts," Adam retorted.

"What facts?"

"Obvious ones," Adam was bluffing, and he abruptly ended the call to avoid elaborating. He had theories, nothing more, and would get no further except through an unforeseen fluke. Charlotte was ashamed to feel glad, but Adam could be right about one thing. She was apparently under Beckett-clan surveillance via their agents Edric and Vanessa.

A cue for Melanie's voice to intervene, and Charlotte waited to hear that being noticed by a wealthy man, no matter what the circumstance, was to a woman's advantage. Definitely Melanie's opinion, but no rebuke came. It seemed that she had finally given up on her daughter, which made a placid autumn evening as bleakly cold as winter.

Even if there were an afterlife, no spirit would return merely to nag offspring, and Polrenek revenants normally restricted themselves to scratching on walls or tapping at beams in discreet yet futile manner. They never displayed pushy tendencies, so perhaps a bereaved daughter had always known she was talking to herself, not Melanie, but still Charlotte felt orphaned and alone.

*

Reluctant to accept her own humdrum findings, Vanessa sighed. "I think Olsen's really a Joseph Colin Smith."

"And that's why he became Rufus," said Charlotte. "Joe Smith would be too anonymous for the film world. His name's got to stand out."

"I guess so." But Vanessa frowned at her inability to provide Adam with proof of diabolical intent behind Olsen's masked identity. "All official and legal, not just an alias he adopted for the time being. I can't imagine why Fenella wanted to get at his accounts, but there must have been a reason. Are you planning to interview him again?"

"After his Adam experience, I'm fairly sure Rufus will never agree to another *Clarion* interview."

Vanessa giggled, but her frustration at the dearth of evidence against Rufus would match Adam's. They were both certain that a criminal was menacing Polrenek, because Adam needed saleable copy to relaunch his career. "I'm positive the Olsen guy's got a secret in his past," Vanessa maintained, "and I'm going to uncover it."

A secret Fenella had presumably learnt, and if it did concern Beatrice Beckett, Charlotte hoped Vanessa would continue to follow Adam down meandering paths that rambled on and on until the journey's original purpose was forgotten.

"Adam says this will be the most incredible story *Clarion* readers have ever seen." Yet Vanessa was more fretful than celebratory. Her parents would want damaging copy buried with Fenella, and Luke Beckett could rely on his pal Conrad Penry to stifle any problematic details. However, Adam was determined to expose a psychopathic Rufus, and *Hawk* hacking might not then remain under wraps. Adam Rigg was the enemy Luke Beckett should fear, not a provincial newspaper.

"Most leads dwindle to nothing in the end," said Charlotte.

Then why was Fenella dead? Why had Nadine also died? Questions probably racing through Vanessa's mind, but ones that stayed unspoken. "Adam swears you know far more about Rufus Olsen than you'll admit."

"Adam can't resist the occasional conspiracy theory," said Charlotte, smiling in a show of tolerance for idiosyncrasies, although after her own half-baked conjecture, she ought to sound less patronizing. Unlike Adam, Charlotte knew that a hunch had to be supported by evidence.

"Edric told Mum he can't even guess what you're thinking."

"Enigmatic, that's me," declared Charlotte. "I cultivate an aura of mystery to disguise the fact I don't do much actual thinking. At the eleventh or twelfth Council debate, your brain shuts down to preserve its sanity."

So Edric and Beatrice had discussed what Charlotte Paxton might suspect. If Vanessa passed on Edric's comment to Adam, he would order Charlotte to seduce the deluded sucker, and grab a copy of the Rufus email to Lambert Freight Transport.

"What's funny?" asked Vanessa.

"Just reappraising my career. I'm off to visit a cottage in windily damp Harbour Way, and then I head for Polrenek's last greengrocer shop, soon to close because of superstore cut-price offers. Was it for this I laboured night and day to get into university?"

"I asked Adam what a bowgle was, and he said poltergeists don't exist. You believe in them?" Vanessa was torn between Charlotte her Mentor and Adam the Omniscient, but then she gasped. "Do you think it might be Fenella? Is she trying to get messages through to us?"

Not from a soggy backstreet, thought Charlotte. Fenella Beckett would insist on haunting a more prestigious address than Harbour Way, particularly if she had somehow latched herself onto a spectral Nadine. "There are always logical explanations for anything that goes bump in the night. Like Adam, I don't believe poltergeists are real." Emphatic words that troubled Charlotte's West-Country upbringing, and she felt apprehensive lest an ethereal world might so resent disparagement, heavy objects would be hurled at her head on entering the spook-infested cottage.

"Fenella was into spiritualism," said Vanessa, as if that made her sister's return from the hereafter more rational. "She went to séances."

"I'm not sure that Gabrielle Henver or her ouija board ever summoned any spirits from the vasty deep to appear in a school's reference library."

"Maybe not," Vanessa admitted, although uneasily. "But it might be different now."

Because Harbour Way was close to the place where Fenella's body had been found? Disquieting for those who lived in the area if every drowning led to a resident ghost.

"Fenella wouldn't haunt random strangers. But I'm not the person to consult, when I don't believe in all that." Yet Charlotte plainly did, as she again worried about offending a possible seventh dimension by her denial of its existence.

"So if there are spirits, you think they go back to a house they knew." Vanessa concluded.

"Too early in the day for me to ponder a cosmos and its inscrutable murkiness. Try Gabrielle Henver. This is her field of expertise."

"I guess so," agreed Vanessa, yet without enthusiasm. "Will it help Adam, if I talk to Gabrielle? She never spoke to me, when I was a kid, but I could tell her I'm helping you research bowgles for the *Clarion*, and Adam can give me other questions to ask. Not that I want to contact. Gabrielle. She's a total bitch. That old hag made poor Adam lose his job."

Not to mention losing Gideon his job too. Charlotte wondered if she would be next on a Henver hit-list, after dispatching Vanessa. "Don't let Gabrielle have too much info."

"Absolutely not. She led Adam on, and then tried to destroy his career, but that won't happen. Adam's so brilliant, all the newspapers will want him. I bet he'll be working on telly before long."

Vanessa would have difficulty hiding her indignation, should she encounter Gabrielle, but the result might be interesting, and Charlotte advised, "You could get her chatting about Farfield, and when she's relaxed, say that Adam's in line for a job on the *West Briton* because of a fantastic scoop. See if Gabrielle starts panicking. She might let something slip."

"Her involvement with Rufus Olsen?" Vanessa's eyes began to gleam at obtaining such a scoop for Adam.

"Those Henvers are all sly," Charlotte said, reviving an old prejudice. "I bet they're into shady stuff that Adam could unearth with your assistance. But don't enlighten Gabrielle."

"Journalists never reveal a source," Vanessa stated, trusting her professionalism would impress Charlotte. "Will I really help Adam, if I interview Gabrielle?"

Vanessa's loyalty belonged first and foremost to Adam, so a reminder that the *Clarion* actually employed her was pointless. She had yet to decode Adam's airy disregard for other people, which was the mistake Melanie had also made in her dealings with men.

"Better not tell Gabrielle you've met Adam. If she doesn't know, you'll get more out of her." But there was no need for Charlotte to tutor Vanessa in dishonesty. Farfield Manor's stern régime had taught its pupils to lie, cheat and bypass rules with merry insouciance. Adam would have thrived at the school.

"I won't let Gabrielle suspect a thing," declared Vanessa.

*

A row of sixteenth-century cottages had once been the draughtily ramshackle homes of fisher-folk and harbour workers, but was now a pastel-tinted, double-glazed centrally-heated wasteland, because second-home owners were snatching up house after house at exorbitant prices few Polrenekers could match. The status symbols would then be left empty for months on end, but Laurel Sutton's cottage was a rare exception: still alive, still owned by permanent residents, last of the former diligent community.

Gabrielle Henver plus ouija board might be better equipped to investigate a scratching bowgle than Charlotte Paxton ever would, but Laurel Sutton, cousin of Sidney, mother of Warren, turned out to be a reassuringly down-to-earth local-government employee, who had had little belief in ghosts until she acquired her own. And one that was expanding its repertoire beyond the occasional scratch.

"It'll answer questions now: a single knock for yes, two for no. Well, that's what Florence Cobb claims. It doesn't talk to me. You should interview Florence. She's an expert on psychic stuff." Words incompatible with Laurel's professionally styled brown hair, neat business suit, and fingernails glinting under satiny varnish. An office was her natural habitat, not a haunted house. "Vermin, I thought first, but the pest-control people maintain there's nothing behind any beam or wall. Florence is trying to get it to move, but no luck so far. I'd be tempted to move instead, but this has been my home for over twenty-seven years. Besides, as everybody in Polrenek knows about the bowgle, I'd have to sell to a second-home owner, and I couldn't do that. I won't!"

"A real quandary," Charlotte commented, hoping no show-off chatty bowgle would attach itself to her when she left Harbour Way.

"Florence said to explore the cottage's past, so that she can access a stronger wavelength, but I haven't found much." Laurel shook her head in irritation. Noisy neighbours were dealt with by the Town Council, but no department tackled noisy ghosts. "Perhaps you could dig up a reason why we're being haunted, Charlotte. The *Clarion* history pages are always so very — so very — so very comprehensive, and Horace Quennell at the Prom Café says you write them."

"For the moment," admitted Charlotte, wondering if she ought to apologize. "I've never come across a traumatic event in this cottage, or any place in Harbour Way, but I'll do more research."

"I can't think why a bowgle should suddenly choose to hang around here." Laurel glanced up at the granite walls and wooden ceiling, as if ghostly fingers would materialize and begin writing an explanatory message. "I haven't had any previous bother, and it's a bit much to get used to, especially after decades of silence."

"Maybe this is a hundredth-year anniversary," suggested Charlotte. "Perhaps your bowgle will leave in January. When did you first notice the scratching?"

"A month or so back. Do you think it'll stop at New Year?"

"Well, it can't be permanent, or you'd have heard the sounds long ago." Taken aback at being regarded an authority on the methods and procedure of strident phantoms, Charlotte forced herself to sound confident, and Laurel did indeed appear comforted. And there was some good news. The bowgle clearly had nothing whatsoever to do with Fenella or Nadine, as it had commenced activities before either death. "Have you been upset recently? Or stressed at work?"

"No," snapped Laurel. "Absolutely not."

She was lying, but without cause. The *Clarion* would never report her son's inadequate surveying skill or any trouble Laurel might have with antagonistic bosses. A haunted-cottage story should bring in helpful spook-eradication tips, but more earthbound matters were none of Charlotte's business, and she ignored Laurel's acerbic tone. "I think the bowgle will vanish as abruptly as it arrived."

Words that Charlotte would want to be told, should psychic phenomena invade her flat, and Laurel began to relax. "You've investigated other hauntings where that happened?"

"A similar one, and the voice just went away." Charlotte could speak from experience at last, since Melanie had left her daughter's mind without even saying goodbye.

Awake in the night, brooding on her problems, Laurel might become conscious of previously unnoticed sounds: a wooden beam expanding and contracting or wind-gusts under roof tiles. Laurel had doubtless created her own ghost, which was an admirably rational, scientific and level-headed conclusion to reach through calm analysis. All the same, Charlotte knew that nothing could persuade her to spend a night inside Laurel's bowgle-ridden cottage.

*

Vanessa was looking perturbed, when Charlotte went into the newsroom, and an explanation seemed all too obvious. "So, you met Gabrielle?"

Vanessa nodded, rueful rather than victorious. "I don't know why Fenella was friends with Gabrielle Henver. She's a complete phony."

"Can't disagree. I never warmed to her."

"She was horrible about Adam." Vanessa's tone condemned Gabrielle outright, and there could be no appeal against that verdict. "She said he's a manipulative chancer, who uses people to benefit himself."

Again Charlotte was unable to disagree. A rare moment when her opinion and Gabrielle's coincided, but there was no need to burden Vanessa with superfluous info. "How did Gabrielle come to mention Adam?"

"She asked if he was pestering my Dad for interviews. As if Adam would be so insensitive!"

Vanessa was affronted by the shameful smear on Adam's noble character, and Charlotte felt glad to have moved beyond adolescent crushes. "Sounds like Gabrielle's got something to hide, and she fears Adam will suss out her guilty secret."

"That's what I think too," declared Vanessa. "You won't believe it, but Gabrielle was actually proud to have lost Adam his job. She said it had been worth putting up with that dreary Gideon. Adam isn't the person who uses people. Gabrielle was describing herself."

"Did she seem anxious?" ventured Charlotte. "Afraid that somebody might target her next?"

"I wouldn't care if they did," jeered Vanessa. "Though Gabrielle got a bit het up when she asked if I'd met Rufus Olsen. Fenella's boyfriend, Gabrielle called him to throw me off the trail. As if Fenella ever went anywhere to meet anyone, let alone boyfriends. Then, Gabrielle was telling me not to confide in you."

"Why? She dismissed me as a clueless nonentity years ago," Charlotte pointed out, smiling with Vanessa.

"Gabrielle's reassessed you. You're clever, with an investigative team on tap," laughed Vanessa. "She doesn't realize they work for Adam."

"What does Gabrielle think his team will learn?"

"Could be her father who needs to worry about investigators." Vanessa shrugged, indifferent to the fate of Adam adversaries. "My Dad says Daniel Henver might be congratulating himself too soon over Mother Trevail's Inn. The Council hates retrospective planning applications, and Henver will have to cough up really big bucks this time."

"Who's on the Henver bribe list?" demanded Charlotte. "Did your father give a name? Or names?"

"Is it important? Adam says local-government stuff is the last word in boredom, and no one reads those pages anyway."

"He could be right, but the *Clarion* has to take an interest in Council matters, particularly when corruption's involved. Would you ask your father what he's heard, even if it's only a rumour or two? We might be able to get Henver's planning application thrown out, and then he'd be forced to rebuild the Trevail Inn. Adam would be so pleased."

"You should talk to Dad yourself," said Vanessa, giggling. "He told Mum it was the first time Edric had dated a sensible girl, and that's high praise from Dad."

But a dull compliment, and one that ought to send Edric hurtling in the opposite direction. Fortunate she already suspected him of a hidden agenda, thought Charlotte, or her day might have been ruined. "I think your father will speak more freely, if I'm not there."

"You mean, I'd be an undercover reporter," cried Vanessa, gloating at her unexpected promotion. "Yeah, Dad will totally forget I work at the *Clarion*. And when he does remember, it'll be too late. Is this a scoop? Could it give Adam his job back?"

"Depends how solid your source's info is." Charlotte tried to be hopeful, but no allegation had ever stuck to Daniel Henver, and Luke Beckett might simply have been airing a prejudice. Yet any chance to stymie Henver was worth pursuing.

"Dad would like to annoy Henver," Vanessa remarked.

"And Conrad Penry will consider making you editor, if the *Clarion* does topple Daniel Henver. Gideon's opinion of Gabrielle is not shared by his father."

"She's horrible," snarled Vanessa. "She's a total lying fraud. I can't wait until Adam gets those disgusting Henvers named and shamed in every national newspaper."

"Well, let's concentrate on a possible *Clarion* story for now." Would Daniel Henver risk petty bribes or comparable small-town misdemeanours? Yet those born wealthy seemed to believe they were above the regulations other people had to obey. Arrogance might lead to a Henver downfall. "Assuming we can prove there have been Council shenanigans, and also assuming Daniel Henver hits the headlines after a *Clarion* scoop, our poor old paper will be evicted from this building. But that's a small price to pay for exposing the charlatan."

"I thought journalists were meant to be impartial," Vanessa commented. "Yet you just can't bear Daniel Henver. You absolutely loathe the guy."

"With a deep and abiding hatred that editorial guidelines are unable to erase." Charlotte overdid the venom in her statement, and made Vanessa laugh. "I won't be content unless Henver rots in jail one day."

"My Dad would second that. He was furious when the bloke tried to become our MP. Already a glut of liars and vultures in Parliament, he said. Did you have to interview Henver at the time?"

"I'd be more inclined to bash that pompous smirk off his face than ask questions, so Adam went instead. Forget *Clarion* neutrality, I couldn't endure Henver's gambit to dupe voters."

"Adam will see the guy never has nerve enough to flaunt himself around Polrenek again," predicted Vanessa, confident in her hero's prowess. "I bet Henver cheats on his wife as well."

"He does," confirmed Charlotte. "He definitely does. So I've heard. Off the record."

"Knew it!" Vanessa declared.

9

Charlotte left the *Clarion* offices and strolled into a mild afternoon, when even the ocean was subdued, making its winter violence seem mythical. A perfect day, tranquil and warm, rare in squally Polrenek: a day to be treasured. Then his voice was calling her name, and Charlotte saw the middle-aged man get out of a brazenly expensive car that matched his bespoke suit. He still had a sleek handsomeness, almost youthfully smooth features, and thick brown hair that ruffled in a sudden breeze. Since childhood Charlotte had thought of him as a monster, and she was surprised he should look so blandly inoffensive.

"Do you know who I am, Charlotte?"

"You're the man who demolished Trevail's Inn: a Grade-Two Listed Building. Would you care to comment on such vandalism for the *Clarion*?" Damn him. He had dark-blue eyes: the eyes she saw in any mirror.

"Straight down to business, just like me." Daniel Henver smiled, and Charlotte fought an unsuccessful battle to hide her resentment. She was nothing like him: never would or could be. "What were you told about me?"

"Little to your credit," snapped Charlotte. "Although as the *Clarion* is strictly impartial, anything you do say will be reported accurately with no editorial criticism."

Daniel laughed, appearing genuinely amused. "I gather Melanie didn't give you a very flattering account of me."

"Did you expect her to?" Charlotte retorted. "What do you want?"

"To persuade you to call off your attack dog. Adam Rigg is becoming irksome."

"He doesn't work for the *Clarion* now. Your daughter got him sacked."

"Which daughter?"

"You only have one."

"Judging by your attitude, I think we both know that isn't true."

A mocking tone, Charlotte decided. His words were an insult to her and also to Melanie. Remaining in Henver's vicinity was betrayal, and Charlotte hurried away, as though she could leave the past behind in a specific place, but Daniel followed her.

"I can keep pace with you. At least, I should be able to, considering the vast sum a personal trainer lifts from my bank account each month. Melanie chose to cut me out of your life. A surprisingly determined girl, your mother. I'd thought she was sweet and gentle, not a latent thunderstorm complete with lightning bolts."

He had told Melanie that his marriage was a dismal failure, on the rocks, practically in a divorce court. Any lie to seduce the romantic teenager, who believed Romeo and Juliet were amateurs compared to them. Well, until finding out that Romeo's discarded wife was in fact current enough to produce his daughter, and only days after Melanie realized the stork was also planning to visit her. She might have been able to fool her seventeen-year-old self a little longer, but Daniel's reaction to the news of an unofficial baby, preparing to gate-crash his existence, brought Melanie face-to-face with reality. Romeo found himself recast as villain, and was swept away by Storm Melanie.

"She ordered me to have nothing to do with you, but I couldn't accept that," Daniel was saying, apparently convinced he had been the hapless victim of Melanie's refusal to tolerate a submissive background rôle in his world. "I never stopped thinking about you, and did my utmost to guarantee your future by paying for a place at the best school locally."

"If you mean Farfield Manor, I went there on a scholarship," said Charlotte, angered by the attempt to con her.

"I created that scholarship on condition you were its first recipient. Told the headmistress your father had been my childhood friend."

Daniel sounded smug, and a temperate day abruptly felt cold. Charlotte had taken pride in being chosen for a free education at Farfield Manor when other pupils, such as Gabrielle Henver, were only allowed to enter its high and mighty premises after parents forked out excessive fees. Yet Miss Polnan, and perhaps the entire teaching staff, knew that Charlotte Paxton had merely been permitted to defile their edifice because of a rich man's self-congratulatory largesse.

"I hated every day I spent in that dump," Charlotte stated, longing to puncture Daniel's puffed-up egotism.

"Yet Farfield could never defeat you. You're a fighter like me. Nothing will prevent you reaching the heights after your *Clarion* stint ends. I wish Gabrielle had the same drive and single-mindedness."

She probably did, but her ambition was to enjoy years of leisure financed by a rich father or rich husband. Charlotte just had to stay working in local journalism, and Daniel would be equally disappointed in her. A simple way to avenge Melanie.

"Well, I'm unable to help you. Nor can the *Clarion*," said Charlotte, to notify Daniel that the confrontation was at an end. "Adam Rigg's a freelance. I can't stop his investigation."

"You can. I know you can," Daniel asserted, his voice implying that they shared a secret. "Rigg's working with your investigative team. It's quite plain that you don't just write for the *Clarion* now. You're also employed by a news organization with far greater clout and resources than Conrad Penry's negligible set-up. He wouldn't fund one investigator, never mind a whole team of them."

Charlotte's celebrated instigative team yet again. Daniel's informant had to have been Gabrielle, and it meant Adam was asking questions that were inconvenient enough to goad Daniel into contacting another inconvenient part of his life. Better to leave him worried, and encourage a little paranoia as well. "I work for the *Clarion*," Charlotte declared. "That's all I'm prepared to say."

"I didn't kill Nadine Napier," Daniel protested, as if there had been an accusation in Charlotte's statement. "Yes, I own the Trevail land, but I've no idea why Nadine would go there. I barely knew that girl, and wasn't even near the site when she died. Your team should concentrate on Rufus Olsen. Gabby thinks he was Fenella Beckett's boyfriend, but that's wrong."

Daniel paused, waiting for Charlotte's response, but there was no need to push him to go on talking. He would say more, either because Daniel had no alibi for the time of Nadine's death, or because he preferred not to mention an inopportune alibi. Another Melanie? Another deluded female under the impression that his divorce papers were on a judge's desk? Almost fun to disconcert him by remaining silent.

"You already know about Olsen," Daniel concluded, mistaking blankness for pokerfaced inscrutability. "You know Beatrice Beckett and Rufus Olsen are lovers."

Confirmation of Charlotte's guess? Or was Daniel also guessing? Charlotte glanced away, hoping to seem nonchalant, a pose shaken when she spotted Vanessa further down the road, but mercifully too far off to have overheard

Daniel possibly slandering her mother. As he turned his head to see what was distracting Charlotte, Vanessa ducked behind a shop door.

"Thank you for your input," said Charlotte, to regain Daniel's attention.

"It's clear as morning light that Rufus Olsen killed Nadine, and Fenella too, because they were going to alert the Inland Revenue to his activities via you. So get Adam Rigg and your investigative team off my back. You'll find I can be very grateful," added Daniel, his manner suggesting there were no problems that money would be unable to remove.

Was Daniel a police suspect, or merely spooked by Adam? Whichever, message delivered, mission accomplished, Daniel began strolling back to his car, and Charlotte walked in the opposite direction, knowing Vanessa would reappear as soon as Daniel drove off. Did he not realize that by attempting to exonerate himself, a resentful gate-crasher had been told he needed to evade police scrutiny?

"What did Henver want? What did he say?" Vanessa asked, breathless after rashly dodging traffic as she sped across the road. "Did he threaten Adam? Did he try to bully you?"

"No, but Adam's got him jumpy. Henver was agitated, and kept on maintaining that he didn't kill Nadine."

"Do the police believe he did?" Vanessa demanded.

"I reckon Henver doesn't have an alibi. Or one he prefers not to name. Anyhow, you can tell Adam that he's hit a nerve."

"Adam will be so glad." Then Vanessa's face lost its excitement, and she started whispering as though not to disturb the placid air around them, "But if Henver murdered Nadine, did he kill Fenella too?"

"I don't think so," Charlotte admitted, albeit reluctantly. She would baulk at a murderous appendage to her DNA, and yet Daniel imprisoned was an attractive picture. "Olsen seems to have been Fenella's sole target, and Nadine was just her collaborator. There's no *Hawk* link to Henver."

"But he's panicky because Adam's onto him?" Vanessa relaxed, despite the prospect of a Polrenek executioner still being at large to roam streets and lanes throughout the town.

"Was Nadine a Henver girlfriend?"

"Maybe. Something's got him edgy."

"What would rattle him?" asked Vanessa, to glean every last detail for Adam. "Did Henver want rid of Nadine because he'd got a new lover?"

"He's sure to have one, whether or not she was his alibi. Anyway, Henver's a businessman, and they're usually in contact with people every hour of every day. Too odd, Henver suddenly deciding to be a hermit."

Vanessa frowned, but came to the obvious conclusion without need for an additional hint. "So he either killed Nadine, or his alibi's somebody he won't name. Could be Henver's scared his wife will divorce him, grabbing half the dosh. I'll tell Adam, and he'll find out."

"Yep, Adam never gives up." Was she avenging Melanie, or acting like an obnoxious child? The latter, Charlotte suspected, but Adam would hound Daniel, and that was a cheering thought. Henver wealth could not buy him freedom from tenacious Adam.

As Vanessa hurried down the Promenade toward Estuary Avenue, she was already gabbling into her mobile, while Charlotte stood at the bus stop, knowing she ought to be ashamed of her vindictiveness. But what else could Daniel Henver expect? Automatic loyalty? Dutiful compliance? Charlotte was a born-and-bred Polreneker, and the town had yet to spawn a saint.

*

Charlotte's phone started to ring even before she had taken off her coat after closing the front door. Adam either knew Polrenek bus timetables by heart, or he and Vanessa had only just finished talking.

"Why didn't you ring me? How come Henver's confiding in you? Are his lawyers going to threaten me?"

"Possibly," Charlotte replied. "Although Henver thought you were still working for the *Clarion*, and I could rein you in. Does it matter? You've got plenty to investigate now."

"Would you have told me any of this, if Vanessa hadn't seen Henver?" In Adam's suspicious mind, a scoop could easily have been filched from him, its rightful possessor. "Have you met Henver before today?"

"No, and I think his secret could turn out to be embarrassing rather than criminal, unless the latest girlfriend's underage." Charlotte went into her front room and sat down, wearied by both Adam's distrust and Melanie's poor judgment in men.

"Was Nadine a Henver girlfriend? She did die on property he owns."

"Would Henver be dim-witted enough to kill her there?"

"Double-bluff?" Adam was doubtful, but could and did rapidly dredge up an alternative explanation. "Henver ditched Nadine by text or email. Minutes later, she saw Daniel on his building site, left her car to harangue him, and he exploded. It was a crime of passion."

"Passion? Daniel Henver? Are we discussing the same guy?"

"You seem to know a great deal about him," remarked Adam, suspicion reasserting itself. "When did you become the Henver expert?"

"Shortly after I began to report on Planning-Committee issues. His applications are smiled through, even ones that should be thrown out," complained Charlotte, indignant again at the annihilation of so many granite structures, some having withstood centuries, only to be replaced by mediocre rabbit-hutch houses needing constant repair. "Take Old Mother Trevail's Inn, for example —"

"I'd prefer to leave it," groaned Adam, having heard innumerable Charlotte-tirades on the subject.

"And look how Henver claimed half his site drawings had been lost by an incompetent Council clerk. Bizarre fluke that only those pages concerning the Inn's demolition should go AWOL from his planning application. Typical Henver to shift blame onto somebody he considers powerless."

"I know, I know," sighed Adam. "You've told me so often, every last detail is etched in my brain. Yeah, a classic Henver dodge, but you couldn't get proof then and you can't now. We win some; we lose some. Let it go. The Nadine case is far more promising. I've got to find somebody who knew what was going on, or at least saw them together. I don't suppose you could have a girly gossip with Gabrielle?"

"You suppose correctly. And after her experience of your cross-examination technique, she'll boycott any *Clarion* reporter who approaches her. Gabrielle clings to a grudge." So did Charlotte. A discomforting reflection that it might be an inherited characteristic.

"I'll dispatch Vanessa for the girly gossip, while I try milking Nadine's husband," decided Adam. "As they were getting divorced, I bet he's sick of hearing laments for the dear departed. Besides, a husband is likelier than anyone else to bump off his wife. He'll be well worth a visit. Why did they split up?"

"Another woman, I gather. But it was Nadine's second marriage, and some people are serial divorcers."

"And some are serial killers," Adam commented optimistically. "I'll track down the first husband too. Who was he?"

"I'm not an authority on Nadine. You'll have to research her yourself."

"Nadine deleted him from her social media, along with Piper. Only posh-house pictures remain. Vanessa might know more. I'll phone her."

And Vanessa might be upset by a reminder that her sister could have been slain by the same murderer, but Adam would never think of that. The call ended abruptly, leaving Charlotte to brood yet again on Old Mother Trevail's Inn.

*

"Just a follow-up chat to be certain I've got the specifics right, and you're happy with what's been written." Charlotte sat down opposite Sidney in his office, and handed him a computer printout, confident that he would approve her account of Tyrrel excellent craftsmanship over decades: *Clarion* praise at its most fulsome, reserved for potential advertisers.

"Yeah, that's all accurate," Sid confirmed, smiling at the manifold achievements of his family and firm.

"Daniel Henver is mad not to employ you on the Trevail site," remarked Charlotte, struggling not to overdo casualness. "He won't get a more reliable company."

"Not sure I want to be associated with him," scoffed sour-grapes Sid. "No better than a crook, that Henver. But he'll get his just deserts one day."

"I can never understand how he fiddles planning permission so easily. Practically the whole town's a conservation area, even alleyways and slithery granite steps. Yet I reckon the Council will backpedal when it comes to reconstructing Old Mother Trevail's Inn."

"And that's why Henver knew he could tear it down."

"The building might have been converted into flats or a hotel. There was no need to send in that demolition gang," Charlotte maintained, as she had done for weeks. "I went to the Town Hall, and studied Henver's original plan. Not a single word or diagram about the Inn's removal. Strange that the allegedly absent bits should relate to it alone, and nothing else."

"Convenient, rather than mysterious." Sid grimaced, shaking his head. "There were far too many regulations and restrictions on the Trevail site to please Henver. He doesn't like being told what to do, and an extra half-dozen houses can be jerry-built now that the Inn's obliterated. Quick money, and then onto his next scheme, while a few more Councillors wine and dine on Henver freebies or get golf-club membership."

"He doesn't joke about cheating the system, does he?" Yet Charlotte knew Daniel would never be that stupid.

"He's no fool. Bribery works, and Old Mother Trevail's was a goner from the start. Henver took that for granted."

Of course he had. Daniel assumed his wishes were law. Losing the chance to become Polrenek's MP must have astounded him. "Did Henver mention being a candidate again in the next general election?"

"We talked double-glazing, not politics. Are these questions for the *Clarion*?" Sidney was hopeful, but felt obliged to add a warning, "Henver will come after you. And how!"

A reality check: one that Charlotte knew she had to accept. "He covers his tracks too well for me to prove a thing, and the high-ups in our Planning Department would close ranks."

"My cousin Laurel might talk to you. Well, off the record at any rate. They're blaming her, and yet Laurel would never lose paperwork. She's the most efficient person in Polrenek, but could still be sacked, thanks to Henver. There are too many Councillors grovelling at his feet. You ever met our Daniel?"

"Once. Briefly. Full of himself. I wasn't impressed." But Charlotte could admire her amateur psychology. The bowgle might have been manufactured by Laurel, as she lay awake fretting and jittery. A triumph of rationality, thought Charlotte. Unless ghosts did exist.

"Henver likes to throw his weight around," jeered Sidney. "Yet he'd have been nothing without rich parents. Our Daniel hasn't done a proper day's work since he was born."

"That's true." A pleasure to belittle Henver, and Charlotte was cheered that his deceit might somehow become public knowledge. "Would your cousin talk to me again? Perhaps we could prove she wasn't at fault."

"Henver would get you sacked as well."

"Not while Conrad Penry employs me." A safeguard that even Daniel Henver's influence could not remove.

*

"The flowers didn't work, Char. Gabby won't talk to me. She's blocked my phone number." Gideon seemed less distraught than indignant at his rejection, and Charlotte was silent, watching rush-hour traffic clog the road outside her Tyrrel window, while she sought a tactful way to suggest that the ex-editor should forget Gabrielle and make peace with Conrad. It was obvious what Gideon ought to do, but his bewilderment left Charlotte uncertain what he expected from her. Sympathy? Guidance? Coaching?

"Sorry," Charlotte said at last, in the absence of a slicker response.

"Talk to her," urged Gideon, as though still in a position to give Charlotte orders. "Tell Gabby she's being unreasonable."

"I doubt that message will endear you to her." Penry conceit would be no match for Henver arrogance. Gideon had served his purpose, and was therefore in Gabrielle's past. A mere bouquet could alter nothing.

"How am I meant to go on?" Gideon enquired, elbows on Charlotte's table to prop up his drooping head. "I've sacrificed my whole life, yet Gabby doesn't appear to care one iota."

"She might have met somebody else," Charlotte offered as encouragement for Gideon to move on. "And he could be the jealous type. So Gabrielle doesn't want to upset him."

"What's she told you?" Gideon was taken aback that a rival could oust him when, in his mind, Gabrielle was branded property.

"I haven't spoken to her for ages. I'm just guessing. I don't know the Henver mob." Gideon's power to sack her had gone, but still Charlotte sounded apologetic. There was always a danger that Conrad might rehire his son, if the Gabrielle split proved permanent. Best to reprise sycophancy, just in case.

"Phone Gabby. Ask her who he is," instructed Gideon. "Get a name."

Assuming the contender existed. If not, Gideon would have to accept that Gabrielle had dumped him for being himself, but a devious lecher in pursuit of the Henver heiress might enable Gideon to exit with dignity.

"Gabby's naïve," he moaned. "Gabby thinks the entire world is as generous and easy-going as she is. Phone her. Warn her."

Charlotte would never equate his Gabrielle with the one she had known, but time should enlighten Gideon. "OK, I'll ring her this evening, and then get back to you."

"Call now," insisted Gideon.

"Not possible. I've got an appointment to interview someone in her haunted cottage, and I'm running late." A convenient excuse that was practically true.

"Is Adam Rigg still chasing after Gabby?" demanded Gideon.

"He never had a chance. Gabrielle wasn't fooled by him. Sorry, but I'll have to dash. Phone you in a couple of hours."

"Ghosts aren't real," Gideon objected, cross at having to wait for vital news. "They're an illusion."

"Perhaps," conceded Charlotte. "But they make brilliant copy."

Nostalgia had Gideon sighing in pensive melancholy, as he remembered bustling around the *Clarion* newsroom. His days would now feel empty, and Gideon might come to resent the woman who cost him a self-image he had overvalued. His road back to fulfilment would entail writing off Gabrielle, Charlotte decided on Gideon's behalf, but another person's life was so easy to tidy up.

*

"Well, if it isn't Charlie Paxton. I bet you can't place me."

Charlotte could, but only because she had knocked on the Sutton front door, and knew that Warren was Laurel's son. A jeans-and-T-shirt-clad man in his stocky twenties bore little resemblance to the skinny boy wearing school uniform, who had gleefully compensated for his diminutive stature with raucous cheek. Cornish dark hair and blue eyes were the only reminders of that impulsive child, once smaller than Charlotte. "Nobody could forget you, Warren Sutton. I trust the years have had a civilizing effect."

"And on you, after your defection to that posh school. My girlfriend Elly says it's a rubbish place anyway. How come you're here again?" Warren had always managed to defuse irate teachers by utilizing a cheerfully forthright smile, and he tried the same tactic on Charlotte: a manoeuvre she had too often witnessed to be taken in by it. Unlike his mother, Warren was presumably reluctant to publicize the Sutton's resident ghost, who would not be a plus factor if the cottage were ever sold, and it might represent Warren's sole legacy.

"I'd like your mother to read the piece I've written, and check she's happy with it."

"That's all?" queried Warren, still smiling but now dubiously.

"What else? Is there a story I'm missing? Do tell me every last squalid detail." Charlotte smiled too, but aware that she was hoping to get Laurel's account of a certain planning application. "*Clarion* reporters are eager for any hot news. You might not believe it, but Council Meetings and school concerts tend to lose their lustre after four years."

Warren opened the door wider to allow Charlotte inside, her ostensible candour temporarily disarming him. "Well, I'm not keen on the idea of press intrusion in our lives and all that, but you'll print the story anyhow, so better Mum does check it. She'll be home soon."

"Your mother works in the Planning Department, I gather," Charlotte remarked, aiming at serene chattiness. "Wouldn't be my dream job."

"And yet you seem spellbound by us," commented Warren, leading Charlotte into the front room through a doorway built for people shorter than they were. "You're writing an article about Sid too. Why the fascination with our family?"

"Less fascination than coincidence. I interviewed the Prom-Café's Hector Quennell for a local-business profile. He suggested I talk to Sid next, and told me there was a bowgle plaguing your mother."

Charlotte's reply made Warren frown sceptically. He would have heard Laurel complain about Henver duplicity, and knew Council employment contracts prohibit discussing job-related concerns with the media. Charlotte could cause trouble, and Warren was cagey.

"Readers love a ghost story," Charlotte continued. "And with the local-business profile, your family's an ideal *Clarion* target this week."

"What's Sid told you?" Warren was still vigilant, conscious that his surveying deficiencies might soon be emblazoned in print for all Polrenek to savour.

"It's pretty much the same for every business in town: expenses high, households cutting back, so fewer opportunities around. But the Tyrrel firm is sure to survive. I mean, things must have been equally difficult at times in the past, and yet three generations managed to keep going. Did you work there straight from school?"

"Unlike your school-pals, I didn't have the option to lounge around," Warren retorted.

"If that's a dig at me, forget it. I made no pals in Farfield Manor, and haven't done any lounging around with other ex-inmates." Her attempt at a wry laugh failed to appease Warren, and Charlotte was grateful to hear the front door open, signalling Laurel's return home.

"Charlie Paxton's here," called Warren, evidently in the belief that his mother might need a warning. "Sid talked to her."

"Yes, he told me," replied Laurel, pulling off her coat as she entered the room. "But Charlotte let him read what she's written, and it's OK."

Had they expected the *Clarion* to lambaste Polrenek-born Warren and his professional shortcomings? Obviously the article would be OK. Charlotte knew her job. "You can both read the piece too," she offered, rummaging through her bag. "I've got a printout here. No pictures yet, but they'll be online and in the paper next Saturday."

"If Sid's happy, that's fine," said Laurel, but Warren took the page Charlotte held and he unfolded it.

"Yeah, this'll be OK," conceded Warren, "But how do we know you won't alter what's here before Saturday?"

"You can trust a *Clarion* reporter's word of honour. Besides, it's late in the week now, and rewriting would take up too much time."

"You forget I knew you at Polrenek School, Charlie Paxton," Warren muttered, as if her name and treachery were synonymous, even though pupil solidarity had meant transgressors never found themselves betrayed to the staff. "I remember those days quite clearly."

"Didn't realize I was so shifty," said Charlotte, tempted to cite a few of Warren's more extrovert moments.

"She was better behaved than you ever were," Laurel told her son with rueful amusement. "What else will be in the *Clarion* next Saturday, Charlotte?"

"Your bowgle, if you approve my copy."

"Mum, there's nothing in the house," decreed Warren. "I haven't heard a sound. And nor did Elly, when she was here last weekend."

"Well, I have. Every night for ages," Laurel insisted. "Florence Cobb hasn't been able to make it move out, but someone might read the *Clarion* and know what to do."

"You'll have plenty of advice," predicted Charlotte. "I can't say how effective it'll be, but we always get a reader response to ghosts."

"They don't exist, Mum," declared Warren. "You shouldn't tell people there's one in here."

"But there *is* something," maintained Laurel, as stubborn as her son. "There's definitely something. And it's got to go."

"That's no reason to stick us on a *Clarion* front page."

"You won't be," said Charlotte. "Next Saturday's front page is almost certainly the Council proposal to switch off streetlights from 11pm to 6am. Your bowgle will be inside, along with a plan to make Fore Street one-way, the final independent greengrocer shutting up shop, and an exclusive interview kindly given by our MP. Again. You can tell Polrenek's a marginal constituency. Oh, and an update on Old Mother Trevail's as well, with our Town Archivist calling for Henver to rebuild the Inn."

Not exactly a polished endeavour to camouflage her wish to reap incriminating gen on Daniel. Adam's battering-ram approach would at least have been straightforward, yet neither Laurel nor Warren seemed to register Charlotte's clumsy effort to appear ingenuous.

"Henver thinks he can do whatever suits him, and saunter off scot-free," fumed Laurel. "I hope he is made to rebuild. There wasn't a word about demolition anywhere in his planning application. I dealt with the paperwork myself, and didn't lose so much as a paragraph, let alone whole pages. The man's a liar, and you can quote me in the *Clarion*."

A bowgle would soon find itself evicted, in Charlotte's opinion. Laurel was no longer sleeplessly brooding on her wrongs. She was now angry, and maybe angry enough to become a *Clarion* source, but still the warning had to be given. "There's probably a bit in your job contract about not speaking to the media."

"How convenient for my boss. Obvious to him, he told me, that I must have put those allegedly missing pages through the shredder. That was a day after he joined the golf-club, thanks to Daniel Henver's sponsorship."

A reward that would be hard to establish as bribery. No doubt Charlotte's expensive education was Melanie's reward for keeping quiet about her child's father. It would not occur to Henver that embarrassment at being conned by him was Melanie's reason for silence. She had been a beautiful teenager, who imagined her life must include an MGM-type happy ending, complete with mansion and wealthy husband. Daniel never did leave the purportedly glacial wife unable to appreciate his self-proclaimed complex nature, but Melanie clung to her daydream. She dismissed him as a false start, while awaiting the riches that declined to come her way.

"No one could prove Henver's lying, Mum," said Warren. "And he'll get retrospective permission. The Trevail Inn belongs to yesteryear."

"I know," sighed Laurel. "But I also know there wasn't a mention of demolition in the plans he submitted. Henver's going to bilk the system."

"They're all like that," declared Warren. "They stick together, and lie through their teeth. I mean, the mistake was mine, not Sid's, but that would be nothing to Henver. Daft of me to try fixing it."

"You saw Henver?" queried Charlotte in surprise, unable to imagine the brash Warren humiliating himself even for a family member. "What did he say?"

"Henver wasn't at his office," reported Warren, the ignominious memory reddening his face. "I was a fool to go there. He wouldn't have taken any notice of me. His daughter got to him, and yet Sid had replaced her friend's windows cost-free."

All the same, Nadine would still urge Gabrielle to notify her father that Sid Tyrrel was a lousy workman. Compelling Nadine to wait for what she wanted would be an unforgivable offence.

"Does the architect still back Henver's story?" Charlotte asked, despite knowing that Daniel was a cover-up master. Both Warren and Laurel snorted in derision, making Charlotte admit, "Yeah, stupid question. Of course Henver's got a yes-man architect."

"Sid was told about houses and flats on the site, but their precise location was vague." However, Gabrielle had then relayed Nadine's Tyrrel gripe to Daniel, and Sidney's chance of a profitable contract was over. Laurel shrugged, accepting her inability to defy an impregnable foe. "Henver will forge ahead, the double-dealing swindler."

"I guess so," agreed Charlotte. Injustice rankled, but life had been unfair since their planet came into existence: a fact that even Nadine Napier ultimately learnt. Odd to feel luckier than her.

*

"Sorry, but I can't get hold of Gabrielle either," lied Charlotte. "Her mobile's switched off. She might be at a concert. Or has got a new phone."

"Keep ringing the number, Char," ordered Gideon. "Only losers throw in the towel. Winners never give up. I never do."

Catchphrases would achieve nothing. He had already lost.

10

New-job eagerness to please had faded. Vanessa made no attempt to seem contrite for her belated arrival at work: a sure sign the novelty of employment was wearing thin.

"All OK?" Then Fenella's fate leapt into Charlotte's head, and she added hastily, "This morning, I mean. Didn't your alarm go off?"

"Hardly split-second timing around here," snapped Vanessa. "You're almost never in the newsroom, and I haven't even met any other *Clarion* reporters."

"True," conceded Charlotte. "But they work from home. Were you following a lead? On the trail of a sizzling scoop?"

"I'll wallop anyone who tries joking with me today," declared Vanessa. "I'm late because I couldn't be bothered getting up early. That's it. So sack me."

"A prerogative I don't have, but you could get me kicked out. Your Dad's pally with Conrad."

"Parents! Total frauds!" growled Vanessa. "You're lucky not to know who your father was."

"I do, actually," said Charlotte. "Why think I don't?"

"Something I heard Fenella — oh, never mind. I misunderstood."

"My father died. Years ago. Before I was born," Charlotte claimed, preparing to lie valiantly. "Mum never got over the shock. Or her grief. She was very young."

"And didn't ever look at another man? That's so touching." Eyes misty with tears, Vanessa sighed at the lifelong devotion of a woman who had, in fact, spent her days pursuing a string of suitors, all deceived by Melanie's smokescreen docility.

"Mum was faithful to her memories," Charlotte stated: an assertion that made Vanessa begin crying in earnest. "Want to go home? You're obviously not well."

"I'll never be well again," sobbed Vanessa. "And Fenella wouldn't have gone out that night either. It's all Mum's fault. And Dad knew. He knew the whole time. You can't trust anyone. Families are just a charade."

They were with Rufus Olsen in the mix, thought Charlotte. "I'm sorry," she ventured.

A banal response, and Vanessa flew at it with prosecutorial vigour. "You're not surprised. Did you know? Does the entire town know?"

"Know what?" Easier to pretend than be brutally honest. Adam would do the deed soon enough.

"I bet people have been laughing at me for years," wailed Vanessa. "Yeah, laughing at how dense I am."

"Why would they? What's the problem?" Charlotte aimed at a soothing tone, but Vanessa continued to glower.

"Haven't you been listening? Dad said Mum's never left yet, but she will this time. I know she will, because Fenella's dead. And you'll put it in next Saturday's *Clarion*." Another betrayal, Vanessa's face declared, tears abruptly driven off by fury.

"The *Clarion* doesn't report marital glitches," said Charlotte. "If that's what you're on about. And things usually calm down. Given time. But don't tell Adam any of this."

"Why not?" demanded Vanessa, instantly belligerent. "Adam's the only person who understands me."

"He's also a reporter in search of material," Charlotte warned, although she knew that Vanessa would refuse to see sense. "You keep mentioning Fenella, and Adam could sell a story about her."

"He'd never do that," Vanessa decreed. "Besides, Mum deserves to be shown up, making Fenella track her."

"Why would Fenella track your mother?" Because of an overheard phone call? A chance sighting of Rufus with Beatrice? One way or another, Fenella realized that Rufus Olsen had a place in her mother's world. While attempting to cause trouble for him, Fenella might also have started to monitor parental comings and goings. It would explain Fenella's journey from home that night, but not her death.

"I won't tell you one syllable more," announced Vanessa, a sulky child cross with her previous best friend. "You don't know the first thing about Adam. He's —"

Wonderful? Ethical? Flawless? Unable to find adjectives fulsome enough, Vanessa abandoned her attempt to describe the perfection that was Adam. A situation Charlotte knew well, having witnessed Melanie bounce in and out of love with superheroes rapidly written off as fallen idols. Maybe Vanessa was destined to tread a similar path, unlike sensible Charlotte.

*

Yes, sensible Charlotte. She was not going to rerun Melanie's life. Sensible Charlotte would never be conned. "No, I can't meet you this evening. Sorry. Got to work."

"Tomorrow?" Edric suggested.

"Busy then too," Charlotte claimed, glad that phone calls were such an aid to lying. "Long hours are in my job description. Council Meetings, interviews, and so on and so forth."

"Sunday perhaps?"

"Perhaps, but people email about Saturday's *Clarion*. I have to respond, and update online articles as well. It'll be worse than usual this weekend, now there's no editor to take the flak. I'll be frantically checking every word, and if Vanessa doesn't show up, I won't have any help."

"Why wouldn't Vanessa show up? I'd heard she was keen to make journalism her career."

"Enthusiasm appears to be waning. Polrenek isn't hot-news territory. But let's talk later on, when I've got more time."

A brush-off: something Edric might not have experienced before, as he could very well be Polrenek's most eligible bachelor. However, his voice gave no hint of noticing that Edric Lambert had been rejected. "You work so hard, us loafers are put to shame. I coast along as the boss's son, confident I won't get sacked, no matter what."

Gideon Penry must have thought the same. "When you like your job, it doesn't seem to be work."

Charlotte's comment sounded reproving, but Edric merely laughed. "Then I guess freight transport doesn't intrigue me. I never wake up eager to speed on winged feet into the office, but neither does my Dad. It's just how we earn a living. You're lucky, Charlotte."

"I know." She was lucky: lucky not to share Melanie's belief in the ideal man who would bring an ideal future with him. Therefore goodbye, Edric. Goodbye to the illusion named Edric Lambert.

*

"Saturday's *Clarion* is shaping up nicely," said Rosalind, as if contradicting a previous speaker. "Conrad will be delighted."

Doubtless an exaggeration, but Charlotte was glad to be reassured. Gideon would have cut her article about Harvest Festivals, but Jethro had dug into his archive, and unearthed evocative pictures of children who were now parents. "I reckon we'll sell at least a hundred extra copies. Jeth's photos are superb, and the Drama Group will be ecstatic when they see his rehearsal shots."

"Your bowgle piece should get some good feedback too," Rosalind remarked, scrolling down the newsroom's computer mock-up: always a hopeful moment. "Everybody in Polrenek has an uncanny tale they're keen to relate. You'll be visiting haunted houses for weeks to come."

"Worth it, if we increase sales. I won't complain, as long as a spook doesn't follow me home."

"That won't happen," Rosalind stated, apparently the spirit-world's spokesperson. "Poltergeists haunt a specific place, and never move house."

"Then I shall report fearlessly and without favour, especially as bowgle activity is said to be caused by humans under pressure. And Laurel Sutton's job is causing her a whole heap of stress."

"Yeah, typical Henver. But his current patsy's a stupid choice. I went to school with Laurel, and can testify she was the most efficient Head Girl since Polrenek got its town charter." Rosalind huffed in scorn at Daniel's poor judgment, when he had had an entire Planning Department to choose from, and one led by a man not noted for integrity. "Sid's the best double-glazer around here, but Henver was too cowardly to risk a chance encounter with Laurel by employing her cousin on the Trevail site."

"That decision wasn't anything to do with Laurel," Charlotte explained, although reluctant to absolve Daniel of gutlessness. "Gabrielle Henver told her father there'd been a mix-up at a friend's house, but the right windows were installed cost-free, so she had no call to trash Sid's name."

"A troublemaker, that Gabrielle Henver," decreed Rosalind. "And now I gather she's dumped Gideon, despite losing him his job."

"Will he be back here then?" After the giddy heights of approval for her attempt to rustle up Saturday's *Clarion*, Charlotte was hurled down to earth with a sickening jolt.

"Alas for Gideon, his copybook remains Henver-blotted, and Conrad isn't in relenting mood. No need to pretend you're saddened by this outcome. I'm certainly not."

"It's hard to warm to an editor who loathes your work," admitted Charlotte. "I'm pretty sure Gideon was on the verge of sacking me, so his departure might count as a reprieve. After all, he gave Adam the heave-ho."

"Gabrielle Henver did."

"Was there a difference?"

"Not then," acknowledged Rosalind. "Adam must have been close to info the Henvers want kept quiet. Or he just annoyed Gabrielle, and she took revenge. While we're on the subject of annoyances, I haven't seen Vanessa for three days. Is she on an undercover assignment to expose corruption in the Pony Club?"

"Regrettably no, and Vanessa hasn't been in touch to explain her absence. I think local journalism was a disappointment."

"Luke Beckett's daughter won't need to earn money." Rosalind shrugged, accepting that wages were the sole reason most people turn up at work each day.

More likely Vanessa knew that if Beatrice's relationship with Rufus had been a factor in Fenella's death, the *Clarion* would have to print something, albeit in circuitous manner. Vanessa's faith was now in Adam, her unreliable champion. However, à-propos Adam —

"Could you ask Conrad about a second newsroom reporter?" Charlotte ventured, hoping the boss would not take her request as an implication that he had no idea how to staff the *Clarion*. "A Council Meeting clashes with the Operatic Society's opening night next Friday, and there's a school recital too. I can't cover several events at once."

"I'll mention it to Conrad," agreed Rosalind, although her mind was elsewhere. "Quite a few businesses have made enquiries about advertising, ever since word got around that you're highlighting a different firm each week. Local traders want to keep in our good books, and that should please Conrad. He'll be even happier if you dig up some dirt on Henver."

"I'll do my utmost. When Al Capone can be toppled by income tax, a planning application might rout Daniel Henver."

An uplifting prospect, and the sole gift Charlotte could now give her mother.

*

"Thought you'd like a complimentary *Clarion* this week," Charlotte said, pretending she imagined Sid Tyrrel might neglect to purchase a copy, despite his starring rôle in local journalism for the next seven days. "Nice picture of you Jeth Kern took."

"I'll never live up to it," Sidney commented, surveying his photo. "Jeth used powerful wizardry to make me look like this."

Sidney was correct, and even his disorderly office had been transformed into a neat workspace by Jethro's magic, but Charlotte's response was ready. "A photographer can only take what's there. And if I'm flattering enough, would you answer a few more questions?"

"About my beauty régime, I guess, going by this vision of me." Sidney shook his head in wonder at the image supposedly his.

"Concerning Daniel Henver. Did he ever claim there was Council permission to demolish the Trevail Inn?"

"It wasn't mentioned. Henver's not that thick. He wanted an idea of what my estimate would be for, say, two hundred average-sized windows. That went OK, so he asked me to come back and do an official quote when the building work began. Then I hear an upcountry firm's in line to nab that contract because Henver's daughter had put the boot in."

"Well, well, Charlie Paxton snooping yet again," observed Warren, from the doorway of Sidney's office. "What does she think we've done that would interest next Saturday's *Clarion*?"

"Charlotte's keen to get Daniel Henver through his planning lies," explained Sidney. "It'd be brilliant if she could prove your Mum never made a mistake, but Henver does know how to cover his tracks."

"Then he'll be overconfident," Charlotte argued, although without much hope.

"His type think they rule the world," griped Warren.

Too right, thought Charlotte. Daniel Henver certainly believed he was invincible, and that regulations were for lesser people.

"Where's his office?" asked Charlotte, wishing she had the nerve to do a little breaking and entering. Adam might not hesitate, so perhaps she ought to pass a Henver control-centre address onto him as retaliation for the *Clarion* burglary. After all, fire was said to be fought with fire.

"He doesn't actually have an office," Sidney replied, saving Charlotte from a possible descent into criminality. "Good idea, I reckon, not to keep paperwork and computers at one fixed address, if you're Daniel Henver. He uses a caravan on whichever site's being developed. Wise, in his case."

"I guess so," Charlotte acknowledged reluctantly.

"Forget Henver," muttered Warren. "The *Clarion* hasn't got a chance of bringing him down."

"You could look at his pal Councillor Glynn though," Sidney told Charlotte. "Glynn bought three fields on the cheap last month, and it seems a Council proposal to build social housing on those very fields will be announced soon, giving him some quick bunce. But I didn't tell you this."

"No bowgle or Henver in the mix," Warren commented. "Not appealing enough for Charlie Paxton."

*

Adam had phoned twice during the afternoon, but Charlotte was loath to contact him, suspecting he wanted her opinion of Vanessa's latest outpouring. However, a visit from Adam might be trickier, and Charlotte forced herself to call him on reaching home, excuse at the ready.

"Sorry, but I haven't got much time. A Council Meeting about the slow-traffic scheme. Everything OK?"

Adam ignored conventional chitchat, demanding instead, "What do you know about Nadine's husband?"

"Which one? Not that it matters. I've never met either of them."

"Two murders in Polrenek, and you haven't bothered with a death-knock visit!" Yet Adam was less sceptical than scathing when he added, "Call yourself a journalist!"

"A *Clarion* journalist," amended Charlotte. "We don't intrude on people's grief, as I'm sure you remember."

"You're in the middle of a Farfield cover-up," declared Adam, making Charlotte laugh. "I said that at the start."

"You're so off-target, you could be taking aim from Australia. I'd grass on all Farfield cover-ups, if I knew of any."

"I've got my sources."

"Ill-informed ones."

"And why are you ditching Edric Lambert?" wailed Adam. "That's what Vanessa told me. Don't you realize sources like him are invaluable?"

"Edric wasn't a source."

Adam sniggered in disbelief, because people were only part of his life when they might prove useful. Any other relationship was pointless. "What did Lambert tell you? Vanessa said you weren't in the least surprised, almost as if you'd known about her mother and Olsen for centuries. Why didn't you ring me the moment you heard?"

Adam was indignant to be so let down, and his self-importance amused Charlotte. "Edric told me nothing. I did a little guesswork, and Vanessa confirmed it. How is she?"

"OK," replied Adam, impatient with a question he saw as an attempt to sidetrack him. "Why shouldn't Vanessa be OK? She's from a rich family. I'm the guy who's unemployed."

"Vanessa might be as well. She appears to have quit the *Clarion*."

"So there's a vacancy? Not that I'd run around for local papers again. Too restrictive, and if you don't escape soon, you'll be stuck reporting slow-traffic zones until retirement age."

"Not so bad a fate as some," Charlotte observed. "Besides, it's a different workplace without Gideon."

"He'll grovel to his Dad. An owner's son can't be ex-editor for long. It infringes the natural order. Gideon will make a comeback."

Then Charlotte might be unemployed too, after her many excuses for being unable to reach Gabrielle, but the problem could wait until it happened. "Re: Nadine's second ex. Much police interest? What's he like?"

"Foul-tempered, abrupt and wary. Terence Piper's got a secret to hide. If not, he'd speak to me."

However, as Charlotte would also hate to be interviewed about her reaction to Nadine's death, she found the widower's attitude quite rational. "Nobody's going to rehash a dreary marriage for your benefit."

"I'm not the person who benefits. That bloke is. He won't have to shell out on a divorce settlement. Keeps the house, his dosh, and gets rid of an unwanted wife in one go. That's what I call raking in the bunce."

It sounded close to a remark the schoolgirl Nadine Napier might once have made, posing as a cynical woman of the world, but Adam was just being himself. "Nadine came from a family that's loaded. She didn't need to scrounge handouts."

"The rich are gluttons. They always crave more," Adam retorted.

"So husband number two is now a prime suspect? And prudent fiscal management the motive? OK, but it doesn't explain why Nadine left her car and went onto a building site."

"Well, maybe she spotted husband number two and his inevitable other woman enjoying a romantic liaison."

"On the building site?"

"Nadine could have arranged to meet him there," Adam said, unwilling to allow commonsense to tarnish his theory. "Petty detail doesn't matter."

"She didn't plan to clamber around piles of rubble," Charlotte pointed out. "Nadine was wearing stiletto heels: very very stiletto heels."

"How do you know that?"

"I saw her, remember. Nadine wouldn't have worn those shoes to wallow through mud on a wet day. She didn't expect to visit the Trevail site."

"So what? Shoes are unimportant," Adam ruled. "She could buy herself dozens more. Greed was the motive. It made Piper kill his wife, and got Nadine out of her car. She saw the soon-to-be ex on a Henver site, and decided there were business deals that she knew nothing about."

Nadine had presumably spotted someone, and that someone could have been Daniel Henver. Hope raced ahead of evidence, and Charlotte's heart sang as she pictured him peering out morosely from behind prison bars. Should two unpleasant people destroy each other, it would be perfect symmetry. Yet Nadine was not the trusting innocent favoured by Daniel, and he was too arrogant to regard anybody as an unmanageable threat. The conclusion was logical, but frustrating.

"You've gone suspiciously quiet," Adam commented. "You've just thought of something, Charlotte. What is it?"

"Rosalind might be able to get you your job back. She's running the show, and we could do with another reporter."

"To chronicle school concerts and fishing quotas?" Adam was disdainful, but he would need money while awaiting his London future.

"I reckon Gideon's stint as editor is history, but even if he did return, you might bond over Gabrielle Henver's cruel rejection."

"Oh yeah," jeered Adam, but he was weighing up possible options.

*

On Saturday morning, various suggestions for poltergeist removal began flowing into the newsroom computer, and Charlotte was encouraged to note the simplicity of bowgle eradication. According to readers, troublesome spirits would depart the moment they heard a drum beat, brooms striking walls, or even loud handclaps. The message was clear. Noisy ghosts were offended when their act was stolen, and they also took a dim view of aroma therapy, in particular if the fragrances concerned were rosemary, sage or fennel.

"Mint too. My grandmother swore by mint," Rosalind commented. "She grew it in window boxes, and never had any bowgle bother. Pass on all the tips to Laurel, and we'll see if they work for her."

Charlotte figured that proof of Daniel Henver's deceit would silence Laurel's cottage more effectively, yet the remedies were inexpensive, and readers had shown greater interest in bowgles than any other *Clarion* story that week. "I could do a follow-up piece on Laurel's ghost-eviction success or failure."

"Talk to other people who've been haunted as well. We haven't had such good feedback in months. I guess everybody loves a ghost story and all its spookiness."

Apart from Adam, who would label the reporting folksy flummery. Adam Rigg had never been cut out for small-town journalism, but he was *Clarion*-trained and available. "Adam hasn't found a job yet. Any chance Conrad would reinstate him?"

"Temporarily, I suppose." However, Rosalind was unenthusiastic, and she grumbled, "Adam made it very plain that the *Clarion* bores him. He'd always be looking for another job, and we need somebody who's committed to Polrenek. I'm glad the Beckett girl sashayed off. She'd be apathetic too."

"Has Vanessa left?" asked Charlotte. "I haven't heard from her."

"Me neither. I assume it means goodbye forever." Rosalind sighed in disapproval at so casual a departure, but Vanessa would soon be forgotten. "Are you thinking about a move, Charlotte? Perhaps Plymouth? Or Bristol?"

"A hint that I should be doing job searches?" Lucky she had expected to face unemployment, thought Charlotte. It was not crushing defeat, just a turn in the road. "Is Gideon making a comeback?"

"He's still in exile, and likely to remain there. Are you another restless Adam, with the *Clarion* merely a rung on the ladder? Is working in Polrenek enough for you?"

"I belong here. It's home."

The correct answer apparently, to judge by Rosalind's smile. If she were asking as Conrad's proxy, Charlotte might have a little job security at the *Clarion*, but until an updated contract was ready for her signature, Charlotte knew better than to relax.

"Conrad's put in an offer to buy this building from Henver," Rosalind remarked, her smile even warmer.

"Is it for sale?" queried Charlotte, hoping to hear that Daniel teetered on the brink of bankruptcy.

"Anything can be bought or sold, if the price is right." And she knew that because millions were residing in her bank account, Rosalind's worldly-wise tone implied. "Ever since he heard Gideon lament a smashed door lock, Conrad thinks Henver might be spying on us."

"Possible," said Charlotte, although she suspected Gabrielle of being the *Clarion* intruder. Yet whoever vandalized Gideon's lock, presumably Henver knowledge had overridden the alarm system and Henver keys used to gain access.

"I bet Conrad will get his way. Everybody wants more money than they've got, even the richest amongst us, and Reynolds's Travel Agency is considering a move when their lease ends here. But if Henver won't sell, Conrad's minded to relocate the *Clarion*. Actually, I guess we could all just work from home, but Conrad wants an impressively big office with his surname attached to bricks and mortar: well, granite blocks in this case."

Rosalind's speculation about a *Clarion* future made Charlotte aware that something lurked in the back recesses of her mind: something significant she had not yet registered.

Conrad Penry wanting a formal base. Luke Beckett's paperwork stored in Estuary Avenue, where it would never again receive Fenella's attention. Daniel Henver's caravan-HQ at whichever was his primary construction project. Therefore, Warren's futile trip to Daniel's office would mean visiting the Trevail site. Where Nadine saw him? Left her car to gloat?

"Is it too early for a discussion about next Saturday's *Clarion*?" asked Rosalind. "Any gossip in the air, Charlotte?"

"I heard that Oliver Glynn bought three fields a month ago, and I've since learnt they were supposedly to accommodate his daughter's pony. The Land Registry confirms Oliver's purchase, but poor pony might find himself restricted to the Glynn backyard, because there's now a Council proposal to buy those fields from Oliver and build housing on them. Pony will be most dismayed to lose his lavish pastureland."

"But a nice profit for Councillor Glynn."

"I'll have to check with Conrad's lawyer, and find out what we can say or hint at."

"Conrad would be thrilled to go after Glynn. And if you can link Henver to the tale, even better. Oliver's a Daniel crony."

That aspect of the saga had not escaped Charlotte, who could hope Glynn might rat on Daniel. "I'll keep digging."

"Just printing facts without comment might be enough. I know what conclusion they're making me draw." Her grin betrayed Rosalind's merry anticipation of Councillor Glynn's imminent disgrace, although she would maintain that *Clarion* reportage scorned vindictiveness.

"I'll get the Glynn version first," Charlotte decided. And she would ask outright how Henver was involved. After all, Daniel seemed to have a finger in every Polrenek pie.

Nadine had loved to ridicule her victims. She would have relished seizing an opportunity to assure Warren that the Tyrrel firm stood no chance of sweet-talking Daniel Henver into any contract. A potential scenario, yet the film that ran through Charlotte's head was produced by imagination, not evidence. Furthermore, Charlotte had known Warren since they were five years old, starting Polrenek School together, and no former pupil had turned into a homicidal psychopath. So far.

"And to what do we owe the honour of your presence?" Rosalind was enquiring, as the newsroom door opened.

Glancing around, Charlotte was surprised to see Vanessa. "Hi there. I thought you were fed up with the *Clarion* and had left."

"I've been working: working hard," retorted Vanessa, truculent rather than apologetic. "Doing research for Adam. He asked me to help him."

"Adam's not a *Clarion* employee," Rosalind reminded her. "Working for him isn't working for us."

An extraneous detail, in Vanessa's opinion, but family wealth meant she could afford to strut out of any job. And argue with a boss. "You were crazy to sack Adam. The *Clarion* needs him."

"An editorial verdict is final," said Charlotte, exasperation having momentarily silenced Rosalind. "No doubt Gideon had his reasons."

"Stupid ones," decreed Vanessa. "Adam's a brilliant journalist. The London papers will pay millions to hire him."

"Well, he'd never get that amount in Polrenek." Charlotte wondered if Vanessa had daydreams of accompanying Adam, should he leave town to chase a metropolitan destiny. Melanie would have already packed her bags.

"The *Clarion* doesn't fund staff members to work for somebody else," Rosalind proclaimed: a ruling clearly lost on Vanessa, who failed to grasp that she had just been demoted to unpaid intern.

*

"This bowgle story's plain stupid," griped Vanessa. "And why do I have to drop by the cottage with you?"

Because Rosalind was likely to order Vanessa to go home and stay there, if Charlotte left the pair of them together. "I thought you wanted to learn about journalism."

"*Clarion* stuff isn't journalism," sneered Vanessa.

"It's local journalism, and our bowgle got us a bigger reaction than the other stories put together."

"You never get mad. Never!" Apparently objecting to a flaw in Charlotte's character, Vanessa flounced down Harbour Way, giving her escort a welcome break from juvenile petulance. Vanessa's safe world had been shattered for a second time by the knowledge of Beatrice's relationship with Rufus Olsen, and everybody around Vanessa ought to suffer alongside her.

Charlotte paused by the corner, and hopeful gulls swooped low in case sandwiches were next on her agenda. Despite the cold wind and sea spray, Charlotte wished she could stand there indefinitely, while a sullen child stamped away, but the breather was a short one. Vanessa had reached the Sutton cottage, and was knocking on their front door with an imperious succession of raps that demanded immediate attention. *Clarion* reporters would normally advance on targets with ingratiating obsequiousness, and Charlotte headed up the road, apologies forming in her mind.

As she approached Laurel's cottage, Charlotte saw the front door fly open, and then there was silence until she heard Vanessa snap, "You look like you've just seen a ghost."

Warren stood in the doorway, his stunned expression gradually fading as he attempted a shaky laugh. "I was expecting Charlie Paxton. Are you from the *Clarion* as well?"

"Sort of," admitted Vanessa, loath to identify herself with provincial trivia after Adam's big-city propaganda.

"Sort of?" echoed Warren. "Either you work there or you don't."

"I double as researcher for a freelance journalist. He edits my raw copy," Vanessa declared, proud to display her mastery of professional lingo. "We'll be moving to London soon."

"While I remain devoted to Polrenek," said Charlotte. Why should the sight of an unknown girl so startle Warren? Like he'd seen a ghost, Vanessa had remarked. Fenella's ghost? But she was hardly going to return from an afterlife, as Nadine's stand-in, to harp on about Warren's surveying limitations. Far-fetched to place him at the Trevail site with Nadine, but even more fanciful to assume he also had a connection to Fenella, enabling him to spot the resemblance between Vanessa and her sister. Yet something had spooked Warren, and that something was not the Sutton bowgle.

"I think it's gone," called Laurel, smiling in relief as she waved them into her front room. "I read the online comments about your article, Charlotte, and went through each room clapping my hands. Then I bought a child's drum, and beat it in every corner to make sure. I've put rosemary and sage all over the place as well. Since then, there hasn't been a sound. I'm so glad I spoke to you."

"The *Clarion* aims to serve its community," said Charlotte, suspecting that Laurel's newfound self-assurance might have solved her problem, rather than drumming a bowgle retreat. "Have your Trevail-site difficulties been unravelled yet?"

"They're not going to sack me. Henver can't prove he applied to demolish the Inn, but they'll give him retrospective planning permission. And that really narks me."

"His sort always win," groused Warren.

"But at least Henver can't use the same trick twice," Charlotte declared. "Incidentally, is he going to build the houses on Councillor Glynn's recently purchased fields?"

"I've heard they had a row over money," replied Laurel. "But my job contract prevents me talking to journalists about any work-related matter."

"Naturally," agreed Charlotte, awaiting additional forbidden fruit.

"I can't possibly tell you that Glynn hung around my office a few weeks before he bought the land, studying how new-build sites are selected. Then, after Glynn's acquisition, his pal Simon Latimer advocates a Council purchase of said fields for what he termed 'low-cost' social housing. But obviously I can't talk about this, or the closed-door chats Glynn had with our Head of Planning, another mate. However, all these manoeuvres could be sheer coincidence. Or possibly not."

"You won't get them, Charlie," Warren predicted, taking comfort in someone else's failure. "They're beyond *Clarion* reach."

"That doesn't mean I should stop trying." Yet Charlotte came from the same background as Warren and, in their world, those with even minor clout inevitably triumphed.

"A *Clarion* summary of the facts might be enough," Laurel suggested, duplicating Rosalind's optimism. "People will read between the lines and suss out exactly what went on. Glynn thinks we're all stupid. He's the complete big-head."

So was Daniel Henver, but he would never be as careless as Oliver Glynn. Only someone exceptionally slapdash would let a Planning-Department employee witness searches that would enable him to exploit insider knowledge of forthcoming Council construction.

"You won't get them, Charlie," repeated Warren, but he was still glancing at Vanessa, his personal spectre.

*

Gabrielle Henver.

Charlotte made an attempt to back away from the window, but too late. She had been spotted, and Gabrielle was waving as though at a friend. Her genetic inheritance did not include Daniel's shrewd appraisal of character.

"Good to meet up again, Charlotte. I'm so horribly alone these days."

"You must be," Charlotte agreed. But it would have proved challenging for Nadine to widen her social circle beyond Gabrielle and Fenella. Other classmates had shunned recruitment as Napier acolytes.

"I feel ancient, with everything in the past," sighed Gabrielle, assuming she required no invitation to enter Charlotte's home and flop onto a front-room chair. "You're the only reliable ex-Farfielder left."

And I've hated you since childhood, thought Charlotte.

"Nadine's memorial service is next month," continued Gabrielle, sighing again. "You'll be there, won't you? And report it in full?"

"The *Clarion* will have coverage," Charlotte acknowledged, deciding she would pay Adam to attend in her place. "Our photographer might have a picture in his archive that could accompany —"

"I've got a photo of me, Nadine and Fenella by the school entrance on our last day there." As she spoke, Gabrielle's eyes began brimming over with tears, and Charlotte was embarrassed not to be a fellow mourner. "This is all so wrong. So cruel. I can't believe they're both gone. Has your investigative team made any discoveries yet?"

"Olsen can be ruled out," said Charlotte, marvelling that anybody saw her as a leader of dynamic investigators. "There's no evidence that he met either Nadine or Fenella."

"But Olsen had to have been Fenella's ex. Nadine was positive," Gabrielle protested, astonishment halting her tears. "Why else would Fenella want to ruin him? Why else get you to delve into his finances?"

"Could be Olsen ditched a friend of hers."

"But Fenella didn't have any friends, apart from me and Nadine," Gabrielle pointed out.

"The answer will come to light soon." Maybe. Should the Beckett marriage officially end. But that was none of Gabrielle's business, and Charlotte added, "I'll contact a police source for their latest gen."

"The killer must be Olsen," Gabrielle insisted. "It's got to be him, but if I go to the police, Olsen might attack me as well."

"I think you're safe from him." But perhaps not from Warren? Charlotte pushed the idea away. "Don't wander up remote lanes by yourself or frequent dark alleys. And get some running shoes."

Gabrielle looked down in wry amusement at her ultrafashionable footwear: decorative but apparently designed as torture implements. The type of shoe that might have been a contributory factor in Nadine's death. "You're so sensible. No wonder my Dad's cross with me. He keeps saying I should be more like you."

"Why?" Charlotte spoke warily, prepared to deliver several emphatic lies, should Gabrielle claim her as a half-sister. "Your father doesn't know the first thing about me."

"Yes, he does, and I wish he didn't," carped Gabrielle, rolling her eyes in mock frustration. "My life would be loads easier, if Dad stopped comparing me to you. The same education, the same opportunities, yet I'm useless. It's particularly bad on a Saturday, after he's read the latest *Clarion*. You're an achiever; I'm not."

"He's muddled me with some other staff member." Subject at an end, said Charlotte's enmity, yet Gabrielle was not to be contradicted.

"My Dad's the most avid *Clarion* reader there is, so I clearly bragged once too often that we were at Farfield together."

Extraordinary to hear Gabrielle Henver maintain that being in the same school year as Charlotte Paxton was bragging material, but too late for phony friendship: years too late. "If your father's a *Clarion* fan, he must have been delighted when you were dating Gideon Penry."

"Gideon!" scoffed Gabrielle. "Somebody to use and then lose, as Dad says."

Was that Daniel's opinion of Melanie too? Despite having long known all about the Henver situation, Charlotte was angry on her mother's behalf. "Gideon quarrelled with his father and lost a job because of you."

"Not my fault," Gabrielle declared, smugly serene. "Anyway, he's got money. No need for him to work."

Nadine's supercilious disdain resonated in Gabrielle's voice, and Charlotte knew exactly how revolutionaries felt, even though Gideon would have a much happier life without Gabrielle in it. "He adored being *Clarion* editor. Gideon loved that job."

So what? said Gabrielle's face, as she addressed a more urgent topic. "You'll never guess who I saw on my way here. Eleanor Yeo! She's got a cheek, prancing round Polrenek like she owns the place. Some people have no sensitivity."

Charlotte recalled a gawkily shy thirteen-year-old girl in Farfield's navy-blue uniform, pale eyes anxious, fair curls restrained in plaits. It was difficult to picture her as the seductive siren who carried off Nadine's second husband. "I don't remember much about Eleanor. Too quiet to make an impact, I guess."

"She certainly had an impact on that grotty Terence Piper, but it's always those quiet women. You can never trust them. Never!" Gabrielle's vilification held an echo of Farfield's abrasive headmistress when rebuking a wayward third-former, but Charlotte was tempted to applaud the alluring Eleanor. Terence Piper's existence would be a permanent vacation, after Nadine.

"Did he get kicked out, and then met Eleanor?" asked Charlotte, hoping Terence Piper had dumped his wife to become a victory notch on Eleanor Yeo's gun-belt.

"Not sure when they got together. You won't believe it, but he packed his stuff and left for Mevyn Village while Nadine was out shopping. Just a note to say he wouldn't be back. Nadine was livid."

Of course Nadine would be livid. Not heartbroken or in despair: merely livid. To her, his departure was an affront, yet absconding spouses were no novelty in Nadine's experience of marital bumps on the road. "Terence Piper was her second husband, wasn't he?"

"And the first one was another scumbag. Waltzed off before a year had gone by. He simply didn't appreciate Nadine, and yet she worked herself to a frazzle, transforming his run-of-the-mill house into a showpiece. Then Piper came along, and precisely the same thing happened again. Nadine's life was an absolute tragedy."

Right up there with Hamlet and Lear, thought Charlotte. At least Romeo and Juliet had had the sense to die before they got around to dream kitchens or double-glazing. But that brought Warren to mind, and Charlotte turned her questions in a safer direction. "Where's the first husband now? Does he live in Polrenek?"

"Moved to Plymouth. Last I heard, he'd been nabbed by some floozy. Men are all the same: liars and swindlers."

Particularly when the man's name was Daniel Henver. Or perhaps Adam Rigg. Gabrielle might have a point, Charlotte reflected. "You could trust Gideon. He'd never have left you."

"I'd do the running off," declared Gabrielle, grimacing. "But you're in luck with Edric Lambert. His mother was Fenella's aunt."

And therefore acceptable, Gabrielle's tone implied. A good catch, who would enable even Charlotte Paxton to infiltrate the very heights of local society. "I'm not seeing Edric any more."

"No!" gasped Gabrielle. "Why not?"

"Didn't work out."

"So Edric's met someone else," Gabrielle concluded. Obviously no Polreneker could be indifferent to golf-club dinners, charity balls and other swish revelries. Hence beyond belief that Charlotte Paxton might voluntarily condemn herself to obscurity. After all, Cinderella never rejects the prince. "I wonder who Edric's dating now? Fenella's sister might know. Vanessa's in your office these days, isn't she? A bit snide and abrupt, that girl. I wouldn't have thought her *Clarion* material. Oh, *Clarion* material! How could I forget? Dad told me to give you a note. Lucky I remembered, or he'd have been even grumpier with me."

"What note?" demanded Charlotte, angry at herself for so nervous a reaction. "What does he want?"

"Nothing, I guess. It's just some info or other." Gabrielle opened her bag, did a trawl through the contents, and then looked up, grinning conspiratorially as she handed Charlotte a small envelope. "Dad must fancy being the *Clarion*'s secret source."

"Not very secret when you've just told me who the sender is," commented Charlotte, reluctant to touch any object that Daniel had held. "What's this about?"

"Not a clue," replied Gabrielle, returning displaced lipstick, mirror and hand-cream to her bag. "Aren't you going to open it? Dad wouldn't breathe a syllable to me. Has he given you hot news?"

"It'd be unprofessional to tell," said Charlotte, resolving to destroy the envelope after Gabrielle left. Daniel's agenda would be to benefit himself alone: not her or the *Clarion*. They were mere puppets.

"Whatever he's sent, I bet you'll find it drearily dull," predicted Gabrielle, any transaction involving her father the last word in boredom.

*

Of course Charlotte opened Daniel's envelope, and found a single-sheet printout of emails from Oliver Glynn. He congratulated himself on having bought three fields cheaply, before the Council plan to build houses in that area became public knowledge. All emails were addressed to *Hi Dan*, who would get the construction contract, Glynn assured him, no problem. Presumably a hollow promise, and *Hi Dan* was out for revenge. As the *Clarion*'s source, Henver could expect anonymity, while Glynn was disgraced. A state of affairs that would please Daniel Henver, and pleasing Daniel Henver had to be avoided. Yet Oliver Glynn ought to face retribution for his attempt to fleece Council Taxpayers. A conundrum that made Charlotte frown.

11

A solidly square granite cottage on the outskirts of Polrenek: that was Councillor Glynn's home. At the back, a high-hedge paddock adjoined his garden, and from the lane Charlotte could see a young girl grooming the dapple-grey pony fated not to become a second-stable owner, should human residences be built on fields ostensibly bought for him.

"Hi," called Charlotte. "You're Poppy Glynn, aren't you? I'm with the *Clarion*, and hoping to interview your Dad. Is he home? Gorgeous pony, by the way. He's a total star. I saw him win his two rosettes at the last gymkhana. Charlie, isn't he?"

"That's right." Poppy swung back long tawny plaits and beamed, happier with praise for the pony than she would be with praise for herself.

"I remember his name because I used to be called Charlie too, when I was young. Now I'm terribly grown-up and known as Charlotte."

"Indeed you are," agreed Oliver Glynn, rushing out of the kitchen and opening a side gate, his plump face and plumper figure enthusiastically alert at the sight of a tame *Clarion* reporter able to provide him with good publicity as devoted family man. "You're here to interview me, I guess. Come in, Charlotte. Tea? Coffee? Wine?"

"I'd like to check something with you, if that's OK?"

"Of course, Charlotte. Always glad to help the press." A prime minister could not have smirked so patronizingly, as Councillor Glynn escorted his visitor through a perfect house, reflecting a perfect life in a perfect world. "We'll go into my study."

Oliver spoke with pride. He was the first Glynn to have a study, the first to buy his daughter a pony, and the first to be known throughout Polrenek. Charlotte found herself feeling sorry for him, as she sat down and put the photocopy of Daniel Henver's betrayal onto a shiny desktop. Oliver picked up the page, his jovial public façade rapidly diminishing with each sentence he read.

"A scam," Oliver announced at last. "Fake news. If the *Clarion* prints any of this codswallop, Conrad Penry will find himself in court. And you will too. Those emails were never written by me. I can prove they weren't."

"Absolutely," agreed Charlotte. "Powerful men have enemies keen to destroy their reputations."

"Exactly!" claimed Oliver. "It's a conspiracy. Yes, a conspiracy to end my political career. Everyone knows Daniel Henver's crooked. He gave you this rubbish to try and force me off the Council."

"I can't confirm a source's identity," said Charlotte. "And your identity is equally protected should you tell me info concerning Henver. But you don't have to worry about his jealousy in this case. Simple to defeat him."

"How?" demanded Oliver, glancing again at his printout doom.

"You take control of the narrative. You turn it to your advantage, and enhance your reputation. Yes, even higher than it already is."

*

"You'll never guess who I've been talking to," Rosalind called, hurrying out from her office as Charlotte opened the newsroom door. "A great honour can be yours. Henver wants to see you, and left his mobile number. Should I treasure the paper it's on? Or reach for a shredder?"

"Do you need to ask?"

"Good choice." Smiling in satisfaction, Rosalind tore up the note she held and dropped remnants into a recycling bin. "Conrad would never permit dear Daniel to force himself on the *Clarion*."

"Then I'll go out my way to avoid Henver," declared Charlotte. "More importantly, I might have our next front-page story. A tale of munificence and public-spirited largesse that rouses even my jaded journalistic heart. Councillor Glynn is donating three fields to the town, so that Polrenek's social-housing project won't exceed its budget."

"Most considerate and most unlike Oliver," Rosalind commented.

"Spoke to him myself yesterday evening. The fields were originally bought for his daughter's pony, but aforesaid pony is just as altruistic, and quite prepared to rough it in a single paddock behind the Glynn house. An adorable rocking-horse-type dappled charmer, who'll look delightful on the front page, alongside Oliver and family. Jeth ought to visit our local philanthropist this very day, and take some poignant photos."

"You've found damning evidence against Glynn," concluded Rosalind, astute in the behaviour of Polrenek Councillors.

"Fairly damning, but Glynn might be grateful enough to count the *Clarion* among his friends, so we could get a few valuable off-the-record tips from him. Anyhow, puff-pieces about integrity are preferable to one that deals with corruption, and it should stop Glynn attempting similar trickery in future. Long live fairytales."

"You understand the *Clarion*." Rosalind said, nodding appreciatively. "We favour happy endings, and Conrad will relish the way you've handled this situation."

Perhaps he would, but Charlotte wondered what sort of person she was, feeling sympathy for an avaricious Councillor while doing her best to overlook Warren Sutton's possible participation in two deaths. Certainly no reporter should allow sleaze to masquerade as benevolence, and were Charlotte not clinging to childhood hatred of Nadine and Fenella, Warren might have been brought to police attention via a *Clarion* scoop. Adam would not hesitate, no matter how much he detested the victims. That was journalism. That was real journalism.

Maybe she ought to rethink her future. Maybe staying in Polrenek was the mistake. Moving to a different town, where Charlotte had no past, might be the solution. Having made herself a model *Clarion* reporter was actually the problem, and no true journalist should ignore a potential lead.

*

"Not you again, Charlie Paxton," sighed Warren. "You'll get my Mum sacked, if she tells you anything else about dodgy Council goings-on."

A cold wind swirled up from Polrenek Promenade to remind the town that winter was fast approaching, and Charlotte wanted to change career with immediate effect. What could she say? Ask Warren had he killed Nadine, before turning his attention to Fenella? "I thought your mother might like to see a printout of the next *Clarion* front page. Oliver Glynn will donate his three fields to Polrenek. He yearns to keep our social-housing costs within budget, and save Council-Taxpayer money."

"How did you manage that?" Warren took the article and began reading it, as he opened the door wider to allow Charlotte inside. She had unexpectedly become a Sutton ally.

"Mum will love to have this. Thanks."

Charlotte went into the hall, morbidly imagining her name added to Warren's hit-list. He led Charlotte to the front room, cluttered with remnants of a sandwich meal eaten before the television, and switched off a quiz programme.

"Free day?" asked Charlotte. "Sorry to disturb you."

"No disaster. I was just weighing up my employment options," Warren announced, his tone suggesting there were copious local-job vacancies.

"You don't work for Sid now?" Charlotte was surprised, knowing that most Polrenek businesses were family based, and Sidney had no children. Warren's future might have been carved in stone from adolescence.

"Isn't it obvious?" retorted Warren. "I cost Sid a load of money, replacing those windows. How could I stay? It's a nuisance though. My girlfriend Elly and I were hoping to get married soon, but we'll have to — Hey, you won't print what I'm saying in the *Clarion*, will you?"

"Not a word without your consent. It isn't the paper's style to have a swipe at people. But Sid didn't seem that bothered. He merely said it was a mistake that wouldn't happen again."

"Yeah, Sid was nice about it. Easier if he'd kick up a fuss," complained Warren, scowling at Sidney's calm reaction to what must have been an expensive blow. "I'm going to pay him for those windows, but he deserves a more reliable worker."

"You must have hated Nadine. I would have been hopping mad at her," ventured Charlotte.

"Who?" Warren spoke absently, still brooding on Sid's relaxed nature.

"Nadine Napier. The windows woman."

"You mean Mrs Piper?" queried Warren, his discomfort at saying the name visible. "What customer would be happy with windows that didn't open properly? All the same, she needn't have moaned to her friends and made them cancel jobs. After all, Sid took full responsibility, even though I'm the guy to blame."

Yet awkwardness overrode resentment in Warren's voice, and Charlotte suspected he might be attempting to dupe her. Time to disconcert him. "Something's puzzled me for days. Why were you so taken aback by Vanessa Beckett? One glimpse of her, and she was saying it looked like you'd seen a ghost."

"Guilty conscience," replied Warren, forcing a grin. "Do the police know what happened to her sister?"

"Fenella hit her head." Or someone bashed Fenella over the head.

"She got her Dad to cancel his order, and then wrote to the Colberts saying Mrs Piper had to threaten Sid with legal action, before he'd replace her windows. That was a total lie. Not one word of truth in it. I went round to explain, but the Colberts had already hired an upcountry firm to do the job. Fenella Beckett was a two-faced bitch."

Spot on, thought Charlotte. Nadine had wanted to punish Sidney, and Fenella the disciple would go overboard to oblige her leader. "Odd: both Nadine and Fenella dying."

"I guess more people than me hated them."

Again spot on, thought Charlotte. Yet if hatred were enough to kill somebody, she herself would have been under arrest in childhood. "You mentioned a guilty conscience just now. Was hating Fenella what you meant? I loathed her at school, and Nadine Napier too, but it never made either of them die."

"They say 'off the record' in films," remarked Warren.

"It's an agreement that I won't name my source, but can use the info to further a story. Why? Are you about to burden me with an off-the-record confession?" Charlotte smiled to disguise anxiety. If Warren admitted being a murderer, he might decide to kill her as well. Then commonsense took over. She had known Warren practically from birth. He was as ordinary as Polrenek. His mother drudged in the Town Hall. His father had been a haulage driver. "Your Dad worked for Lambert's, didn't he?"

"Yeah. What's that got to do with the price of tin?" Warren was nonplussed by the sidetrack, before adding hopefully, "Will you ask your boyfriend to give me a job?"

"Edric Lambert isn't my boyfriend, but he might remember your Dad, so you ask Edric for a job. My mind went off at a tangent."

"Oh." Warren was mystified, but Charlie Paxton had been a minor character in school, and so her ramblings could be dismissed.

"You were talking about off-the-record stuff," prompted Charlotte. "Why did you think a ghostly Fenella Beckett might have come back to haunt you?"

"Because I didn't warn her. I should have, but I didn't," said Warren, rueful and yet defensive. "I'd been walking along the beach until it got dark, and then climbed up those lifeboat-station steps. The granite's always slithery there, but was even worse than usual that night. Thick soggy moss, and seaweed as well, so of course I slipped, walloping a knee which hurt like hell. I was limping along the Prom, when Fenella Beckett came out the shadows. She seemed to be following a couple who'd just gone by, and didn't notice me. But next thing, we were face-to-face, and naturally I glared at her, ready to bellow a few choice words, but before I had the chance, she went bolting off, headed for those steps. And I didn't yell a warning about the danger. Not a single word.

Serve the bitch right if she breaks her neck, I thought, and hobbled on home."

Charlotte could picture the scene as clearly as if she had witnessed it. Trailing Beatrice along the lamp-lit Promenade to spy on a *rendezvous* with Rufus Olsen, Fenella was confronted by an irate Warren. She had gleefully repeated Nadine's Sidney-slander from a distance, but dealing with the consequences in person was a very different matter for spineless Fenella. If her imagination had made the same journey as Charlotte's, then Warren could be Nadine's killer, and he was fast approaching her. Fenella had panicked, and taken the nearest escape route.

"Was anybody else on the beach?" asked Charlotte.

"No. Hardly ever is, at that time. It's why I went there. I was trying to plan for the future. I can't get a job in Polrenek now."

"Why not?"

"Everybody knows everything about everyone else here."

"People envy us living in such a close-knit community." The perfect *Clarion* reply made Warren look scathing, and Charlotte sought a less propagandist answer. "Better chance of being a big fish in a small pond."

"Better chance of all the other fish remembering your stupid mistakes. I mean, one startled glance at Vanessa Beckett's face, and the local press is at my front door."

"None of this will be printed. We're speaking off the record," Charlotte reminded Warren. "Anyway, sounds as if Fenella could have had a fall on those steps, and hit her head."

"Which would be my fault. I'd shout a warning for anyone else." Warren's remorse seemed genuine, but he might admit to understandable rancour against Fenella in the hope of diverting Charlotte from Nadine's death. Simpler to accept his testimony. The alternative would be problematic: too problematic for Charlotte.

"If you had shouted, Fenella would still have run off." Especially if Fenella thought she was fleeing Nadine's killer.

"I guess you're right, but —" Warren shrugged, apparently unable to fool himself. "They were horrible people though, the whole pack of them. That Mrs Piper tore into her husband, even when I was there, screeching on and on about a new conservatory. Said he was a miser, and Terence didn't like it one bit."

"Have you told the police?"

"The police? Why would I talk to them? Why would they bother talking to me?" Warren demanded. "Windows don't come into it. Anyhow, I bet the bloke's thankful to be free of that shrieking nag. Has he got an alibi?"

"Presumably, or the police would have hauled him in for questioning, and they haven't."

"He deserves a rest after that wife. There hasn't been much in the *Clarion*. I thought it'd be headlines forever. Have the police got a suspect? Or theories about what happened to Mrs Piper? Or anything?"

"Not that they're sharing, although a husband will always be prime suspect." Charlotte decided to check Terence Piper's alibi. Possibly home-wrecker Eleanor Yeo? Lying to shield her lover? More importantly, the task might stop Charlotte reassessing Warren's account of events on the Prom.

*

"I'm nowhere with the Nadine/Fenella murders," groused Adam, disappointment his sole reason for visiting Charlotte's flat. "I was sure Olsen had to be the killer, but info from Vanessa probably rules him out. She told me in strict confidence the guy's had an affair with her Mum."

"Not altogether honouring that strict confidentiality to reveal your source's identity," Charlotte said, amused.

"You knew it already, and telling a *Clarion* reporter stuff is like telling nobody." London was Adam's future, while Charlotte putrefied in the provinces, recording anniversaries and Council brawls.

"Has Terence Piper got an alibi?" asked Charlotte. "I've heard he and Nadine were arguing all the time. She called him a miser."

"And why would that make him kill Fenella? The murders are connected. It's glaringly obvious." There had to be a frenzied psycho at large in Polrenek to boost Adam's career. No London editor would be interested in small-town domestic slaughter. Such stories were routine.

"Fenella might have had an accident," Charlotte offered. "I spoke to the police, and they appear to accept that she fell on those steps. You know how slippy it gets there with the moss and seaweed."

"Someone could have pushed her down onto rocks. Just as lethal," Adam maintained, his hopes reliant on the existence of their local assassin. "And that same someone killed Nadine. I've gone through all the scenarios with Vanessa. Not that she's much use."

So Vanessa could soon be dropped. Better for her in the long run, as she might eventually grasp, but reaching equanimity wasted years. "Is Vanessa helping you full-time now?"

"She doesn't need wages. A Beckett isn't short of cash." Adam grinned, happy to utilize whatever financial support was available on his Fleet-Street quest. "Besides, I deem her a source, and we've got to humour them. Isn't it why you were busily cultivating Edric Lambert?"

The situation might actually have been Edric targeting her, but Charlotte had gained access to the Beckett household via him, and that brought responsibility with it. "You shouldn't exploit Vanessa. She's very young."

"So was I, several centuries ago."

So were they all, once upon a time, and Vanessa would survive. Most people did. "Yeah, we seem doomed to meet at least one slimy fraudster along the way."

"It's how we learn," Adam agreed, content with his rôle in furthering Vanessa's education. "Have you got any info out of Gabrielle yet?"

"None," replied Charlotte, picturing Adam's face if she told him that Daniel Henver had voluntarily become a *Clarion* source.

"Gabrielle's got the answer," Adam insisted. "It's why she blocked my mobile. Put some pressure on her. Remind Gabby that she's next on a killer's hit-list."

Adam sounded almost euphoric at the prospect of Gabrielle's corpse adding zest to his copy, but she might not be the person in closest proximity to a murderer. High time Charlotte reminded herself that she was still a newsroom journalist, albeit without an investigative team on standby, and more than high time that Charlotte began researching Eleanor Yeo, the Farfield-Manor Jezebel who had bewitched Nadine's susceptible husband.

*

Nearer Plymouth than Polrenek, the ostentatious Tregerne House had recently bid farewell to its patrician past, and become yet another hotel after being purchased by Raymond Yeo of Polrenek. Tregerne's staff-member list was headed by his daughter, and Charlotte dialled the phone number beside Eleanor's name.

"Hi. Tregerne House. Eleanor Yeo speaking. How can I help you?" A professional voice, aiming at simulated friendliness.

"I'm a reporter with the —"

"A reporter?" Eleanor demanded, suddenly apprehensive. "What do you want? Who are you?"

"Charlotte Paxton. From the *Clarion*. You might not remember me, because I was years ahead, but we went to the same school."

"Of course I remember you, Charlotte," said Eleanor, relaxing. "You didn't grass on me for sneaking home when I should have been out by the games field, frozen in a north wind, at some hockey match."

"I appear to have been a rather lax sixth-former. I was talking to Vanessa Beckett, and she recalled similar negligence on my part. Anyway, I'm ringing to ask if you'll do a *Clarion* interview." Charlotte awaited further suspicion, but Eleanor was more taken aback than guarded.

"Interview *me*? Why?"

"Because you're helping Tregerne House reinvent itself, and we're inclined to demolish old buildings around here. I know Tregerne isn't exactly *Clarion* country, but you live in Polrenek, don't you?"

"Not now. Mevyn Village."

"Close enough. You won't want me disturbing you at work, so perhaps we could talk one evening or at the weekend?"

Too obvious? Would Eleanor figure out that a reporter might have more interest in Nadine's widower than a revamped mansion? There was silence, and then a showy rustle of pages being turned, before Eleanor spoke again, attempting to imply that her schedule was one hectic appointment after another. "I've got space in my diary this evening. Would that be too short notice?"

"It's ideal. Oh, and could our photographer visit Tregerne?" added Charlotte, to reinforce her newborn fascination with the hotel and allay any misgivings Eleanor might develop. "Pictures make such a difference to any feature. I expect you already know Jethro Kern."

"Doesn't everybody? He'll love the house, and there's a walled kitchen garden we're restoring for our restaurant." Free publicity would please her father, and Eleanor was no longer cautious, which made Charlotte hate the deception. Yet an article about Tregerne would be written, and the Yeo family's Polrenek background should render it *Clarion* material.

"Interesting project, a kitchen garden," commented Charlotte. "You must tell me all about it during the interview."

"We plan to grow our own veg soon. People love organic stuff these days, and I expect the rain has washed any old tin-mine arsenic from Tregerne's soil by now. But you won't mention arsenic, will you?"

"The *Clarion* never does. Our cafés would be empty," replied Charlotte, making Eleanor giggle. She assumed they were fellow conspirators.

*

Mevyn Village required shelling out on a taxi, as buses were few and far between even in daylight hours. Stupid, thought Charlotte, going to such expense for nothing. The police would have investigated Terence Piper, and he was unlikely to confide in a reporter about the split with Nadine.

"Pick you up later, Charlie?" enquired Spike Deacon, another revenant from Charlotte's primary-school days, yet he was still recognizable with his snub nose, apricot hair and freckles.

"Yeah, in an hour or so." And if there were no sign of Charlotte Paxton at that time, inform the police that Terence

Piper was a murderer. Perhaps she ought to get the taxi turned around and head home. Then Charlotte sat back, deriding the imagination she had borrowed from Adam Rigg. He would claim Charlotte was following her journalistic instinct, and Adam had great faith in journalistic instinct, but she grouped it in the same category as Gabrielle's ouija board. No instinct had told Charlotte that Nadine would die minutes after they spoke, and presumably the ouija board had been equally silent.

"Number 28," said Charlotte, as Spike's car began to slow on the approach to Mevyn Row.

"Oh, Elly's place. It's at the far end. Last house."

"You know Eleanor?" queried Charlotte in surprise. It felt almost uncanny that the opposing sides of her two very different worlds had somehow managed to combine.

"Elly's my best customer. I'm always ferrying her up and down and to and fro. She loses her nerve at driving tests, and Warren doesn't have a car. It's made things difficult for them: him in Polrenek and Elly at the back of beyond."

"Warren?" echoed Charlotte. "Not Warren Sutton?"

"That's right. You remember him from school, don't you?"

"Yeah, but isn't Eleanor involved with someone else? It's what I've heard, at any rate."

"Me as well. But don't tell Warren. He thinks Elly will marry him. Much too good to be true, if you ask me. For Warren, I mean. The Yeo nobs are wallowing in dosh. Elly's Dad owns Tregerne House, and it's only one of his hotels. Warren just isn't that lucky."

Spike was laughing, and Charlotte smiled in reply, feeling sad for Warren. Terence Piper could be a generation older than Eleanor, but the Yeo parents might still regard him a more appropriate suitor than Warren Sutton, currently lacking employment. Unless they considered their daughter a naïve child held captive by the hypnotic sway of cunning seducer

Terence, whose wife died in mysterious circumstances. Hopefully Eleanor had sense enough to leave her parents serenely unaware that Terence Piper existed, although any subterfuge would soon be brought to an end. Polrenek gossip about the liaison was already circulating, as Charlotte's presence in Mevyn Village testified. Yet, whatever the Yeo attitude to Terence, any great expectations that Warren Sutton might have were probably doomed.

*

The Napier wealth had mattered greatly to Nadine, giving her a status otherwise unachievable. Of course she would marry rich men, and yet there was little sign of Terence Piper having splurged money on a love-nest. Eleanor Yeo was living in a granite two-up-two-down at the end of a terrace lining the single road that encompassed Mevyn Village. A dilapidated engine-house chimney was the only other building visible: sole souvenir of an epoch when the tin mine would have provided jobs for Mevyn and surrounding district. Even on a dark night, past loomed over present, making the terrace seem toy-town dwellings, instead of real homes.

"Glad to see you again, Charlotte." Words that Eleanor Yeo might recant after questions concerning Terence revealed the visitor's objective. Eleanor was twenty, but looked younger: her delicate fair prettiness reminding Charlotte of both Melanie and Beatrice's deceptive flaxen fragility. Such women were tougher than they appeared. "I don't usually meet anyone from school now. I was unhappy the whole time, and will never ever attend a reunion."

"Me neither. I didn't make any lifelong friends there." A statement to distance herself from Nadine Napier, and persuade Eleanor they could bond over hatred of Farfield

Manor. "Three repellent bullies in my year made life an utter misery."

"I had more trouble with the staff," said Eleanor, not realizing she was supposed to ask Charlotte to identify that detestable trio, so Nadine's name led straight onto second-husband Terence.

"Beautiful cottage," declared Charlotte, dutifully admiring the granite fireplace inside Eleanor's seventeenth-century home. "One thing I'd like to ask. Well, it's a bit intrusive, I know, but —"

"Money!" laughed Eleanor, perhaps deliberately sending them in a direction she would prefer. "That's no secret. Dad paid a few million for Tregerne, but I expect the Land Registry can provide more detail. Needs work, Dad said, but the building will repay me."

"I was surprised it only dates back to 1875," Charlotte remarked, accepting Eleanor's detour. "A mine owner who wanted to flaunt his wealth, but had no idea how soon Cornish tin prices would collapse. A lesson for us all, as our old headmistress might have said."

"She would; she absolutely would. And this row of mine-waste cottages, thrown up for the peasantry, will last longer than Tregerne House, as they're loads easier to maintain. Changing a light-bulb in the hotel is a big deal requiring ladders, but here I just reach up without even standing on a chair. I love this place, but poor Warren has to bow in doorways to avoid clobbering himself."

"I didn't realize you were Warren's Elly, until Spike Deacon mentioned it on the way here," said Charlotte, grasping her opportunity. "Polrenek rumour links you to another man entirely."

"Terence Piper." Eleanor sighed, her face wrinkling in boredom. "I've never even met him. He bought the old Mevyn

Counthouse just after I came to live here, and all Polrenek jumped to conclusions."

Assuming Eleanor had told the truth, not a single dastardly fact about Terence Piper was up for harvesting that night, and Charlotte would have to settle for a two-page *Clarion* feature on Tregerne Hotel as the only result of her journey to Mevyn Village. Unless she went to Terence's Counthouse home? Knocked on its door?

"Dad wants to get more Tregerne stuff online, and print some leaflets too," Eleanor was saying. "Could we use your *Clarion* article?"

"I'll have to check with Conrad Penry. Should be OK though." The idea of her words being reprinted anywhere would once have thrilled Charlotte, but she was busy attempting to conjure up an excuse that might disarm Terence and get him talking. *Clarion* curiosity about former counthouses? Yet why select Mevyn's? There were several closer to Polrenek.

A flurry of raps on the front door brought Charlotte back to reality, and sent Eleanor dashing into her hallway, able to recognize a welcome visitor's signature knock. Despite Eleanor's testimony, Charlotte hoped that coincidence would somehow produce Terence Piper, but the voice she heard was Warren Sutton's: a very flustered Warren.

"Spike says he drove Charlie Paxton here."

"She's doing an article on Tregerne House," replied Eleanor, as if soothing a fractious child. "Charlotte's OK. The *Clarion*'s OK."

"You don't know Charlie," argued Warren. "I was at school with her."

"So was I. It really is OK. The Napier crowd were awful to Charlotte at Farfield. She hated them all."

Hence Charlotte is on our side. That was the inference behind Eleanor's statement. On their side against Fenella?

Nadine? The world? As a sixth-former, Charlotte had kept quiet when school rules were flouted and that, in Eleanor's opinion, meant the *Clarion* could also be trusted. Warren had told his Fenella story, and it remained off the record, yet he was still anxious. There had to be more than an accidental fall perturbing him.

A whispered consultation in the hall, and then Eleanor led Warren into her front room. "Spike's here to drive you home, Charlotte, but waiting a few minutes won't bother him. I'll ask Dad to show you his Tregerne deeds. The early ones are handwritten on what looks like parchment. You'll love them. And Dad knows far more Tregerne info than I do. You ought to interview him, not me. I'll arrange it."

No doubt because Dad knew nothing of whatever Warren feared Eleanor might inadvertently disclose to a *Clarion* reporter. But journalistic optimism lives on.

"Off the record?" suggested Charlotte.

"You've got her imagining stuff," Warren informed Eleanor. "She thinks there's some big secret, and there just isn't."

"Charlotte was asking about Terence Piper," said Eleanor, her words hurriedly jumbling together. "You know, Warren, the guy Polrenek gossip says is my boyfriend. The guy who quarrelled non-stop with that horrible wife of his, even when you were around."

"Mrs Piper blew her top, howling and shrieking at him like an endless tornado. Enough to put anyone off marriage permanently," Warren added to Eleanor, making her smile. "And I reckon you won't print that in the *Clarion*, Charlie."

"Conrad Penry would deem arguing spouses too commonplace even for the *Clarion*," agreed Charlotte.

Warren was tentatively grinning. Best to leave them confident they had sidetracked her, and Charlotte stood up to indicate she accepted their hints that Terence Piper might be a suspect worth investigating. Whatever Warren had or had not done, Eleanor believed they were in no danger from Charlotte, because Charlotte had hated Nadine Napier. Therefore, Charlotte would automatically support Warren. Just as Eleanor herself was doing.

*

"You're still in great demand," said Rosalind, when Charlotte arrived at work the next day. "Daniel Henver seems to think I neglected to pass on his phone number to you. I told him I gave it to your assistant, but he was suspicious, and demanded your contact details. I became very fluent on employee-privacy regulations at this point, and it didn't half annoy him. I gather minions ought to recognize their humble rank, and never dare thwart the mighty Henver."

Yet Daniel would not tolerate his rebuff, and Charlotte resolved to ignore any calls coming from an unknown number. "Henver will get bored and go away."

"Didn't sound like it. Must be your local-business profiles. Henver can't understand why you haven't approached him. He wants a puff-piece lauding his multiple heroic deeds," scoffed Rosalind, delighting in her power to withhold newsprint from a man loathed by Conrad. "Wish I'd thought to mention his defeat at the last election. Henver shouldn't be so haughty. Not that I'd oblige him if he grovelled."

It was Charlotte's fault that Daniel assumed he could expect her to obey his orders. She ought to have torn up the Glynn emails, not used them to create a *Clarion* front-page story. But if Henver had been angered by Oliver's strategic wriggle off the hook, then that was Daniel's problem, not Charlotte's.

"Any sign of an Adam understudy?" asked Charlotte, endeavouring to evict Henver from her mind. "Or maybe Adam's comeback? A vintage-car rally clashes with the

Harvest-Home treasure hunt this weekend, and I can't get to both events. There's a Chamber of Commerce get-together in the afternoon as well."

"Oh, you find a replacement to help out." Rosalind wafted the task away as though it had become as tiresome as a buzzing fly. "Or phone Adam. At least he knows the job. But tell him no pay rise, no byline, and he's a freelance. Make that very clear."

"OK," said Charlotte, taken aback by the unexpected responsibility. Adam would be a convenient choice, yet his London ambitions might mean he saw returning to the *Clarion* as a backward step, if not downright failure. In Adam's imagination, he had left Polrenek far behind him.

*

"One or two freelance jobs, that's all," Charlotte bargained, hoping the phone would mask eagerness to halve her workload. "No extra money, I'm afraid, but it'll only be for a few weeks. Until I find someone permanent. You're not off to London tomorrow, are you?"

"Not *tomorrow*," Adam replied. "But how come you've got the clout to offer jobs? Has Conrad made you acting-editor or what?"

"Or nothing. Rosalind's busy, so she's gone in for a spot of delegation. You'd be doing the *Clarion* a favour." Charlotte made herself sound meek, but knew that Adam would need funds, whether or not he ended up in London. "You have an opportunity for journalistic glory this weekend, and can choose between the vintage-car rally or a Harvest-Home treasure hunt."

Adam groaned at the abrupt downgrading of a London career already established in his head, but money was money. "OK. I'll take the cars, in preference to screaming kids."

Just to help temporarily. By the by, have you come across anything new on the Nadine murder?"

"No," Charlotte stated.

"I'm still gleaning stuff on Rufus Olsen, but he won't talk to me," Adam remarked, too casually.

"I think you can rule him out as the Polrenek serial killer," said Charlotte, but that would mean Adam giving up on a potential scoop with no stand-in suspect.

"Then who did murder Nadine? And Fenella too? Got any hunches worth following?"

"None," declared Charlotte. "You forget I inhabit a world of fêtes, anniversaries and Council Meetings."

"What about Nadine's husband?"

"Which one? There were two."

"Why are you hedging?" Adam demanded. "Terence Piper's got to be prime suspect. Don't tell me you haven't had a look at him."

"He dumped Nadine awhile back, and is of no interest to the police, so alibis presumably abound. That's all I know."

"You haven't heard anything on a Farfield grapevine?"

"There is no grapevine in my case. When I left school, I gave the door a good slam. Ask Vanessa about grapevines." But that might lead Adam straight to gossip concerning Eleanor, and eventually to Warren. Charlotte needed to change the subject. And quickly After all, journalists had gone to prison, rather than betray a source. "Does Vanessa still think she's going to London with you? Incidentally, how is Katlyn?"

"Her? Oh, she's fine." Nothing more to be said on so insignificant a topic, it seemed. Adam's attention was elsewhere. "I gather Terence Piper ditched Nadine for one of your Farfield chums: Raymond Yeo's daughter."

"Piper would be the slain victim, if that were true. Nadine would have throttled him with her bare hands. She had to be a megastar, not the sidelined wife. You've heard Polrenek gossip at its wildest and woolliest. Terence Piper moved house around the same time as Raymond Yeo's daughter. They both went to the Mevyn area, but separately. I checked it out. No story there." Charlotte spoke to divert Adam away from Eleanor, but had Terence discarded his wife for another woman, the vendetta against Rufus would have been Fenella's mission alone, without input or help from Nadine, who would be focused on her own revenge.

"Something big is behind all this," Adam said, piqued by fortune's refusal to cooperate. "I just know it. Every instinct I have tells me so."

"The mystery is why Nadine left her car and went onto a building site. Solve that, and you can probably name the killer." An assignment to keep Adam busy. And ineffective, as police officers had yet to locate a witness or any relevant dash-cam footage.

"You could be right," admitted Adam. "And she wouldn't have seen either Terence Piper or his girlfriend there."

"Daniel Henver owns the land," Charlotte pointed out, conscious that she could rival Nadine when it came to vengeance. "And he'd be alone in his caravan-office that day. All work had had to stop on site, remember, while the demolition of Old Mother Trevail's Inn was investigated."

"Henver could have had an affair with Nadine, but she threatened to go public and end his political chances." Adam spoke slowly, yet with replenished hope. News that a Parliamentary candidate, albeit an unsuccessful one, had engaged in homicidal rampages the length and breadth of Polrenek would be certain to further Adam's own aspiration. "Nadine confided in Fenella, and so Henver had to silence her as well."

"Possible," said Charlotte, pleased that Adam too could picture Daniel as villain. "Henver's been complaining about you and your questions."

"It adds up," conceded Adam, ready to convince himself. "Henver thought he could get away with murder, then the guy realized I was a danger. That's why he told Gabby to boycott me."

As Adam was living with Katlyn Kyle, any father might tell his daughter to keep her distance from a philanderer, but Charlotte preferred Adam's analysis. "Henver controls the family finance, and I don't think Gabrielle's ever had a job. She's got to obey him."

"I'll doorstep Henver again." The plan of campaign made Adam's voice grow warmer as he visualized byline after byline. "If I get him angry, Henver's bound to blurt out incriminating stuff sooner or later."

"Good idea, but don't forget that vintage-car rally," pleaded Charlotte. "You only need stay an hour or so. Jeth Kern will be there too."

"Yeah, yeah." An absent-minded reply, but the prospect of quick money should help jog Adam's memory.

And perhaps Daniel had killed Nadine. It was as likely a scenario as any other.

*

"Yet more messages from Henver," said Rosalind, as she strolled into the newsroom where Charlotte was trying to liven up her account of local disputes concerning waste collection. "I didn't bother to record details, but the bloke clearly doesn't give up at the first obstacle."

Nor did Charlotte when her obstacle was Daniel Henver. "He'll work out that the *Clarion*'s got no interest in him. I've just deleted another of his emails unread, so you should be left in peace very soon."

"Why is he so eager to contact you?"

"Might be a complaint about Adam, who's certain Henver killed Nadine Napier. And when Adam starts to pester, he's unrelenting."

"In that case, there'll never be a mention of Adam on any staff list, if he does stage his *Clarion* comeback," decreed Rosalind. "Easier to disown a freelance: a nameless freelance. No bylines for Adam."

"He won't mind. London's his goal."

"But you're happy to stay in Polrenek?" A question, yet Rosalind ploughed on, not requiring an answer. "Conrad's decided to appoint you editor. Well, reporter-cum-overseer, rather than monarch of all you survey. Pretty much the way we've been managing recently. A little more money comes with the promotion, but not riches. OK? Want to be our new Gideon?"

"It'd be a great opportunity." Each day on the same track until her retirrement? Charlotte was staggered at how dull that felt, even though she had never seriously considered leaving Polrenek. But what more could life offer her? "Are you and Conrad sure I'm the best candidate?"

"You wouldn't have been chosen, if we had doubts." Rosalind so obviously believed she was delivering good news that Charlotte forced herself to look and sound enthusiastic.

"It's incredible, especially as I thought Gideon was about to sack me a few weeks ago."

"He's in our past, and it was a mistake giving him the job. You understand Polrenek. You understand the *Clarion*."

Yes, Charlotte understood the *Clarion*. Years of Council Meetings and summer fêtes and school concerts were ahead, like a trap closing around her. Yet Charlotte had been very certain that she was on the right career path when a *Clarion* job came her way.

"You and Edric can begin making plans now," added Rosalind, slyly teasing.

Even worse. A Polrenek happy ending. Domesticity with a man the town would think her lucky to attract. What was wrong with Charlotte Paxton that she wanted to run in the opposite direction? "Edric and I haven't bothered getting in touch lately."

"He'll be back," predicted Rosalind. "I know for a fact he isn't seeing anyone else. You've definitely had an impact on him. His mother told me. I went to the same school as her."

Rosalind was visualizing a Polrenek road map, with Charlotte's route and destination highlighted. It would also have been the outcome that Melanie craved for her daughter. Charlotte ought to be celebrating. "I hope Conrad hasn't made another mistake, because I feel overwhelmed," she said, sternly informing herself that promotion was always advantageous.

"We liked your handling of the Glynn business. No lawsuit bluster from him after hard-to-substantiate allegations, and Polrenek won."

A good tactician, but a slipshod reporter. The *Clarion* portrayed a fantasy town, and Charlotte was colluding in the myth, yet only a fool would turn her back on regular wages. She was not Adam. She was level-headed. And prudent. "It's an amazing chance," Charlotte said firmly.

*

Her front door within sight, and also in sight was Daniel Henver getting out from his flash car to storm terrain that belonged to Melanie. Gabrielle must have told him the address, but she was unlikely to be notified of Charlotte's parentage in return. "I've been waiting here almost an hour," complained Daniel. "And I never hang around for anyone. Your secretary ought to be sacked. I left half-a-dozen messages with her. Emails too."

Did he think Melanie's daughter would leap to attention at his command? Charlotte glanced across the road towards her flat, Melanie's flat, and was angry that his car should be in the vicinity. "What do you want? Why are you here?"

"To give you another front-page story," replied Daniel, ignoring the hostility in Charlotte's voice. "You dealt brilliantly with Glynn. Making the guy lose bunce will get to him more than anything else."

Charlotte wished she had torn up the evidence against Glynn, even though Council-Tax payers would have been cheated. Pleasing Daniel Henver was intolerable.

"There's security-camera footage that you ought to see," he continued, taking a laptop computer from his car. "We'll go into your place."

"No," said Charlotte. Melanie had often worked overtime to pay the mortgage on her flat, and Daniel's presence would pollute each room.

"OK, get into my car then."

"No," said Charlotte.

"Your mother's decision to cut me out of your life," claimed Daniel, seemingly entertained by Charlotte's obstinacy. "But you're like me, even so, with more spirit and determination than Gabby will ever acquire. OK, we can study the film right here, and you're going to be very interested. It's doorbell footage."

Daniel was aiming to strike back at yet another foe, but Charlotte could prevent him using the *Clarion* for reprisals. Whether he chose to search online or in a print version of the paper, Daniel would read nothing about whatever she was expected to publicize. No wonder Gideon had so enjoyed his authority to wield power.

Opening the laptop, Daniel put it down on his car's passenger seat, and a film began running. Naturally he would have the best security system, which meant a clearer-than-usual picture told Charlotte that she was looking at the Trevail site presumably shot from Henver's caravan-HQ. Charlotte also saw two figures facing the camera. They turned as a woman came into view with the unsteady gait of somebody in high heels crossing boulder-strewn ground. Hands on hips, Nadine obviously started to harangue Warren, perhaps employing the same mockery Charlotte had so often known. He marched off disdainfully, but a furious Eleanor swung her bag at Nadine's smirk, and sent her tumbling sideways into rubble. Eleanor delivered a second blow via bag to Nadine's head, and leaving the casualty prostrate, ran after Warren out of camera range.

"Why haven't you shown this to the police?" demanded Charlotte.

"It should go to my mobile as well," Daniel replied, not even feigning defensiveness. "I handed a phone in. Not my fault it's kaput. Anyhow, the girl's accomplice is called Warren Sutton."

As Charlotte knew. But in her opinion, Raymond Yeo would be the actual target. Had Daniel wanted to buy Tregerne House? Or did Yeo undercut him on some other building project? Whatever Daniel's motive, no doubt he intended Charlotte to harass a father with allegations against his daughter, the story then backed up in *Clarion* headlines. Not while Charlotte had a say in the matter.

"Films are easily faked."

"I promise you this film is the genuine article."

A Henver promise? He was overlooking his promises to Melanie. "How many copies have you got?"

"There are no copies. This is the one and only."

He was probably lying, but Charlotte picked up Henver's laptop, using both arms to hold it securely against her.

"You're investigating Ray Yeo? What's he done?" Daniel asked, too eagerly. "You need copies of the recording to put pressure on him? Take all you want."

"What I want, what I'll do, is destroy your computer's harddrive. I'll replace it and return the laptop. If you object, there'll be a *Clarion* piece about your illicit dealings with Polrenek Town Council. I have several sources, and the article should end your hopes of becoming an MP."

Charlotte expected aggression, not amusement, but Daniel was smiling. "It's incredible how alike we are. I feel positively proud to have such a pugnacious daughter. You do realize you'll obliterate evidence concerning a friend's death, don't you?"

"Nadine Napier was no friend of mine."

"Good for you," chuckled Daniel. "A tedious girl. I could never fathom why Gabby wasn't bored rigid by her. Keep the laptop. It's a gift."

A gift! Charlotte would accept no gift from him. His computer was going to be returned. Indeed, returned by courier, and hang expense. Charlotte hurried across the road, fearing Daniel might follow her, but he made no effort at pursuit. Even so, locking and bolting Melanie's front door felt close to a narrow escape.

Charlotte loathed the idea, but Daniel could be right to say she resembled him, and now they were sharing a secret that the police ought to know. Yet Eleanor's rage was triggered by Nadine's spite towards Warren, not any accusation of luring a second-husband away from the marital home. Eleanor and Warren could have laughed at that. Nadine's malice was the cause of her own death, and it seemed almost logical, almost like justice, that she had been hoist by the Shakespearean petard. For a split-second, Charlotte was back in school, hearing the same derision, and sorely tempted to aim both fists in her tormentor's direction. It would be a gratifying memory to have had the bravado to fling a hefty bag at Nadine Napier's contemptuous snigger.

Hatred of Daniel and Nadine should be irrelevant, but the fact inevitably lurked behind Charlotte's judgment. What did or did not occur on a Polrenek building site, what was or was not said, however events transpired there, Nadine would stay dead. Yet intervention with possibly false evidence might hurt living people.

If anyone except Nadine Napier were the victim, had Charlotte's informant not been Daniel Henver, she might still have considered handing the film to police officers. But Eleanor's life appeared far more valuable than Nadine's ever had, so Charlotte would act as jury in the case. She was *Clarion*-trained after all, and Nadine's petty ill-will against Sidney Tyrrel, against Warren Sutton, against a Polrenek firm remained reprehensible.

Fenella's death? Using the same analysis, Charlotte was compelled to believe Warren's version. He had given his off-the-record account to distract Charlotte's attention from Eleanor and the Trevail site, yet Fenella had so often repeated her controller's deceitful embellishments to a smidgen of truth, she would have good reason to dodge any encounter with Warren. The authorities seemed content to agree that Fenella had died because of an accidental fall, and Charlotte thought they were probably right.

All would be well in the *Clarion* world.

12

"Hi, Charlotte. A mind-numbing vintage-car rally has received sky-high praise, my lustrous prose sent to your laptop, and now I'm done here." Adam stood by the newsroom door, a hand extended palm-upwards, indicating that immediate payment would be welcome. "Edit to your heart's content. I'm off to London next week."

"You've got a job?" asked Charlotte, feeling sadly staid.

"No job yet," Adam admitted. "But I'll have somewhere to live. Vanessa's stomping back to college in a mood. Kids are meant to be traumatized when their parents split up, but she's throwing a tantrum because hers are still together."

So Luke Beckett was either an extremely tolerant husband, or unwilling to submit himself to Polrenek gossip. Whichever, Fenella's war against Rufus Olsen might have succeeded, if the aim had been to preserve her parents' relationship. "Is your girlfriend vanishing to London with you?"

"She doesn't want to disrupt her career plans." Adam shrugged, his own career plans far more important. Maybe Katlyn had finally developed some acumen, and Vanessa might also remove her blinkers as infatuation waned, but Adam would survive.

"Oh well, at least I know that Vanessa's left the *Clarion*," Charlotte remarked. "She didn't bother to tell Rosalind."

"Vanessa could never be a journalist," declared Adam. "She's got no perspective. Much too wrapped up in herself. One moment she's livid that Dad isn't kicking Mum out, and five minutes later Mum's to blame for not running off with another man. Vanessa appears to think a third-option compromise was chosen to spite her."

"She'll calm down," Charlotte predicted. "Vanessa was very meek and mild at school. She'll revert to her true nature ultimately."

"Talking of natures, yours is rather secretive. I've picked up rumours that you've had several meetings with Daniel Henver. Is he a source?"

"Henver!" laughed Charlotte.

"Sorry. A moment of madness," Adam conceded. "What did he want?"

"To curry *Clarion* favour, I guess. The next general election must be a Henver priority, if he still sees himself strutting around Westminster as Polrenek's future MP."

"Yeah," sighed Adam. "Yeah, makes sense. Turns out he did eventually produce an alibi for Nadine's death: a young extra-marital alibi. But keep tabs on him. Henver would do anything to get what he craves."

So would Adam, who was readily abandoning job and girlfriend to chase ambition. Charlotte knew she would never take such a gamble, and found herself envying Adam's recklessness. "No need to warn me about Henver. I'm well aware that he's a sham."

"If you stumble on stories the *Clarion* won't touch, let me know." Adam was faking indifference, but he would be on his own in London, even with Vanessa providing accommodation, and any story was better than none.

"OK. Copy too sensational for Polrenek will be sent your way."

"I'm giving up on Nadine Piper. It's a waste of time. I bet the attack was just a robbery gone wrong. Some random guy chanced to be passing through town, and he won't ever be caught. But if you do get a lead —" Adam paused hopefully, and Charlotte's reply was automatic.

"No problem, although I figure you're right. Unless Henver's alibi is bogus, the culprit won't be arrested."

"All decent stories fizzle to nothing here," grumbled Adam. "I bet the police are right about Fenella too. An accident. Naturally, an accident. Typical of Polrenek. Reporters haven't got a chance in this town."

"And that's why people are happy to live here," said Charlotte, forcing a grin at Adam's disgusted tone. "Not everybody wants their street to be a crime-ridden area."

"The *Clarion* wouldn't print a word anyhow. You'd have front-page headlines about the summer festival instead."

"And Polrenek would thank us."

"That's the problem with a backwater," griped Adam, rolling his eyes in vexation. "This place prefers fantasy to news."

"The *Clarion* mantra," said Charlotte.

*

Five years earlier, being *Clarion* editor would have delighted Charlotte, but now felt like surrender. She was also in collusion with Daniel, which further diminished what ought to count as progress. Somehow Charlotte had to stymie Henver, although if he did have a copy of the Trevail footage and used it to put pressure on Raymond Yeo, an expensive gaggle of lawyers would surround Eleanor. Warren needed equal protection from Daniel, and the same support might be available to him if he were a Yeo son-in-law. But to be smiled on in that affluent milieu, Warren had to find a job, a career.

*

"What do you want *now*?" Warren slumped against the cottage doorframe, as though a mere sight of Charlotte Paxton could drain all energy from him. "This is practically persecution. Why are you here again?"

"To offer you a job. You're still looking for one, aren't you?"

Warren glared at Charlotte, plainly suspecting an attempted joke against him. "What job? With Lambert's?"

"No. *Clarion* reporter. I need somebody who can start at once. It's the Mayor's gold-wedding anniversary today, and if you tag along, I'll show you how to gather info. There's a sea-shanty concert this evening as well."

"But *I* can't be a *reporter*," said Warren, stunned by the speed of so drastic a change in his prospects. "I can't."

"Why not? It's just asking questions and writing down the answers," Charlotte pointed out. "You were there when I spoke to your mother. And then you read my bowgle stuff, didn't you? That's how it's done."

"But I haven't written anything since school," Warren protested.

"I check copy before it's printed. Don't you want a job? I thought you and Eleanor were hoping to get married soon."

"Well, yeah, but —" Warren paused in confusion as an entirely new image of himself began to infiltrate his mind. "Anyhow, you can't waltz around, offering people jobs. You don't have the clout."

"Actually, I do. I'm an editor now. Turn up at the *Clarion* office by two o'clock this afternoon, and you're on Conrad Penry's payroll."

"But my mates would never believe *I* was a reporter," declared Warren, presenting the insurmountable barrier between him and a journalistic career. "Nobody would believe it."

"You'll have press credentials as proof," said Charlotte.

"Has this got something to do with Vanessa Beckett?" Surprise was wearing off, and Warren's distrustful nature took over.

"This has everything to do with Vanessa. She's left the *Clarion* to go back to college, and I'm on my own in the newsroom, so another reporter's got to be trained right away. Your choice. Take the job or don't. Talk it over with Eleanor." Who trusted Charlotte, and might also suggest to Warren that her father would almost certainly prefer a working son-in-law to one possibly deemed a shiftless layabout. Odd that the prominent Raymond Yeo could be an unwitting ally in Charlotte's battle against Daniel Henver.

"Why pick on me?" asked Warren.

"Why not you?" said Charlotte, noting that he was now more bemused than suspicious. "Two o'clock. Don't forget."

*

"Is anybody lined up to replace Adam yet?"

Rosalind was making conversation as they ate a sandwich-lunch in her office, and Charlotte wondered uneasily what Conrad would be told of his new editor's decision. Time to recruit Eleanor's father again. "Warren Sutton needs a job, and can begin here straightaway. He's going to marry Raymond Yeo's daughter soon."

"Ray's girl? I heard she'd dumped Warren for that Terence Piper." Rosalind's frown was less disapproving than perplexed by the discrepancy between sources, even though she knew Charlotte's information was likely to be more accurate than local gossip. "Has Piper been arrested? Did he kill his wife?"

"No." Too definite, and Charlotte modified her answer. "I don't think so, anyhow. The police have accepted his alibi, and I'm not going to quarrel with them. But don't worry about

Eleanor being enthralled by a possible murderer. She went to live in Mevyn Village just ahead of Piper buying the old counthouse there, and that was enough for Polrenek. Trust me, Warren and Eleanor are an item."

"Does anybody in this town manage to keep a secret from you?" asked Rosalind. "Not a complaint. It's why the *Clarion* pays you. I hope Elly doesn't let Warren down. Ray's inclined to regard lack of riches as a character flaw."

"Eleanor won't care. She and Warren are a loyal couple." They had to be. The alternative could destroy them both.

"Good. I'd hate to have Warren moping around the newsroom, bewailing a broken heart." Rosalind was amused, which doubtless meant Conrad would approve. The job had become Warren's to reject. "His mother was good at English in school. Her talent might be genetic."

"As a kid, Warren wrote most fluently on the subject of pirates and their activities. Startlingly vivid descriptive power. And he'll know every marital twist-and-turn in Polrenek, which is a definite plus at the *Clarion*. Warren won't criticize the Mayor's great-niece to her second-cousin-twice-removed. And it'll give me time to find another candidate, if Warren moves on. Is that OK?

"The editor's decision is final," Rosalind commented.

*

More doubtful than she had seemed about Warren's readiness to serve the cause of local journalism, Charlotte was heartened to see him in suit-and-tie waiting outside the *Clarion* office. "Hi there, Warren. I wasn't sure you'd turn up."

"Mum came home for lunch, and I told her what you said. She informed me I'd be mad not to take a chance, in case you weren't joking."

"I don't joke where the *Clarion*'s concerned. It's my bread and butter. Yours too, if things work out. What did Eleanor say?"

"She doesn't know yet." And never would, to judge by Warren's chary tone, if he had fallen for an April-fool joke at the end of October.

"Well, let's hope she's no objection to *Clarion* reporters. When do the pair of you plan to get married?"

"We thought perhaps around Christmas, but then —"

But then Nadine and her windows had intervened. Now there was even more about Nadine to trouble him, and Charlotte hurried on, "You still could have a Christmas wedding. Or is it to be an elaborate gala on the French Riviera with military-type preparation, thousand-pound dresses and a million guests?"

"Actually, we were thinking more of an elopement. Go to some registry office or other, and tell her family afterwards. They'd want a huge gathering with hordes of people, but Elly hates a fuss. So do I. We both prefer —" Then Warren gasped, recalling exactly who his listener was. "I should have said 'off the record' before I spoke. You won't print our plans in the *Clarion*, will you?"

"Your secret is safe with me." All secrets he and Eleanor had were safe with Charlotte. Daniel Henver was the threat. "Did I tell Mrs Babbage who put that rotten apple in her desk before the half-term holiday?"

"Spike Deacon's idea. I was led astray." But the recollection of those shared childhood years made Warren relax. Charlie Paxton had been trustworthy then, and might still be a team player.

They were approaching Victory Hall, a granite oblong less triumphant than severe, hidden behind Polrenek's main street, which kept holidaymakers unaware of quiz nights, film screenings and other local jollity. Not the most picturesque venue in town for a party, but it was owned by the Council, and their frugal Mayor would almost certainly have been able to get a discount for his family festivities.

"Just follow me," Charlotte instructed Warren. "I'll be harvesting anecdotes for the paper, and amassing names too. You'll pick up the routine in a jiff. Oh, and refuse all alcohol. Don't swallow a single drop, but food's OK. You can fill up at these celebrations, and save good money on your next meal."

"They'll think I'm gate-crashing," muttered Warren.

"I'm a veteran gate-crasher. No call to worry. Mayors need the *Clarion* as much as we do."

Warren at her heels, Charlotte strode into the midst of a perfect-family fiesta, spoilt only by Councillor Dirk's reign as DJ. Despite the racket, everyone was smiling, and everyone was united: an illusion due to revert to petty quarrels and even pettier jealousies, as drink began to wield its power. Yet by then Charlotte would have gleaned details of an ideal *Clarion* gathering, confirmed by Jethro Kern's photographic proof.

The Mayor rushed up to greet Charlotte, and ensure some excellent publicity: a move that took Warren by surprise when his hand was enthusiastically shaken as well. He had yet to realize how imperative a flattering *Clarion* article could be in local-government circles, but would soon learn. Councillors were always eager to cite their latest accomplishment, and had been known to pursue Charlotte in the street to clarify a specific point. Wedding anniversaries were playtime in comparison.

After competing with Dirk's din for a high-volume chat with the Mayor, Charlotte glanced around for another target. Then she froze. Daniel Henver was strolling towards her, his smile sardonic as he noticed Warren.

"So this is the reason you returned my laptop, complete with brand-new hard-drive," Daniel remarked. "And me labouring under a delusion that Ray Yeo's daughter was the Sutton true love."

"She is," snapped Charlotte, conscious of Warren's alarm that Daniel Henver should refer to Eleanor. "Meet our latest *Clarion* recruit."

"Conrad Penry hired *him*?" For Daniel, the world contained two ranks only: success and failure. He was successful; Warren was a failure who ought to languish in hopeless misery, not swan through the town as a reporter.

"Mistake to write people off. Their next job might present them with chances to hit back." Utterly frustrating, but the more unpleasant Charlotte was to Daniel, the more amused he became.

"I'll do my quaking when Sutton's made *Clarion* editor," said Daniel. "By the by, I gather Penry's inept son has been given his marching orders. Who's the editor now?"

"She is," replied Warren, pointing at a tight-lipped Charlotte.

"Of course she is," declared Daniel, beaming as though the news added to his standing in Polrenek. "Penry's managed to acquire some sense at last, and promoted the only *Clarion* employee with real talent. Charlotte, your next move will be to London and a national daily."

"I'm staying right here in this town," Charlotte retorted. "And I've got work to do. Come on, Warren."

"How does Henver know about me and Elly?" asked Warren, trailing Charlotte as she stamped away. "And why are you so angry with him? What's going on? You were like a three-year-old spitfire."

"I simply can't bear the man," replied Charlotte, trying to appear rueful. "You've just witnessed an example of how not to handle Polrenek grandees, but Henver deserves it. He treated you and Sid disgracefully. He was plain wrong."

"Yeah. But working for the *Clarion*, don't you have to soft-soap people?"

"We do," admitted Charlotte. "That's why it's best to avoid all Henvers. I was at Farfield Manor with his daughter, and I hate her as well. Luckily Conrad can't abide them either."

"But how come Henver knows about me and Elly?" persisted Warren. "And what's that got to do with you, his laptop and a new hard-drive?"

"Nothing," declared Charlotte. "Nothing in the least. Some stories don't pan out, but even then journalists never reveal a source, so I can't explain. Henver's just picked up town gossip circulating around you and Eleanor. He's jealous of her father's success, so probably keeps an eye on Yeo concerns."

"Henver seems to know you very well," Warren remarked.

"I've only spoken to him once or twice. The guy's doing a pally approach in case he gets another shot to be our MP. Ask him about his political hopes, if he bothers you again. Dangle the possibility of a good *Clarion* write-up, and Henver will be putty in your hands."

"Does that advice apply to him alone, or to all-comers?" Warren made an attempt to sound jokey, yet there was guardedness behind his question.

"No specific advice on how to treat any Polreneker," Charlotte replied, with an equal effort at airiness. "Trust to instinct. You're certain to cope with Henver better than I do. I'm not even halfway polite."

"And yet he likes you," observed Warren.

"Then I guess he likes bad-mannered people. If you have a problem with Henver, tell me, and I'll deal with him."

Warren frowned, wariness shadowing his face. "You think he could cause trouble? Trouble for me?"

"Henver's got no influence at the *Clarion*," said Charlotte, shirking a direct answer. "Come on. We've still got to talk to the Council Leader. Smile. And keep that smile in place.

Clarion reporters attend these functions, no matter how drear, with a friendly grin cemented on their lips."

"Unless they run into Daniel Henver. How did you get hold of his laptop? And why return it?"

Warren might make a good reporter after all, thought Charlotte, if he automatically zoomed in on transient yet significant detail. "People give you loads of stuff. Printouts and memory sticks are thrust at you almost every day. Conspiracy theories abound as well."

"Did Henver give you a laptop?"

"No, of course not. Bt if he had, *Clarion* policy dictates that any gift goes straight back. Forget Henver," said Charlotte, spotting Jethro as she scrutinized guests for potential copy. "There's our photographer herding the Mayor's grandchildren for a group picture. Do you know Jeth Kern?"

"Everybody knows Jeth," replied Warren. "How did you get Henver's laptop? And what was on the original hard-drive?"

"Sorry, can't tell you. As I said, reporters never risk disclosing a source."

"Henver's a *Clarion* source?" demanded Warren, taken aback.

"Him!" Charlotte grimaced, before remembering her own words on the fixed-smile policy. "Henver's no type of source. He's a non-story."

"Why isn't Henver mad with you for removing that hard-dive?"

"He can't afford to alienate the *Clarion*."

"Was there a film or something, Charlie?" ventured Warren.

An emphatic headshake was her attempt to end the subject. Warren was dubious and still had questions, but Charlotte plunged back into the crowd, her route leading them strategically close to Councillor Dirk's endeavour to blast the area with drum-beast hell. Even better, Oliver Glynn was nearby, and he had been watching Daniel speak to Charlotte, the journalist Glynn now regarded as his ally.

"What did Henver say?" Glynn demanded, hurrying to Charlotte's side. "Has he given you any more printouts?"

"Don't worry, Councillor. Henver didn't mention you. No story here."

Oliver was smiling in evident relief as he moved away. So there might still be shady Glynn dealings that Daniel could reveal, and Charlotte would encourage Warren to conclude Henver's laptop had had a part to play in Councillor Glynn's unprecedented rôle as Polrenek benefactor. Simple to suggest Warren consult his mother about additional Oliver transgression.

"He thinks Henver tipped you off?"

"You can always hint that Henver's to blame for everything. No one in Polrenek will doubt you," declared Charlotte. "Well, a word with the Council Leader, and then back to the *Clarion*. We've done our duty here, and a Mayoral shindig can't wait until the weekend's print edition, so an online acknowledgement is required this very day."

Charlotte would show Warren how to transfer copy onto the *Clarion* website, before hustling them both out to that night's sea-shanty concert. Henver could be written off as stale news, not worth discussing.

Yet should Daniel chose to resurface with his security-camera footage stored on another device, Charlotte would tell the police how he had withheld evidence, even though she was just as guilty. Her journalistic days might end, especially if Daniel counted as a source, but wrecking his life would be worth the loss of a *Clarion* career. Daniel was mistaken to assume that Melanie's daughter took after him. Unless Charlotte was equally spiteful?